MW00916991

ZEUD

& the Prophets of Atomic Fire

A Reemergence Novel

Chris Philbrook

Designed and illustrated by Alan MacRaffen

Also by Chris Philbrook:

Reemergence
Tesser: A Dragon Among Us
Ambryn: The Cheaters of Death
Fyelrath & the Coven's Curse
Tesser: A Father Enraged
Zeud: & the Prophets of Atomic Fire

Colony Lost

Elmoryn - The Kinless Trilogy
Book One: Wrath of the Orphans
Book Two: The Motive for Massacre
Book Three: The Echoes of Sin

Adrian's Undead Diary
Book One: Dark Recollections
Book Two: Alone No More — Book Three: Midnight
Book Four: The Failed Coward — Book Five: Wrath
Book Six: In the Arms of Family — Book Seven: The Trinity
Book Eight: Cassie — Book Nine: The Dealer of Hope
Book Ten: The Last Resort — *Coming Soon:* No God

Tales from the World of Adrian's Undead Diary
Unhappy Endings
London Burns
Only the Light We Make
The Shed
An Ill Wind
The Other Side

Short Fiction:
Resurrections: A Short Story Collection

*Don't miss Chris Philbrook's **free** e-Book:*
At Least He's Not On Fire:
A Tour of the Things That Escape My Head

Table of Contents:

Prologue 11

Chapter 1: Zeud 17

Chapter 2: Seamus Drake 25

Chapter 3: Tapper Special Agent Henry Spooner 33

Chapter 4: Laurie Drake 39

Chapter 5: Tapper Special Agent Abraham Fellows . . 45

Chapter 6: Hamza Totah 51

Chapter 7: Zeud 55

Chapter 8: Seamus Drake 61

Chapter 9: Tapper Special Agent Henry Spooner 67

Chapter 10: Zeud 71

Chapter 11: Tapper Special Agent Abraham Fellows . 77

Chapter 12: Seamus Drake 85

Chapter 13: Zeud 93

Chapter 14: Mr. Doyle 99

Chapter 15: Tapper Special Agent Henry Spooner . . . 107

Chapter 16: Laurie Drake 115

Chapter 17: Zeud 123

Chapter 18: Zeud 131

Chapter 19: Hamza Totah 135

Chapter 20: Tapper Special Agent Abraham Fellows . 145

Chapter 21: Tapper Special Agent Henry Spooner . . . 153

Chapter 22: Belyakov. 161

Chapter 23: Fiona Gilmore 167

Chapter 24: Zeud 173

Chapter 25: Tapper Special Agent Abraham Fellows . 181

Chapter 26: Hamza Totah 187

Chapter 27: Fiona Gilmore 197

Chapter 28: Zeud 203

Chapter 29: Seamus Drake 209

Chapter 30: Tapper Special Agent Henry Spooner . . . 217

Chapter 31: Doctor Hillary Tidwell. 225

Chapter 32: Fiona Gilmore 233

Chapter 33: Zeud 243

Chapter 34: Tapper Special Agent Abraham Fellows . 251

Chapter 35: Tapper Special Agent Henry Spooner . . . 259

Chapter 36: Seamus Drake 267

Chapter 37: Fiona Gilmore 273

Chapter 38: Tapper Special Agent Henry Spooner . . . 281

Chapter 39: Zeud 291

Epilogue: Zeud 301

About the Author. 308

This book is dedicated to my small, but amazing contingent of Australian readers and supporters. Jason, Leanne, Keith, and Sarah first and foremost.
May the insane spiders that rule your continent eat you last.

**Patreon Patrons, who rock the Casbah,
and help make it all happen**

Trinity Members
Joni Marcks
Tabitha Burcham
Tim Feely
Tracy Guinther
Trish Volpe

Fire Team Members
Denis LaFortune
Joan MacLeod
Roger Venable
Brandon Kirk
Rich W
Tony Lord
Steve Murphy
Danette Norrid
Russ Berner
Theresa
Roger Patterson
James Spence
Jimmy Evitts
Jenyfer Conaway
James Trudel
Jamie DeAnn
Malinda Gibson
Susie Taylor
Leslie Moss
Stephen Glasgow
Autumn Dempsey

AV Club Members
Sunnita Tardy
Kelly Dingman
Chris Fagan
Colleen O'Malley
Michelle Cooper
Jenny McBride
Jesse Eldridge
Mingo Vidrio
Sean Hammond
Patrick McCurdy
Connie Nealy
Mitzi Marshall
James Black

I'll be your Huckleberry Members

Prologue

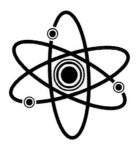

They were never going to be closer to where the spell would work best. Seamus, Laurie, and their followers had to act fast, or they'd be taken away, spirited back to the land of safety.

"Now," Seamus said to his wife after looking out the window of the speeding passenger van.

"Stop the bus, I'm gonna be sick," Laurie said after slipping a tiny piece of Alka-Seltzer under her tongue. She tucked her blonde bangs behind her ear so when the foaming action kicked in, it'd be more visible. She leaned forward in the seat, preparing to present her false illness.

The Japanese bus driver and tour guide both looked over their shoulders at her. The tour guide—an older man, a local, with glasses that had a crack in the corner of one lens, and a smile that said he didn't care about that crack—shook his head in apology.

"No. No," he whispered. "We can't stop here. We are in an area the security forces forbid it. No stopping. Too much radiation."

She felt the foaming action of the tablet bit build in her mouth and she pushed her tongue forward to massage some of it to the front.

"But," she said, then let the foam trickle out to run down her chin.

"She's having a seizure!" Seamus screamed. He stood up beside her and acted like she was about to explode. "Stop! She has to get fresh air! Quick!"

The driver panicked, and disobeyed the guide's wishes. He pulled the large van over without a word. Most of the young, morbidly curious tourists watched on as the young couple had their faked medical emergency. None stepped forward to assist however. They instead chose to gawk, and make more commotion. The driver of their large passenger van hit the lever that opened the door, and the summer heat rushed in to do battle with the vehicle's air conditioning.

"Okay, okay," the guide said, getting to his feet the moment the van stopped moving on the shoulder of the road. "But very quick. Very quick. We will be arrested if we stop too long."

"Are we at risk of radiation poisoning?" a young redheaded woman with an Australian accent asked him as Seamus helped Laurie down the aisle towards the front exit. "If we stop too long?"

"Yes. Yes," the guide said as the young couple walked by. "Check your Geiger counters and measure your exposure. We will be okay, but we cannot linger."

"I just... need a second," Laurie said through labored breaths then pushed more white foam out of her lips on the side the tour guide stood on, and nodded with feigned weakness.

"She just needs a second," Seamus said sternly, hammering the point home with the guide and driver.

The married couple slipped past the end of the aisle and down the small stairwell to exit. He took the first step off the bus onto the Fukushima Prefecture road and turned to help his wife. Once she was down, he adjusted the straps on his backpack. If they had to run... he didn't want to drop all the materials and supplies they needed for the next few days.

"Come, sit on this guardrail, Honey," Seamus said,

helping her to the side of the road where the rail of steel was. He peeked out of the corner of his eye through the windows of the van and made eye contact with several others of his inner circle. He winked as he and his wife got to their first "destination."

Half the passengers remaining in the bus leapt to their feet and bolted. Some went to the back of the large van, hitting the exit plunger and jumping into the road while the other group surged forward, pushing the confused tour guide back into his seat as they went.

"What is happening? What are you doing?" the guide asked, incredulous.

"We came to help," Hamza said, leaning over the driver, using his bulk, shaved head, and Middle Eastern heritage as a collective weapon for intimidation. "We have magic that can erode the radiation. We're the heroes, my friends." He reached to the keys of the van, and turned the vehicle off as the male driver shook, then froze in fear. Hamza took the keys, and with a smile, and a wave, jumped off the bus with them.

"Got the keys?" Seamus asked him as they united in the breakdown lane.

"I do, Seamus. As you instructed," Hamza said, holding them out towards his leader.

"Good. Chuck them down the road as far as you can. Get their phones too, and do the same. Make a friendly suggestion about them forgetting where we got off, too. But hey, don't hurt them."

Without replying Hamza turned and jumped back into the passenger van's side door. He leapt up the stairs and held out his palm.

"What? What do you want now?" the tour guide demanded, his face stern.

"Phones. Just gonna put some space between you and your precious Samsungs," Hamza said.

"No, no," the tour guide said, shaking his head.

"Look," Hamza said, elevating his tone to a fake

snarl, "I'm not gonna break your precious Final Fantasy game machines. I'm just going to slide them down the road a hundred meters or so. Give us a few minutes to start what we came to do."

"How do we know you won't kill us?" the guide asked.

"Because," Hamza said, rolling his fingers in a specific geometric pattern to summon the roiling, impatient magic inside his soul, "we would've killed you and taken your bus this morning." On the last sound of the last syllable Hamza's palm erupted with a foot-tall pillar of white flame. The heat from the fire turned the air inside the small bus arid in an instant, and he smiled as the two Japanese men flinched and called out in fear. "But, my friends, we are not those people. We are here to do good. Now please, let me borrow your phones for a few minutes. Once we're gone, you are welcome to drive up to them, or walk up to them. I leave you with the agency to make that decision. We would also ask that you forgot where we left your presence. We don't want to be stopped by security forces on the eve of fixing the radiation damage here."

Hamza looked down at the flickering, wavering flame, and let his eyes melt into the brightness. He could feel a slow, searing pain on the surface of his eyes, and he relished it. He was creating magic. He was creating something that could affect the real world, made out of the ethereal power than ran just beneath the surface of mundane reality.

The sensation of the pain wasn't something to shy away from; it was something to celebrate.

He let the magical flame in his hand go out and the two men grabbed at their pockets for their phones.

"Thank you, my friends," Hamza said, and departed the bus. Once on the road surface, he underhanded the phones like bowling balls down the center line as far as he could. As the phones slid away, he gesticulated with his hands, wagging them in a wave to conjure telekinetic force. The phones slowed, then his magic hit them, and they jumped forward as if someone had yanked them with a rope. He made them go for a good twenty meters further than they would've without magic, then he stood, happy.

"You're getting quite powerful," Seamus said to him before pulling his glasses off to clean them with his shirt. Hamza could see the pride in his mentor's eyes.

"I am, thanks to you and Laurie. You've learned so much, and then taken the time to pass it on to others. I'm so glad we all met, my friend."

"Crazy, right? And here we are, in Japan, about to save a little piece of the world."

"Let's go," Fiona, the Australian member of their ten-person party said. "More buses will be through soon and we really can die of radiation poisoning."

"Fiona," Laurie said from her seat on the guardrail as if Fiona was a child, "We've the magic to remove the radiation from our bodies as well as the land. That's why we're here. Together, we're going to cure this tainted place for the people who call it home, and when we're done here, we'll go to Chernobyl, then Six Mile Island, then Kazakhstan, and we will make it all clean again. We might as well be angels walking the earth."

"Yeah," Fiona said, looking at her feet, then at the tall and charismatic Seamus with an awkward smile. "I still think we should move. No sense risking anything, yeah?"

"Fiona is right," Seamus said to the group as he smiled at her. He turned to the passenger van and waved to the two frightened men inside. "I'm sorry!" he called out. "But you'll appreciate this much later! We're here to rescue this land!" He turned to his group of spell casters with an even more charismatic smile. "Let's get going everyone. We need to get closer to the center of the reactor if we're going to make this work."

They hooted, they hollered, and then they jumped over the guardrail to sprint to the massive chain link fence that cordoned off the Fukushima nuclear quarantine area.

They were going to fix the world.

Chapter One
Zeud

The Mediterranean sun hung in the sky, dropping its light and warmth down on Zeud, dragon of fire. She enjoyed it in human form, naked, on a reclined patio chair beside an Olympic sized pool filled with gently lapping cerulean waters. The breeze blowing over her Greek island was soft, and it evaporated any sweat from her skin before it accumulated. The only time she did sweat was under the hot sun, in human form. Otherwise, heat and flame caused her no discomfort or damage. Down the cliff beyond the pool she could hear the sea lapping at the shores below, and the tiny pup-pup-pup noises of the feet of two men jogging in the sand.

The closest thing to Heaven I'll ever see. Each and every day should be just like this. Nights as well, she thought with closed eyes. *The warmth of the sun, Kiarohn's cool breeze, loving and loyal friends at my side, and much peace, the world over. All seven dragons have returned to do the good work, and I am happy. It is good to be me, right now. Perhaps more than in a very long time.*

"Something to drink, Lady Zeud?" a familiar voice said nearby.

"Kemala," Zeud said with sublime joy, and opened

her eyes. Approaching her was Kemala, her closest aide and ally. Dark of skin, born in Indonesia, the tiny woman was strikingly beautiful with bright blue eyes, and a radiant smile. She was heading towards Zeud from the massive single-floor mansion the dragon owned on the private island.

"Lady Zeud," the woman said with love in her eyes. "I've made tea, and your favorite; ouzo, arrived on the boat last night."

"Ouzo then," the dragon said. "You know me so well. And thank you. Are the kitchen staff working on lunch? The boys will be starving when they get back from their run."

"Yes, Lady Zeud, the chefs are hard at work. The younger man's appetite has grown considerably since your arrival here on the island however. I had to dispatch the yacht to procure more food from the mainland this morning. He especially enjoys something called, 'Hot Pockets.' He seems to eat a package of them between most meals. The locals must be most pleased with our current stay with all you're spending."

"Ah, yes. Abe is a growing boy, eating away some feelings he's been forced to experience. This is a good sign. Henry came here to help Abe, and it seems to be working. Abe wasn't eating at all last month, and now look at him. As far as the locals are concerned; excellent. Greece is suffering economically, and I am awash in human wealth. Allow me to funnel much of it back into their pockets. I have all I need after all."

"You are very generous. And Abe does seem much better," Kamala agreed. "He has started to take his fiancé's phone calls. Have you done magic to help him?"

"I have no skill to do such things, beyond my radiant personality. And poor Alexis," Zeud said. "Having a damaged spouse must be traumatic. To see them suffer, and then to suffer as a result... And to accept that their going away for a few months to heal is necessary? Awful for a human in a relationship. I fear their love might not be enough to carry them through this."

"With all the lovers you've had over your lifetime, Lady Zeud, I would imagine you would be no stranger to awful experiences."

"Yes, well... It is a unique challenge to live forever, and to love things that do not," Zeud said before running her hands across her warm skin. *Life is about endurance. No matter the species. I was fortunate enough to be born as one of Earth's dragons and thus ever-living. A gift, and a curse.*

"I would not wish for it," Kemala sighed. "I want only a long and healthy life, once. There is too much wonder about what comes next for me."

"I see, my dear. I'm happy to see you are not in a hurry to get to the end of this story, to find out what comes after. You are dear to me."

"And you keep your secrets about what comes after, Lady Zeud. I still say you know what comes after death. You are a dragon, after all. What secrets could you not have learned in all this world's time?"

"Many, Kemala. Many," the redheaded woman said, then stood up. She felt the fine fabric cling to her naked back. She had sweat. "But not all of them. Too many souls on this world, each with their own way to live, each with their own secrets to keep. I'm sure you keep secrets from me. We all keep them. What we hide from shame or greed, or whatever it be, keeps us warm at night."

"Ha, yes they do. I'll fetch a tray of ouzos for you and the men. They are returning soon?"

Zeud drew her attention away from Kemala and tuned her powerful ears into the distance. Over the sound of the rolling surf, she could hear Abe and Spoon talking as they ran. The sound of their feet hitting sand grew the tiniest bit louder as she listened. They were heading back.

"They'll be at the stairs to the cliff in a minute."

"Perfect. I'll return with your beverages, and some

light snacks."

"We wouldn't want to ruin their lunches, after all," the dragon quipped.

"Just one package of Hot Pockets. If there is nothing else....?"

"Perfect as always, my dear. I appreciate your presence," Zeud said, and walked over to the pool's edge to dip her toes in.

Kemala nodded in a half-bow, and walked back to the massive home perched on the cliff of the Greek island.

I do love her. A gift to this world, that one. Zeud's toes dipped into the water, and the refreshing coolness slipped between her toes. Well, might as well take a short swim before they get here. Abe gets uncomfortable when I'm naked in front of Henry.

Zeud smiled again, leaned forward, and plunged into the pool.

*****

"When do you go back to active duty?" Zeud asked Henry. She put a small piece of hard bread covered in olive tapenade in her mouth and chewed. The bright, vinegary food tasted delicious. *It's always better when it's eaten where it's from.*

"Well, Z, two more weeks before Tapper wants me back. I'm checking in at their new Istanbul location. Opens the week after I get there," the agent in swim trunks said. Drops of water fell off the shorts to the stone patio below, and trickles ran down his temples to his chest from his dark, short hair. He used a small white towel to mop the moisture up. "Director Fisher wants me to oversee the first few weeks of their operations. Help them get going."

"That's terrific," Zeud said. "What of you, Abe? Any thought about what's next for you?"

He shifted in his patio seat and started to reply, but

didn't. He shrugged.

"Be honest, man," Henry said to him. "No one is asking you to make a decision."

"Yeah but I need to make one," Abe said to his friend. "Spoon, you've been good to me since Boston. Too good. Helped me out of a rough spot there, then holding my hand as I went through Quantico, and starting out as a Tapper agent, and now. Now you're holding my hand again while I grab hold of my balls and come back to reality." He took off his glasses and rubbed the bridge of his nose.

"Dude," Spoon said and leaned forward to scoop the same tapenade onto the same bread, "No one deserves to be the hero all the time. It's too much heavy lifting to do alone. And believe me, after all the shit that went down in London, and on the Isle of Lundy, you don't *need* the help I'm giving you, you *deserve* it. Know the difference."

"So, pep talk aside," Zeud said, "You don't owe me an answer, Abe. I'm just trying to support you."

Abe smiled; the first smile she'd seen come out of the man that didn't originate from an inappropriate joke out of Henry. "You are doing so much for me. This island is perfect. It's quiet, there's no media, the sun shines all the time, the food is great, and all of your staff are insanely helpful and kind. It's like being on respite."

"That's what it is meant to be for right now," Zeud said. "For as long as you need it, you are welcome here. Leave and return as you see fit. Also, Alexis is welcome too. How is she?"

"She's... you know," Abe muttered.

"I don't actually," Zeud said to him. "That's why I asked about her. Are you not okay talking about her?"

"No," he said. "It's just that, you know, she's working a lot, can't get away to speak of. She's not happy, and I'm not making it any better being here. I mean, that's part of it."

"You being here?" Spoon clarified.

"Yeah. After my trip to England, I wasn't back in America that long before coming here. We haven't really seen each other in… months."

"Book a trip to see her?" Zeud offered. "I'll gladly cover the cost. I'll reimburse her salary if needed. My bank accounts are very old, and very deep."

"I bet they are. How long have you been collecting interest?"

"Since the idea of money was invented. I find it important to have a foothold in the society of the species of the day."

"Species of the day? That's creepy. And uh, yeah, maybe," Abe said, then a gradual smile slipped out. "Yeah let's have her take a few days off. I'll call her later this afternoon after she wakes up and we'll figure out when and where she can meet up. Maybe London—" his face lost the smile when he said the name of the city. "Maybe not London. Maybe like, maybe Portugal. Or um, Berlin or something."

"Whatever you like. We shall let no ocean of Fyelrath's stand between the love you share," the dragon of fire and passion said with glee. "Speak to her, and inform Kemala of whatever you need arranged. Money, plane tickets, security, whatever you need. She will see to it all the details are taken care of."

"That's my lady," Spoon said, and leaned over to give the dragon a kiss. She leaned in to match, and Abe smiled again.

"Calm down you two. You're creeping me out," Abe said and then laughed.

"My island, my rules. Now, if you'll excuse me, I love taking to the sky for a good fly after a swim and a meal. Let the sun warm my scales."

Spoon and Abe watched as the woman stood and disrobed without modesty until all her skin was exposed. She turned, and ran around the pool towards the cliff.

She started her shift into dragon-form ten feet short of

the edge, and dove off into the open air above the shore.

Her limbs snapped outward; her arms growing in length and thickness as her legs did the same. From her back two massive crimson wings—not membranous like a bat's, but feathered, like the mythical phoenix—grew, and caught the wind buffeting upward from the cliff. Her neck lengthened and her head grew. Her extending mouth filled with massive white fangs, and deep in her scale-covered belly, the fire that she was ignited.

Zeud, dragon of flame and heat, fastest, brightest, and most incendiary of all her kind, flapped her wings and rocketed into the sky with glee over the ocean. In the air as she flew, tiny specks of ash rained down from the sky.

Chapter Two
Seamus Drake

"Just a little closer," Seamus said as he stopped at the corner of a small convenience store in what had been suburban Fukushima Japan. The pounding heat and humidity of the Japanese August pulled the moisture from him as if he were being squeezed like a sponge.

Abandoned in the wake of the tsunami, and then the reactor meltdown, the city had become a debris-ridden, poisonous graveyard. The silence choked all semblance of life from the world; even the birds had left. Maybe they were trying to escape the heat.

"We're at 1.9," Laurie said to him after consulting her Geiger counter. "We should be at 2.0 microsieverts before we set up the ritual. That'll be high enough for the magic to take hold. I think."

Behind Laurie in the wood-strewn alley stood the other six people in their posse of wizards, witches, shamans and spell casters. A rogue's gallery of faces from around the world had come together under Seamus' flag at his family's ranch in Idaho to learn stronger magic, and try to fix some of the many things that were wrong with the world.

Fixing Fukushima would be their first true miracle.

Fiona coughed once, then twice, then several more times before doubling over, and putting a palm against the side of the empty store. Hamza stepped to her side and offered a kind hand on the back.

"Are you ok?" he asked her.

"No, I'm not. The purification spell… I don't think it cleared me of the radiation earlier. My lungs are on fire," Fiona said before another coughing fit took her body over.

He looked at her pallor, and limp limbs. *She does seem ill,* Seamus thought. "Okay, we're close enough. Let's find a place of the earth and set up the ritual."

"That field that we thought would work as a second option should be two streets over. Near the school?" Laurie said.

"Yeah, yeah. That'll work well enough," Seamus said, nodding. "Fiona," Seamus added with a warm smile, "Are you able to make it there, and then do the spell with us? We can wait if you need time."

"I," Fiona started, but paused when she saw Seamus' smile, "I think so, yes. Let's get it done."

"Great. Hamza, please give her all the help she needs. Give her another purification spell. Everyone else, we need to move fast before they get to us. By now the van has reported us as having run off, and the security forces will be responding."

"Hopefully our following the road before cutting inland will mislead them long enough," Laurie said. "And remember. If we get arrested after, it doesn't matter. We're saving hundreds of thousands of lives today. Let's go everyone. Hamza, Fiona, catch up after you're done with the spell."

"Yes Mrs. Drake," Hamza said with a small nod of his bald head.

Seamus checked both directions for cars or pedestrians, and the sky for helicopters before leading the group out into the street. It wouldn't do to be caught by some overzealous, ignorant police officers so close to getting their ritual up and running.

I can't believe we're so close to saving so many lives.

*****

Seven stones, all a perfect seven pounds, one each to match the ring of stones in the German forest. One each to match the dragons of Earth, and one each for the continents of the world they sought to rescue from atomic ruin.

Seamus and Laurie designed the spell to draw upon the eternal energy of the dragons alongside the raw primordial power that the baby dragon Astrid poured into the world. Once her energy flowed, it belonged to aether—the air, the water, the earth and fire—and they could harvest it, cultivate it, and turn it into whatever it was they pleased.

And it pleased Laurie and Seamus to wield great magics that made the world a better place for all.

"I am so glad that we met each and every one of you," Seamus began in the small park, overgrown by tall grasses. "For without so many souls carved from the same diamonds made of space dust, we would not be here in Fukushima, collecting our power as one, and repairing the damage caused by man."

"It gives me great honor, Seamus," Hamza said from his place between Laurie and Fiona. "Let our unity teach the world how to live in a better way!"

"You're so right," Laurie said to him. "We are the future. We are the physical embodiment of unselfishness. Here we are, away from our families, away from safety, on the fringe of real, true, lasting danger, doing it all to give land and health back to the people it was taken from. This is what love is," she said with a jubilant smile. "This is the way of the real, true future."

"Well said, my love," Seamus said. He ignored Fiona

flinching. "Now, as we've planned and practiced, let us join hands to complete the circle and begin our spell."

They did as he bid them to, taking one another's hands into their own. With each grasp, with each press of warm palm to warm palm, with each exchange of frightened, excited expressions, the fledgling wielders of magic felt their collective power grow. The energy was infectious; crackling electricity in the air that danced invisibly between them, triggering pulsating heartbeats, ecstatic smiles, and endless euphoria.

In just seconds, the entire gathered group had their eyes closed, and their bodies swayed back and forth in gleeful, wordless unison.

"Now, speak the words of the spell in your language of power to the stones you stand beside. Call upon the aether. Call upon the quintessence, call upon the dragons and Earth, call upon it all, and let us set this land free of the curse we beset upon it," Seamus said.

Seamus began the magical intonations as those arrayed in the circle did the same.

"It is I, Seamus Drake, calling out to the magic of Astrid, the magic of Earth, and the celestial energies of the universe wide," he began. With each word he spoke —and each word his fellows spoke in their own native tongues—Seamus felt the power of their collective spell grow. "I beg of you a dram of your power. A single dose of purity to empower me, and my family in this circle we have made here in Fukushima Japan."

He let his words pour forth into the universe, and listened with his inner mind's ear as the invisible winds of magic picked up around them. He felt them ruffle his pant legs, and shirt sleeves, and his dirty blonde hair. Bereft of heat, or warmth, the winds were a physical and emotional sensation that defied natural words; only magical ones could describe it.

Beside him Seamus could sense that his people were in the same state of transcendence. Like him, their bodies swayed back and forth — hands clasped — and their voices issued forth a steady stream of the same message he said. That they each spoke different languages gave their spell even more power. They were united in their differences, and that was essential for the spell's success.

"Now, sanctify the stones," Seamus said.

At the center of their group, naked in every way stood Hamza. At his feet was a white and blue porcelain vase filled with water they had just harvested from glaciers in Greenland. Ancient water; trapped below for thousands of years, older than human civilization, older than human pollution; perfect for cleansing the stones. The vase was no recent thing either; it had been stolen by the group from a museum in Turkey, and was also thousands of years old.

Hamza began to chant in Persian. Low in tone, slow in its pacing, the words matched his deliberate steps as he carried the vase to each of the stones in the circle. Composed of the same materials as the ancient, pre-human stones in the German forest, they were a representation of the dragons, and thus, representations of the elements that they were the embodiments of. Tokens of Earth's building blocks.

They were the perfect vessels to purify, then use to absorb the destructive radiation permeating the world here.

Hamza took his handled vase and poured a precise amount of water, measured by the speed and duration of his pour. As he did, he punctuated his actions with another, new mantra in his native tongue. Seamus knew the words were declarations of clear intent; a wish for the stones to receive the clean water, and a wish for them to be as pure as what ran down their sides.

As the rest of the group watched on, each chanting their own repetitive spell-words, the power of their collective magic grew. The ethereal winds picked up speed, blowing their hair and clothes even more furiously, though the world around them stayed still; leaves lay where they were, grass stood tall and straight, and papers continued to rot in the open air.

The storm of magic disturbed only the magicians, and the radiation it drained from the air, soil and water.

Hamza poured the water atop another stone, his naked body unaffected by the growing maelstrom.

Three purified stones became five, and as the seventh stone took the final drops of old, frozen water, the clouds in the sky above evaporated, leaving the blue sky revealed. The near to full moon hung in the great distance, watching their acts without emotion.

"And so it shall be, so we shall clean, so the world shall persevere. Allow us to funnel this darkness through our power, and into these receptacles so that they may removed from this place, and sent away to the void for all time," Seamus said.

The wind stopped, the gathered wielders of magic simultaneously ceased their chanting and the movement of their bodies. Stillness remained in the small park they'd chosen to do their spell in.

From all sides along the visible horizon between the trees and buildings a white-yellow sunrise appeared. Dimmer than the true sun above it cast a growing heat.

But not heat... something else. Something the physical body couldn't sense. Nearby, where the group had piled their clothes, their radiation-sensitive Geiger counters turned on of their own accord and started to tick, faster and faster. Faster and faster until their tiny needles were buried well beyond the point of danger, shaking like an earthquake rattled them to their electronic cores.

The bodies of the men and women involved in the ritual did the same. They shook, roiled and quaked as the stones at their feet, between their bodies absorbed the encroaching tide of radiation. It funneled amongst them like an invisible river of pure caustic — almost sentient —

energy, licking at them as if it were flames made material.

I have never felt more powerful, Seamus thought as the horizon's glow dimmed, and the tide of radiation soaked into the stones. *I have never felt better about being born.*

Seamus opened his eyes, and his exultation disappeared.

Instead of seven glowing stones, he had a group of glowing friends.

Irradiated, and somehow… infected by a twisted side-effect of their spell, they each had become luminous, their skin alight with white and yellow energy. Those with open eyes issued forth spikes of angry flame that flickered as they looked back and forth at the people they stood hand in hand with. Fear, anger, and… thrill were on their faces.

Seamus looked down at his own luminescent body, then to his wife Laurie at his side. She'd already turned her frightened gaze to him. Her eyes burned like white coals, casting up ribbons of magical, irradiated flame.

"You are so beautiful," Seamus said, and his voice vibrated the ground at their feet.

Then the stones at their feet exploded, and many of them died.

But some of them… became more.

Chapter Three
Tapper Special Agent Henry "Spoon" Spooner

Zeud lie on her back beside him under the red silk sheets in the plush bed at the center of the expansive bedroom they shared in the palace she owned on her Greek island. She slept a deep sleep, free of worries and concerns.

Spoon sat on the side of the bed, free from the concern of trying to sleep.

In hands worn from too many years of rough living he held his Tapper issued phone, and a paper letter from Tapper's leader; Director Fisher. Spoon read the letter from his boss in the dim light of the dragon's opulent, ruby colored bedroom. After finishing reading the letter for the tenth time that early morning, he sighed for the tenth time, and hung his head low.

The tired agent lifted his head, and started the eleventh reading of the letter, but paused when he felt a warm, gentle hand on his bare back.

"Read it out loud. Perhaps the words will trouble you less when you share them with me," Zeud whispered.

He smiled. "Fisher wants me to leave the field and take over managing special agent operations back in New Hampshire. I'd be managing more of the selection, training, equipment, and big-picture stuff of it all. It'd be a big raise too."

"What would you spend more money on? Guns? Body armor? Your job gives you everything you'd spend money on," she sighed.

"That's the truth. I guess the thrill comes from being able to mold the future of the agency? Teach kids to do the job better?"

"That sounds boring," the dragon said with her own sigh. She rolled onto her back, pulling the sheets that covered her off.

Spoon paused to look at the curves of her body, and how her red hair curled against the red pillowcase as if she'd been staged for a photo shoot. *She's perfect.* "I am afraid I'll get bored. I'm afraid I'm not the leader Fisher thinks I am."

"Well my dear, you are a leader unlike the vast majority of people who claim to be leaders. Men and women have followed your example for your entire life, am I right?"

"I guess. But not like a boss. Team captains earn their leadership positions by playing well. In the airborne people follow you because of your rank. They have to listen," Spoon said with a laugh.

"No, they don't. And I am sure that you can list a hundred stories in the military of when you, or someone close to you ignored a commanding officer because they were a giant pile of accidentally promoted shit," she said, adding her own little laugh. "Or perhaps promoted in great error, but on purpose."

"You got a point there," Spoon conceded. "Are you

saying I should take the job? Leave this lifestyle of danger and romance behind me? Trade it in for babysitting kids who think they're the Special Forces version of Harry Potter?"

"I would never, ever tell you what to do," the dragon said, locking eyes with Spoon. "I would never presume to tell any living creature I care for how to live their lives. I would counsel you to follow your passion. Long term, or short term, discover what you truly want, and pursue that dream with every ounce of your being. I will want you in my life no matter what you choose."

"You have a way of being inspiring, and uplifting while showing no effort in the process, you know that right?"

"Because despite my appearance to the contrary... I have been at this 'living thing' for more than a few trips around the sun," she cooed. "And I think it has something to do with being a dragon. We inspire via our presence whether we want to, or not. For you... it's a conscious decision."

Spoon leaned in and kissed her on the lips. *She's always so soft, and warm. Always warm. I love that about her. It is a little sketchy she essentially has her own little cult though. That's weird.* He broke the kiss and sat back up on the side of the bed. He looked at the cell phone in his hand as the taste of her faded from his lips. She rolled away and over to her side, ending her part in Spoon's late night emotional debacle.

I don't know where this is going, and I don't know if I care how it ends, but I'm glad for tonight, and I'm glad for tomorrow, he thought as he looked over his shoulder at her. *Sleeping with the enemy is one thing, but sleeping with a dragon...? Jesus, what has my life become?* He looked at her again. *It became awesome.*

I fly around the world working for a non-profit NGA with global jurisdiction that's owned by another dragon.

I hunt monsters; real monsters. I rescue families, and I do it all wearing a leather bomber jacket that's bulletproof, fireproof, resistant to magic, while bucking out .45 slugs from an enchanted Sig Sauer pistol. Shit, I just spent a month in Mexico fighting the cartels that crossed tunnels with a massive goblin burrow and teamed up. I tackled drug-running goblins.

That sounded cooler on paper, than when I actually think about that. Drug running goblins isn't the same as daemons from across the Veil.

Every ten year old boy in the world wants to be me and half the girls do too.

He looked over his shoulder once more at the dragon. Her human body's chest rose and fall with the gentle pace of good sleep. Spoon looked down at the letter with the official offer from Director Fisher and he shook his head.

"And she's so right about the money thing. I haven't spent money on anything since Tapper hired me. Not today boss. Not yet," he whispered to his phone.

Spoon got to his feet, and tapped the button on his phone to call the Director's office. He had to give Fisher the bad news.

Spoon slept well after that.

*****

"Wake up," a man's voice said to Spoon.

Why are you excited? No, I'm not getting up.

"Spoon, wake up. Some weird shit is going down," the same male voice said. "You gotta see it."

Don't you have somewhere else to be? Whoever you are?

"Spoon, dude. Wake up and watch the news," the voice said again, and a blinding bolt of light shot across his closed eyelids.

"FUCK OFF," Spoon barked as he tossed the red sheet off his body and sat up. He opened his eyes but saw nothing in the bright light for several seconds. He recognized the laugh that came from the double French doors leading to the balcony on the side of the massive bedroom he was in. "Abe, I swear to God I'll shove every single one of your Magic decks straight up your ass if you don't close that curtain."

"Don't flirt with me," Abe shot back. "No but really the news is crazy. There was a massive explosion inside the irradiated area in Fukushima, and then all of a sudden, the Geiger counters there zeroed out. The boom has the markings of magic all over it. I woke up when it happened."

What? "What does that mean?" He rubbed his eyes as Abe pulled the curtains mostly shut.

"It means something big, loud, and magical happened in Japan, and then all of a sudden; Boom. Radiation gone. Someone, somehow, managed to do something to eradicate all the contamination there using magic," Abe said, ecstatic.

"This is the most excited I think I've ever seen you."

"You should see me at a big Magic tournament. Not only do I make top eight on the regular, I'm a celebrity when people find out I can actually cast spells. Living the dream if you can forget about the cosmic horror sleeping under the Isle of Lundy."

"You need to get out. Some fresh air would do you good."

"Going to Magic tournaments is getting out. No fresh air to be had at most tourneys though. Butt crack is an issue. Don't be so angry because I woke you up. And get dressed. I guarantee you Tapper is going to be called in to help with this somehow. I want to be part of that if it happens. I'm gonna email Director Fisher and see if he can get me on a plane."

"What about Alexis?"

"What about her?"

"Weren't you going to try and spend a few days with her in Portugal or something? You ditching her?"

"Shit," Abe said, deflating. "I did. I don't want to miss

out on that."

"Well, part of being an adult is correctly organizing your priorities, Abe. I suggest you make your fiancé a priority."

"You're starting to sound like Mr. Doyle. And I will. I'm still writing Fisher though. This is... this is the closest thing to a miracle I think we've ever seen."

"A hot shower after three weeks fighting the Taliban in the mountains of Afghanistan is the closest thing to a miracle there is," Spoon said. *I can still feel that water on my skin. So good. Soap porn.*

"You would know. Alright, cool. Look at the news, man. We're gonna be a part of this, I promise you," the younger Tapper agent said as he strode across the room, electrified by his excitement.

"Hey, Abe."

He stopped. "Yeah?"

"Does this mean you're feeling better? You back in the game?"

Abe grinned ear to ear and nodded. "Put me in, coach." He opened the double mahogany door to the dragon's bedroom and left. It shut with a quiet click on his heels.

"Fuck yeah. My man."

Chapter Four
Laurie Drake

Four days, four souls remained. One day for each of the survivors of the ritual had passed. Her husband Seamus, Fiona, Hamza, and of course, her.

Four... scarred souls.

Possibly no longer human souls. Human enough to bury what remained of their fallen friends in the field near the small convenience store, however.

Now, they hid. Having fled on foot for miles to get away from the site of their ritual—and the resulting explosion—they found a building with a small warehouse filled with food attached. Abandoned because of the contamination, the packaged food inside the building was keeping them alive and fed. They didn't worry about getting sick from the food. What had happened to them could do no damage they explosion hadn't.

Sleeping on pallets covered in scrounged mattresses wasn't the best solution for rest, but they didn't seem to need much of that anymore....

"What now, my friends?" Hamza asked as he paced from one dock door to the next. "The helicopters still fly overhead, and we hear more and more vehicles returning each day. We should step into the world as heroes, as we are."

"He's right," Laurie said to Seamus. "We come out into the public eye, and take credit for what we've done. I don't understand why after four days we're still hiding here, like criminals on the run."

Seamus watched her as she finished, then looked at Hamza and Fiona. He seemed to examine each of them for how they swayed on the idea of going public. Hamza's and Laurie's positions were evident, but Fiona avoided eye contact with him, instead turning her attention to a pallet of prepared fish snacks sealed in plastic wrap.

"Maybe because we're criminals?" Seamus finally said.

"Two of us are for it," Laurie said. "I'm sick of hiding. I'd like a hot meal, and running water. I don't care about taking credit. I just care about getting back home so we can figure out what's next. See what's wrong with us, and get it fixed by... someone?"

"Who is gonna fix us? What hospital will take us? I'll tell you what's next, Laurie," Seamus said with honey-coated words. "And I'll even tell you why."

"Yes my friend," Hamza said. "It is time to lead us once more." He slapped his hands together and rubbed them with eagerness.

"You all... feel different now, right?" Seamus began. "Like... warmer? Maybe a bit more energetic? A nervous energy, right? I'm not wrong. Just take a second to feel inside you. Fiona, how do you feel? Tell me, physically, how is your body?"

She turned her eyes back to Seamus and blinked several times as she did what he asked. "I guess I feel great," she said, then smiled. "Scared, sort of hungry, but on the inside, I do feel warmer like you said. Kinda steaming, actually."

"Exactly. Hamza? The way you've been pacing, and

doing push-ups and chin-ups tells me you have far, far more energy than you've said aloud. Search yourself. Feel what's within. Tell me, friend," Seamus said, using Hamza's habit of speech, "tell me about the fire raging inside your chest right now."

Hamza stopped pacing and dropped his chin to his chest. Laurie watched as the man's chest inflated and deflated as he took deep, powerful breaths. The pace of the breathing picked up in the silent warehouse as the man searched inside his presence for the fire Seamus told him to find. Hamza snapped his head up, and he wore a massive, shocked grin.

"My friend, I sense it. I feel great fire within. A new fire." He placed both palms on his chest and seemed to feel it with his fingers. He looked down, then back up at Laurie. "Can you not feel it too?"

You're both crazy. "I feel jittery, like I've been eating crap junk food for four days after watching most of my best friends die in a giant magical explosion. I'm more sad than anything."

"Laurie," Seamus said as he stood. "I haven't been able to sleep."

"I know. You get off our mattress every night and disappear for hours on end. It sucks. Makes me feel damn alone when I don't want to."

"This fire... the fire I'm talking about," he said, patting his chest the same way Hamza did, "It keeps me up at night. Like a furnace that will never shut off. Never cool down. Never give me a break."

"You sound a little off, my love," Laurie said. "I love you, dearly, but this sounds unwell. We need to go home. We need to get back to a centered place where we can recuperate."

"Laurie," he said with that same sickening, charming tone he used when he needed something done by someone else, "I know this sounds crazy in a week of beyond the beyond cray-cray, but I do need you to take this seriously." He stepped closer to where she sat on the mattress side. "Close your eyes. Envision your inner-space. Turn on the part of you that can sense the heat, and believe in yourself. It's that easy."

You're a condescending idiot, and somehow I still love you. "Okay. Fine." She closed her eyes and obliged him. Laurie took a deep breath and imagined what her insides would look like if she were sitting there with her skin peeled off. Morbid as it may be, the gross physical vision helped her remain detached from the idea that her husband was leading her on a wild goose chase about her own body.

Laurie peeled away the muscles like layers of red clay until her ivory-white ribcage was displayed. Under the bone in the spaces between she saw her lungs inflating and deflating in concert with her actual breath, and somehow, in their movement she also saw the pulsating beat of her heart.

"Do you see it?" Seamus asked her in the dark beyond her closed eyes. "Can you feel it?"

"Not yet."

"Keep looking."

"I will," she replied and did so.

Laurie imagined a seam opening down her sternum that allowed her ribs to split in two like the shell of a clam, or a cracked walnut.

Her vision halted as an intense burst of pink-yellow light erupted from behind the parting bone, setting free an invisible vibration on a magical level that shook the whole building and caused the other three people in the room to wobble on unsteady feet.

The energy that leaped out wasn't expected, and she gasped. Her eyes stayed fused shut so she could remain in the vision with the sun inside her body.

"You found it," Seamus said.

He's smiling, I know it. "Yes. What… what is it?"

"When I sneak away at night, I'm experimenting with

using it. It's... well, I think it's radioactive magic, and I think we each have a ton of it inside ourselves."

She abandoned the vision and looked at him. In her breast she felt the heat he'd spoken of remain. Now, it seemed like she'd never be able to unfeel it, or ignore it.

"The purified stones we used... they failed in the ritual. Maybe they weren't big enough, or clean enough, or they had flaws that we didn't see, but they didn't work as receptacles for the radiation. I don't know why, but the last thing I remember seeing was the seven stones exploding. You know they should've remained for proper disposal. That was the second half of the ritual we had to work on so hard. But here we are; broken stones, broken lives, and up until now... broken spirits. But you know what, we did it. And instead of having to dispose of seven irradiated stones filled with waste energy, we *absorbed that energy.* Turned that radiation into concentrated power using magic," Seamus said.

Does that mean? Laurie slid off the mattress and strode over to the pile of shredded fabric that were the remains of the backpacks that belonged to her and Seamus. They were torn up and mostly destroyed in the explosion. She started rifling through the ripped pouches, looking for something.

"What?" Seamus asked her.

"I need a Geiger counter. Anyone? Where the hell are ours?"

"I ran them dead," Seamus explained. "Batteries are gone."

"Take mine," Fiona whispered, extending her small Geiger counter in her frail-seeming hand.

Laurie jumped up and took the device from the younger girl's outstretched hand. She also noticed when Fiona looked to Seamus for approval. She turned Fiona's reader on and held it against her own chest.

Nothing. Normal amounts of radiation.

"There's no radiation inside us," Laurie said,

confused. "Shouldn't this thing be going crazy?"

"It's in there," Seamus said. "Envision it, and let a little out."

Laurie did that. She closed her eyes for a moment and imagined that great flash of sunlight bursting from inside her chest.

The reaction from the Geiger counter was instantaneous, and frenetic. It clicked like a playing card in the spoke of a ten year old's speeding bike, and beeped a cascade of alarms. It did this until Laurie stopped her vision of the flame within. The digital readout dropped fast to just an elevated level, and then trickled to normal.

"What the hell...?" she muttered.

"We are batteries of magical radiation. Sunfire," Seamus said, proud. "Children of the Atom. Prophets of a new energy. Creators of the new world, if we master the power inside us." He held his hand aloft, fingers together and pointed at the ceiling. He exhaled a measured breath and his hand erupted into a pillar of white-hot fire. In Laurie's hand Fiona's Geiger counter went crazy once more.

"We are Ifrit," Hamza said. "Men of fire. Men and women of fire," Hamza corrected himself, looking at Laurie and Fiona.

"What's an Ifrit?" Fiona asked.

"Like... demons made of fire," he explained. "Old stories in the Qu'ran. But we are not demons. We are angels. Heroes made of holy flame."

"And we cannot be made into weapons," Seamus said. "And we cannot let them know what we can do. Because if we've learned anything about the people of this world... it's that they can't handle something they don't understand, and there's no way they'll understand what we've become. Do you think they'll let four people filled with all the radiation from an exploded nuclear reactor just walk free amongst the public?"

Maybe he's right.

Chapter Five

Tapper Special Agent Abraham "Abe" Fellows

Abe and Spoon sat in two wide leather seats in the plane. They were on opposite sides of an equally wide aisle near the cockpit. Both had a window view of the tarmac sliding by faster and faster.

"I told you," Abe said to Spoon as the private jet thundered down the runway. "I told you we'd get sent to Japan."

"We aren't getting 'sent' to Japan," the tired agent said. "You volunteered yourself to Fisher, and he sent your ass because you tricked him into thinking you were fucking Conan or something. And, I might add, he's sending me along with your ass at the crack of dawn because I'm the hero of this story."

"Conan is badass, this is true. I'm not sure about the hero thing though. I think my journey is far more appropriate. Fallen hero, internal turmoil, perseverance, ability to overcome. I've got the plucky sense of humor, clean good looks, and the hot fiancé too."

"You pretty much just described me," Spoon replied. "Be honest about that. And, I might add, we're riding in the private jet owned by my *dragon* girlfriend. Which by, the way, she is letting us use for free, for Tapper business, because she's fucking amazing."

Spoon laughed as the plane tilted back and got elevation. The pilot had the plane at a forty-five degree angle in seconds, and they were powering upward into the Greek clouds and above as Athens disappeared below.

"Speaking of which, where is your girlfriend?"

"Cockpit," Spoon explained. "She's learning to fly a plane."

"A dragon is learning to fly a plane? What's the logic in that?"

"Z says she often flies at a hundred and fifty miles an hour, give or take. Faster if she pushes herself, but it can be taxing for long trips. This plane can fly at five hundred miles an hour, give or take. If she wants to fly to Japan, she can do it the slow way flapping her wings for a few days straight, or sitting on her ass in a leather seat while jet fuel gets the job done."

"Ahh, I see. That does make a remarkable amount of sense."

The plane leveled off at what might've been their cruising altitude, and the two men undid their seat belts. Abe leaned over and watched the Mediterranean below as they sped southeast towards their first refueling stop. The long flight had them headed to Dubai first.

"I've never been to Dubai," Abe said. "I hear it's hot."

"Well, you're not gonna find out when we get there," Spoon said back to him. "All we're doing is getting gas and taking back off again. They won't even let you out of the plane onto the tarmac."

"What about with our Tapper IDs? Can't we just

trump their rules?"

Spoon shrugged and twisted the cap off a tiny bottle of Jack Daniels. "If it's not official business, we really ought not to flex that kind of muscle. Foreign governments are notorious for freaking out over that shit. Dubai isn't considered terribly progressive, either."

"Bummer." *Man, I really wanted to see Dubai. It's so dry there. Unlikely some enormous, cosmic horror resides beneath the sands. Unlikely, but possible. Anything's possible. Shit. What if there was something beneath the sands?*

"Just let it go," Spoon said before downing the bottle in one go. "I need to talk her into letting me smoke on the plane. I mean, dragon of fire is basically the dragon of smoke, right? You'd think she wouldn't mind me lighting up one cigarette in the lavatory, right?"

"Her plane, her rules," Abe said. *Dragon's rules. The only rules that really matter on this world.*

"So what's the plan on the ground? Fisher says I'm the ranking agent, but to give you free reign. So, king of mine, how shall you reign?"

"We land, check in with the local authorities to see what's changed since we took off, then we touch base with Tokyo's Tapper agency. We grab one of their black SUVs—because we're ballers, and that's how we roll—and then we head to Fukushima blasting dubstep out the windows."

"That's about a three hour drive," Spoon said as the plane banked for a gentle turn. "I'm sure it'd be easier to have them meet us at a smaller airport near the quarantine zone."

"Maybe. I guess I just thought we'd be better off driving a truck up."

"You think we need an armored SUV to encounter people who helped removed radiation from a disaster area?"

"What if it was a giant monster that eats radiation for dinner and special agents for dessert?"

"I guess that could be, sure," Spoon said before tossing the empty nip bottle with solid basketball mechanics into the tiny wastebasket at the front of the cabin fifteen feet away.

"Imagine what that monster would shit?" Abe said with a laugh. "I'd give it diarrhea. For sure."

"You call Alexis yet? We bugged out the island pretty fast. You find time?"

Fuck. "I haven't yet. She knows we're on the move. I'll use the satellite phone in a few minutes. I'm thirsty." He laughed again to hide the growing spike of shame and picked up his empty plastic cup. "Vocare potum," he said in a gravelly tone with magic on the mind. The cup bubbled up with his favorite yellow, carbonated drink as he looked at it, and when the level of liquid reached the lip, he let the sustained spell cease. The magic faded like the steam from someone's breath in the winter. He sipped the evoked Red Bull and pretended like everything was okay. His heart raced in his chest like an engine off its moorings.

"Is your magical Red Bull any easier on your digestion than the real deal?"

"I doubt it. My understanding of the spell is that you get what you expect. I expect Red Bull to be bad for me, so... I create Red Bull that's probably not the best thing to drink."

"Why not make a... kale smoothie or something? Fruit juice, or just frigging water?"

"I like myself? I enjoy eating and drinking tasty things."

"You're also a caffeine addict."

"Says the guy that's trying to talk his girlfriend into letting him fire up a butt in her airplane's pisser," Abe shot back with a grin. "We have our vices."

"Ain't that the truth. Can you make a decent sized whiskey with that spell of yours? These nip bottles aren't gonna last me until Dubai."

"Anything I've tasted, I can make."

"Here," Spoon said and tossed Abe one of the remaining small bottles. "Make me a tumbler of that and I'll stop talking smack about your target shooting scores in the Tapper break room."

After Abe caught the bottle in his free hand he sat his drink down. He unscrewed the cap, took a deep breath, and sipped a tiny mouthful of the fiery whiskey. *Oh fuck that's awful.* He coughed, put the cap back on, and threw it Spoon with a bit more force than was necessary.

Might've been on account of Spoon's laughter.

"Gimme," Abe said, leaning forward and gesturing at a glass tumbler sitting on the walnut shelf just below the oval double window near Spoon. Spoon handed his friend the glass. "Vocare potum," the mage said, and his conjured fluid grew up from the bottom of the clear glass until there was an inch of it. "Here you go."

Spoon took the glass back with a relish. He tipped it up and downed the entire contents in one gulp.

Then he frowned.

"This is... flat cream soda," he said.

"That's right," Abe said. "And now we know who has the power in this relationship. Talk shit about *me* in the break room. I'm a legend, bitch. Now, after I return from the bathroom — where I will not smoke a cigarette — I will entertain the idea of making you your whiskey using my prolific magical power."

"I thought we were friends," Spoon said with a shake of his head.

"We are. This is what guys do to their friends."

Abe got out of his seat and turned towards the rear of the cabin. He gave his best friend a grin and a wink and strode away. Twenty steps down the wide aisle, past a few couches, and the core mini-bar under siege in the aircraft he found the bathroom door. Abe flipped the metal handle and pulled the door open, then entered the tiny lavatory. It smelled of lilacs.

As soon as he closed the door with a click, his breathing accelerated and he burst out into a sweat.

"Goddamn it. Fuck off, Abe. Why didn't you just call her? Why, why?" he whispered to his reflection in the small mirror. "Just call her. Just tell her. She'll be disappointed, but she's tough. She'll be okay. It'll be alright." He made a fist as if he were going to punch the mirror, but didn't. He gripped the side of the sink with both hands.

But the lack of the punch and the whispered words weren't helping his nervous system, and they certainly weren't quieting the storm of doubt, and self-destructive thoughts coursing in a maelstrom inside his skull. The thoughts and the storm were regular for him now. He let go of the sink and held one palm out. He looked at the lines on it in the mirror and steadied his breathing to speak a simple spell he had devised on his own since the events in England. Only he knew of the spell.

"Vocare sanitatem," he whispered to the spirits of the healing winds that he had reached out to in order to build the power for this spell, and a small off-white, rectangular tablet popped into existence sitting in his hand. He popped the pill in his mouth and turned the faucet on. He downed several handfuls of water to swallow the pill, then sat on the tiny restroom's toilet.

"Get a grip. Get a grip. Get a grip. Get your head in the game. Stay focused. Stay strong."

Abe looked at his face in the mirror, and wasn't sure he could do any of that for long.

Chapter Six
Hamza Totah

This fire inside my body will eat me alive if I don't set it free, Hamza thought to himself in the dark of the warehouse they hid in. He sat up from the mattress covered with a thin sheet they stole from a nearby apartment and he felt the skin of his chest. *I am so hot, burning like the top of the woodstove in my father's home.* He pulled his fingers away and looked at his dark skin in the dark room.

I know my fingers are almost burnt. It does not cause pain. So strange. Wait... what?

The tips of Hamza's fingers were becoming visible in the dark. No light grew in the room to illuminate them. The tips of his fingers started to glow with cherry-red light, caused by a sudden, tremendous surge of heat in his chest and shoulder. The searing pain moving in his body made his heart race, and triggered a lizard-brain pulse of euphoria.

Hamza managed to not leap up, screaming for joy, but he couldn't help the smile that escaped.

The energy growing inside him—inside his chest, inside his hands, and deep inside his mind—tickled at the little boy Hamza once was that craved power . It teased his selfishness with flashes of heat, and magical energy that tantalized, and spurred on passion. In the corner of his imagination he heard faint voices call to him in the squeaky voice he'd carried until puberty. The voice was an insult to the work he'd done to become a man he was proud to be.

"You are a god," his thirst for power whispered.

"No," Hamza said. "I am but a man. One who has mastered his childish ways. I know my power has changed, but I will not be mastered by that power. I shall remain the king of the palace of my body."

The little boy inside him grunted like a piece of candy had been offered, and then taken away.

"Away with you, young child," he whispered in the dark room, lit only by the glowing heat inside his fingertips.

He didn't feel a presence leave, for the presence was only in his imagination. Hamza nodded at his success in sending the immature thoughts away and returned his attention back to his glowing fingertips. Even at arm's length he could feel the raging heat on his face.

He focused his attention on the heat, and the physical presence of his hand in front of him. He searched out the inner sensation of the bones in his wrist, then his hand, then his fingers. As he realized them—felt them consciously—Hamza absorbed the incredible, molten steel heat coming from his skeleton. In a dim way, he could tell that the rest of his bones were the same; wellsprings for godlike fire.

His fingers glowed brighter with the realization, and he slid off the mattress to stand. Naked, he stood near the center of the abandoned warehouse, looking with glee at both of his glowing hands.

"Hamza?" A groggy Seamus whispered from the mattress he shared with his wife Laurie. "Are you... glowing?"

"I am, my friend," Hamza said back in a joyous

whisper. "The fire inside me rages more than ever. I feel it... wanting to escape. I wish to set it free."

"Everything we did was to contain that radiation, Hamza. You can't set it free," Seamus said. "We need to keep that fire inside us. We have to protect the world."

No, no. "You're not listening. I want to *use* the fire. Set it free from inside me in a way that I can do good with it. I seek to control it, not loose it like a feral dog. I am no arsonist, or terrorist."

"Like... how?" Seamus asked, sitting up. "How do you plan on using it?"

"I am... I wish to *become* the fire in total. Not a container for it. Not just a mere vessel to hold it, or one that has been tipped over to spill what is inside it. I wish to *become* the fire."

"How would you do that and not spill all that radiation again?" Seamus whispered.

"I don't know yet, but with your help, I think we can put this inferno we've captured to good use," Hamza said, staring at the red tips of his fingers. "Are we now immune to radiation? If we house it, then it must not affect us, right?"

Seamus nodded, but Hamza could tell Seamus didn't really know.

"Then we are perfect for traveling into more of these radioactive places. We can fix all the world's worst nuclear contamination. Chernobyl?" Hamza shook his head in the dark room, lit only by the fire in his hands. He lifted his eyes to Seamus as emotion welled up within. "We can change the world, my friend. We can be bigger heroes than we ever thought possible. Not just a clan of misfit magic users buying coach plane tickets to travel around, trying to save the world. We can be like gods. Bringing great life back. Wiping away impurity for a better future."

"We'll be outcasts," Seamus posed. "They'll hate us because we're dangerous. And what if they try to weaponize us? If we go home, the United States government will—without doubt—try to bring us in for some kind of military indoctrination if they find out who we are and what we might be able to do. Lord forbid we try to travel anywhere else and they catch wind of us."

"Let them try to stop us. The people will stand with us," Hamza declared. "We are the heroes. We will show them. We will build support within the science and magic community. We will show them we are in control."

"I hope you're right. You're talking about trying to set the power inside us free, Hamza. Let's get that under control and figured out before we storm off looking to tell people about it."

"Yes, my friend. Yes. I shall work on spells to harness our newfound strength. I will not sleep until I have mastered magic to master the Ifrit I wish to be. This is my life's work now. My purpose."

"You're a strange one, brother. But I treasure you and everything you've brought into our lives," the leader of their group said to Hamza, and in the dark, Hamza could see the man's warm smile.

Almost warmer than the fire in my hands. "I treasure you too, my friend. We are brothers, for now and always. Bonded by magic, blood, and now fire."

"Sleep. We need to be bonded by sleep, now that we *can* sleep. No good spells are concocted in the middle of the night on no rest."

Hamza laid back down and watched as the crimson glow in his hands faded.

He smiled.

The heat remains within me. I am blessed by the fires.

Chapter Seven
Zeud

"Boys," the dragon of fire said as she exited her plane's cockpit. "Landing was good, yeah?"

"Smooth as silk," Spoon replied from his cushy chair, eyes closed as if he were waking from a nap. "Didn't spill a drop of my whisky."

He's a little drunk. Bet he got Abe to make him whisky. "Abe, smooth touchdown?"

"You know, it wasn't bad. I thought you dealt with the crosswinds adeptly, and there was just a smidge of jar when the wheels hit the tarmac. I'll lift the eight card, but to get a nine you really need to stick the landing at the end of the floor routine."

"You're a harsh critic," she said with a smile. "Hate to see what's required for a ten."

"I've been described as being difficult in more than one way."

"Did you make my Henry whisky, Abe? You know he has a fondness for it. One might say a weakness," Zeud said as she slid into Henry's lap. He almost purred at her.

"I am afraid I have no idea how to make alcohol," the agent said with a shrug. "I am not a distiller."

"Ah, perhaps not in the traditional sense. But I do

know that you have mastered a spell to that end. Vocare potum, I think are the words you say. 'Call beverage,' I think is the translation. Your spell speaks to your true self."

Abe's face burned a bright red, and he flipped his palms up. "Yeah about that...."

"Z, babe, lay off the kid. I intimidated him into it," Spoon said with no hint of a slur.

"No, you didn't," a female voice from the back of the plane said.

Abe and spoon turned to look over their shoulders at the appearance of a new speaker. The small women wore a flowery, thin fabric shawl over her shoulder. It covered the plain white dress under it and ran to her hip, where it swirled around to the back. Pretty with remarkable, bright eyes, and a smile that spoke of wit and of intelligence, she looked at Spoon, then wagged her finger to scold him.

"Kemala? Were you here the whole time?" Spoon asked her, shocked. "Where?"

"I was. I saw and heard everything. I will give you a list of what I require for my silence when Lady Zeud has left our presence."

"You're extorting us?" Abe asked her. "Where the hell were you this whole time? I looked in every nook and cranny on this plane. No way I didn't see you."

She ignored his question. "Well applied and infrequent extortion is a way of life for many. While I adore Lady Zeud, she doesn't pay nearly what I require to support my extended family," Kemala said, then winked at Zeud.

"I pay slave wages," Zeud confirmed. "She'll get what she needs out of you both. And now, we're at the hangar. Japanese nuclear regulatory people as well as some police and army men are awaiting us."

"No Tapper people?" Spoon asked her.

"There's no Tapper office in Tokyo," Abe said as he

got to his feet. "They've resisted the idea of any kind of organization that has multinational jurisdiction over their territory, with little to no way to hold that group accountable. I mean… makes sense. We're here right now with special, one-time-only permission. Which means no support from the company, or a shiny black SUV."

"Correct. I am still trying to figure out what your collective obsession is with large, black vehicles."

"Compensating for small penises," Abe said as he looked out the plane's oval window at the group of locals clustered together like a pack of anxious lemmings.

"I can totally see that," she said, and winked at Spoon.

"You shut up with that. Not my fault I'm Irish," Spoon said and poked her in the rump, signaling he was ready to get up. "Small but powerful."

"Fertile," Zeud corrected. "The Irish tend to be fertile. Not sure about your level of power. But that being said, let's grab our bags and get off the plane. It would be improper to keep our hosts waiting."

Within a few minutes the dragon and her two human friends were departing down the stairs. Kemala remained behind to organize affairs.

*****

They didn't know it, but Zeud, Spoon, and Abe were heading towards the Fukushima quarantine zone in a large van that was owned by the same tour company that delivered the people they sought. The same as that bus, the air conditioning blasted against the drenching August heat and humidity.

"So a group of morbid tourists hops out of a tour bus after faking illness, and within hours, this explosion happens, and the radiation goes buh bye," Abe said. "And, geographically, the explosion is within walking distance of where they got off the bus….? I say we head straight there, and start looking for body parts smeared on the sides of buildings."

"Explosion's epicenter is in a small park. We'll need to check some trees, if they're still standing," Spoon quipped. "I think these people tried to save Fukushima, and got blown up in the process."

"Failed spells often have catastrophic consequences, especially ones done in concert with other spellcasters. Too many moving parts, too many possible errors. Did you know Tapper's magical training area deadens extreme spell failures?" Abe said. "Keeps agents-in-training from burning themselves alive, or turning their feet into hooves by accident."

"Assuming we are right about them, I wonder if these people we seek might've fared better in whatever they came here to do if they had coordinated with Tapper?" Zeud posed. "Do you suppose they were good people? Or nefarious?"

I hate this fake cold they've invented. Enjoy the warmth, humans. It's good for you.

As they drove away from the last areas of safety, people standing by the side of the road held signs written in Japanese and English, all praising Zeud, and her presence. They danced, and laughed, and jumped for joy when their van sped by.

"Does it get old when people fawn all over you?" Abe asked Zeud over his shoulder from the front row. "Everywhere I've ever been with a dragon, it's all that happens. Like hanging out with Justin Timberlake. I can't handle life when people focus too much attention on me."

"I am used to it," Zeud replied with a sigh. *Pretty countryside, ignoring the urban sprawl of the island. Why do they continue to make so many children? Eat up the land.*

"Do you like it?" He added as he turned his attention to the suburban landscape slipping by.

"At times, I have lived for it. Temples were built in

my name a hundred and one times. A thousand and one. I was prayed to. Sacrificed to. Worshipped in no uncertain terms, and yet... all things pass. Change is the only constant. I have spent millennia in hiding too. Doing what must be done with no attention at all."

"When was the last temple for you built?" Spoon asked.

"Maybe a hundred years ago."

"Is it still around?" Abe asked.

"I think so. It should be, unless the island suffered some kind of calamity."

"Where is it? When did you last visit it?" Abe turned to her and asked.

"No comment," Zeud replied. "Not an important piece of my life, or my world now. Like all the other places made by hand or claw, it shall fall in time, consumed by the endless raging fire that is the passing of long years."

"Nothing escapes time," Abe mused. "Except maybe dragons."

"Oh it'll get us soon enough, in the big picture of things. One day the sun will grow, and then shrink, then consume the Earth, and as its custodians, we shall perish with it."

"Who put you in charge, anyway?" Abe asked her. "How do you know you're Earth's custodians?"

Now now, tsk tsk. A boy who has seen such horrors you would think would choose to ask smaller questions. "The great powers that manage all things, I suppose. Something or someone more important than dragons. God, perhaps. I don't recall exactly who, or what they were. It was so long ago. I can say, that I know without question, that it is my role in this existence to stoke the flames of this world, or quench them as need be."

"Feel it in your bones?" Spoon asked beside her.

Zeud reached over and took Henry's hand into hers. She pressed his palm against her stomach, just below her breasts. She watched his expression as he felt what she wanted him to.

"Whoa. It's pulsating. Crazy hot. Is that the fire inside you?"

She nodded. "I don't feel my duty in my bones. I feel it inside my chest, and belly, and throat. I feel the fire within. It tells me what I must do; who I am, and why I am here. My purpose burns within, and when needed, it burns without. I am fire made flesh."

"The temples are just a fringe benefit then, eh?" Abe quipped.

Zeud smiled as their police-led caravan crossed into the quarantine zone. A shiver went down her spine.

"What was that? Are you cold?" Spoon whispered to her.

"No... I am... I dislike radiation. It's a kind of fire I am ill-suited to deal with."

"And yet you still came," Spoon said.

"Custodian, remember? Sometimes that means dealing with unpleasantries of a terrifying nature. Additionally, Abraham said the radiation was gone. What could I have to fear?"

Chapter Eight
Seamus Drake

"I can't believe you stole a radio from one of those army trucks," Laurie said to Seamus.

"We have to be able to hear what's going on. The only way we're going to escape the Quarantine Zone is if we can figure out which way to head."

"It is getting very busy out there," Hamza said as he returned from the warehouse's offices, where the only windows were. "Three military trucks drove by in the last hour. That is how many drove by all day yesterday. I see men with rifles."

"They're searching," Seamus said. "For whoever did what we did. I know it." He scratched at his sternum. Inside he felt the growing warmth of the energy they'd absorbed. With each passing day—each passing hour, really—the intensity grew. *It hurts.*

"What if they find us?" Fiona asked no one in particular. "We haven't hurt anyone."

"They'll arrest us for trespassing, and if we're lucky, and keep our stories straight, they'll let us go," Seamus said. "But we'll have one chance, and that will only work if they aren't already searching for us because we hopped the bus."

"They're looking for us," Laurie said. "We know they're looking for us because we broke their rules getting off the bus. But now, they're looking for our dead bodies."

"You're right," Seamus said. "Which means our only choice is to escape and evade. Which will be easier... with this radio!" He held it aloft to celebrate his triumph.

"You should not have taken it, my friend," Hamza said. "It was bad enough I took those two men's phones and threw them. Now they know people are near where you took it. That's why there are more army trucks here. They know someone is around this place, stealing things."

"Look, I did what I thought was best to get us out of here to safety."

"Where will we go once we get out of the Quarantine Zone?" Laurie asked him. "There's no way they're going to let us just get on a plane in Tokyo. Our entire plan for what came after the spell hinged on its success, and us not being batteries of radiation and fire. One out of two isn't bad, Right?"

The group sat with that realization for a few quiet minutes.

A squawk from the radio Seamus stole from the Japanese army vehicle tore the quiet from its unassuming home atop a crumpled, slanted cardboard box. Someone spoke in Japanese. Others replied in the same.

"Fiona, what are they saying?" Seamus asked her.

"Hold on," she said, and listened. "They're moving in more forces. Ten more trucks with civilian buses. Food, water, logistical stuff to set up a permanent footprint. They're talking about restoring electricity soon. Scientists, and a security team for foreign people, too."

"Foreign people?" Seamus asked. "Who?"

Fiona shrugged. "Until they talk about them, I don't know."

"Well, listen," he added.

"I am," Fiona replied, looking at him with an expression that begged for patience, and forgiveness.

Several minutes passed, each filled with torturous radio silence. Seamus started to pace in the warehouse, kneading his hands and scratching his chest. *The heat... it's getting worse.*

The radio kicked on again, and they all turned to it. Eyes darted from the speaker to Fiona, and back again.

"There it is. Two Americans, both work for Tapper," she said.

"Oh fuck us," Seamus said. He punched a hole in a cardboard box and didn't notice that the torn edges smoldered black from his angry touch. Tiny wisps of smoke curled upward.

"Oh no," Fiona whispered, and all turned to her. She'd heard something worse than the arrival of two magically trained agents.

"What?" Laurie pressed. "What'd they say?"

"Two American and... and the red dragon."

"Zeud? Dragon of Fire?" Seamus practically shouted. "The single dragon that happens to be immune to flame and heat? The exact thing that we're becoming? You gotta be kidding me."

"They know of us," Hamza said. "Somehow. But are they coming to help us, or capture us? Or perhaps remove us? The presence of the dragon cannot be a coincidence."

"It can't be," Seamus agreed. "We have to move now. Like, right now. Steal a truck, or something. Is there any way we can shut down their radios? So if we do something they can't report it?"

"If we release the energy inside us, it could be like a... a what do you call it? A magnetic pulse. Might work on some of their electronics long enough for us to escape out of the Quarantine Zone," Hamza answered.

"We're not far from the main road. A few miles at most. Then a twenty minute drive before we can switch vehicles," Laurie said. "We're going to be fugitives."

"Let's just worry about getting a vehicle, and getting out of the zone first," her husband replied. "We have spells that can obscure our facial features a little, and we have plenty of Yen we stole from store cash registers around here to buy whatever we need. Or bribe anyone, for that matter."

"I can be ready to leave in a minute," Hamza said. "My spell to release the energy within is... close enough to work a little. Enough perhaps to scramble their electronics."

"Prove it to me, Hamza. Like you've proven yourself to us a hundred times. Let's move, everyone. We're gonna steal the first Army vehicle we see, and get the hell out of here once and for all. Next stop, freedom and French fries."

"I'd love a French fry," Fiona said.

*****

Alright Laurie. Same as last night. And Hamza... You gotta get the timing on this perfect.

Seamus watched as his wife went to the corner of a three story apartment building that the local vegetation had overtaken to wait for the vehicles they heard approaching. In her hand she held one of their Alka-Seltzer tablets so she could pop it in her mouth for the foaming effect that worked on the van. All she needed to do was stop the car for a few seconds.

On his hip behind him was Hamza and then Fiona. Hamza whispered in his native Persian tongue; he practiced the words of the spell that would poke a tiny hole in the essence of his body, and let out a fraction of the energy they were containing. He was sweating from the concentration.

He needed to release just enough energy to fry their radio, and hopefully not the vehicle.

And please don't hurt anyone. Please to the spirits and Mother Earth herself... don't hurt anyone.

The approaching cars came from out of their view behind the building, but Seamus watched as Laurie crept closer to the sidewalk, and the sound of engines and tires. She popped the tablet into her mouth, and stumbled forward.

"Get ready for her signal," Seamus said to Hamza.

Hamza stopped his whispering, and Seamus felt the man's presence stiffen with resolve. *Or maybe that's anxiety.*

Laurie continued over the sidewalk and into the narrow street of the Fukushima suburb until she stood — on false, wobbly legs — in the dead center. She held her hands out to stop the trucks or vans that were headed straight at her. She faked a cough, and spat white foam on the pavement.

"That's the signal," Seamus said to Hamza. "Do your spell now before they call it in."

"Yes my friend!" Hamza shouted extreme excitement. He bolted from the spot at Seamus' hip and ran around him towards the open street where Laurie stood. White specks of foam slipped over her lower lip as she accelerated her show.

Like an Iranian Superman, Hamza ran, then slowed in a strange strut into the road beside her, grabbing the seam of his shirt at the buttons, and tearing it wide open to reveal his chest. He screamed, voice ululating in crazy pitches and tones as he thrust his sternum at the vehicles Seamus couldn't see. His face was locked into a mouth-open grin that didn't speak to his calm. He looked like a zealot.

That's a suicide bomber right there. No one is going to see that and think any different.

Hamza's voice jumped up and down, wavering in volume and pitch, and Seamus' mind tilted and jarred as the energy in his friend's spell spilled out into the world, askew, and out of control.

What the fuck?

Images of flames, fires, infernos, ash and magma blocked out his vision from bottom to top and the rest of his body equally left the reality they were in; he felt the heat of the fires he saw on his body—inside his body—and it...

I feel good. I feel great. I feel triumphant!

Seamus went down in a heap on the ground as the euphoria triggered by Hamza's spell became too much for his consciousness to bear.

Behind him Fiona fell to the ground as well, and in the street ahead Laurie collapsed from the same orgasmic malady. However, an entirely different thing happened to Hamza.

Chapter Nine

Tapper Special Agent Henry "Spoon" Spooner

The woman standing in the road stopped the humvee at the head of their small column as well as the small touring bus they rode in. The driver of their vehicle and the man and woman assigned to be their translators leaned forward as the brakes halted their progress. They chattered back and forth in an alarmed tone, jabbing their fingers at a woman standing in the center of the grassy, dirty street just beyond the lead vehicle.

The blonde tilted at a strange angle, clutching her stomach and reaching out to ward away the vehicle ahead of her.

"Holy shit," Spoon blurted. "That's one of the women from the group that hijacked the bus. Something-Drake."

"Laurie," Abe supplied as he stood up in his seat. Spoon watched as he pulled his suit jacket open and pushed the right side of it back, exposing his holstered sidearm. As his hand dropped to the pistol's grip runes carved into the wood there emanated faint light. His fingers didn't shake.

No hesitation. Solid.

"Something is strange with the woman," Zeud said.

"Yeah she's foaming at the fucking mouth," Spoon replied.

"No," the dragon said, freeing the red hair from her brow to fall down into her face. "Something is wrong *about* her."

As Zeud spoke a strange man with darker skin ran into the street from an alley. He barked a litany of words in an Arabic tongue Spoon wasn't familiar with as he tore at the seam of his button-down shirt. Something red was beneath the fabric, and the Army Airborne veteran with time served in Afghanistan wasn't about to see the detonation that he knew was coming.

Bomber.

Spoon ducked down immediately to put some form of cover between his face and inevitable hail of shrapnel headed his way. As he went to a knee he tried to grab Zeud to pull her to the floor, but her draconic power prevented him from moving her body even an inch. Where his hands grabbed the emerald colored blouse she wore he too froze solid, preventing his flee for cover.

He saw the insanity.

The bald man with coffee colored skin with the now-torn off shirt revealed a hairy chest with roots buried in what looked to be skin made of lava, complete with bright fissures and dark surface spots of presumably cooler flesh. His eyes… were alight with an inner fire that pierced and flickered, like stars in the night sky, if they burned just a dozen yards away.

Spoon saw all this for a fraction of a second before the euphoric man… exploded.

The cracks showing through to the stranger's molten interior erupted outward in a 360 degree explosion of beams made of yellow-red energy. His body disappeared at the nexus of the calamity, but the near-light speed energy he released caused havoc.

In perfect unison with the blasts, Zeud leapt over the seat beside Spoon, and dove forward.

The lead humvee just a few yards from the epicenter took several of the energy lances front and center, tearing the engine block, hood, and passenger compartment into shreds. The force of the strikes tossed the heavy military truck up and over on its side and shoved it away as if weighed no more than tiny Matchbox toy.

The higher beams shot over the exploding humvee and hit their touring van through the windshield, slicing through the cabin, and wasting everything it hit.

Everything but Zeud.

Somehow she knew what was coming, and her prescient leap to the front of the van allowed her to get her human-form dragon body between the incredible power released from the man and the people she cared about.

She was unable to get to the driver, and their translators and escorts at the very front, but she was able to block a beam heading down the center of the bus that surely would've annihilated Spoon or Abe, or both. Zeud took the blast directly to the chest, obliterating her blouse and scorching the skin beneath. The power of the strike pushed her backwards several inches and left her darker toned skin reddened and raw. Spoon caught a sideways, behind the chair glance at her face, which had twisted into a shocked grimace.

Oh fuck no. You hurt her? I'll wreck your rectum you fucking Hajji prick, Spoon thought, slipping back into an earlier, more jaded version of himself. *Didn't think that was possible.* He drew his side arm as another volley of smashing energy beams tore through the cabin above his head, shredding the windows, roof, and cooking the air until breathing it in caused terrible pain, and made it impossible to breathe at all. Spoon covered his mouth with his left arm and tried to stay down as beam after reckless beam of bizarre magical energy smashed through their transport. The intense light shut his eyes then, and all he had left were the grinding, crackling sounds of the destruction, and awful heat.

A hand grabbed his arm just below the armpit with tremendous strength, and then he was yanked aloft. He soared upward and diagonally for a full second before he opened his eyes. He hung from one of Zeud's hands, and Abe hung from the other. She had grabbed them and jumped, and now the trio were skyrocketing out of the van below a hundred feet up and away where she landed on her feet, on the roof of a small apartment building. She let them go and the two men dropped to the hard gravel roof.

"Stay here," the half-naked dragon barked at them, then ran to the building's edge and dove off in the direction of their assaulted convoy and the man who exploded.

Abe and Spoon exchanged a worried glance, and ran to the building's edge to see what would happen next.

Chapter Ten
Zeud

Don't shift yet, she thought as she soared downward through the storm of energy still pouring forth from the strange man who was exploding in the street. Her trajectory was almost straight down, so when she landed, the flipped over humvee would be between her and the bizarre threat to her friends. *I wish I could've saved the people at the front of the van.* She leaped the ten foot standing width of the humvee on its side using her immense draconic strength and landed on the soles of her $2,000 Gucci sneakers.

The bottoms of her shoes sizzled against pavement that had become almost molten.

The urchin of power stood wavering in the center of the Japanese street thirty feet ahead. The beams shooting out of his chest were dimming, wobbling in the visual spectrum, and the insane, grating, chemical, energetic sound faded as well.

The woman?

Just a few feet from where the Death Star stood was the woman who'd been the catalyst for the violent ambush. On her back, shaking with violent tremors, the lady's body had taken on a crazy luminescence the same as the interior light that came from the man who'd blown up. Her clothes smoldered where they hadn't been destroyed by her friend's spontaneous combustion.

She's about to blow.

Zeud ignored the man whose energy was clearly running down and dove towards the woman on her back.

If I can cover her body, with my body before she blows up...

The half-naked dragon went horizontal as she launched the remaining few yards to try and bottle up the ticking time bomb on the ground. She extended her slender arms so as to grab the woman who glowed like a wall-fixture in Satan's living room. She landed on the woman's convulsing chest, and wrapped her arms and legs around the stranger's writhing body, containing her.

She's absolutely thrumming with power....

And then she blew up.

No different than the explosion from the man, the energy tore out of the woman, smashing up into Zeud's chest, thighs, arms, legs, and face with the power of a thousand burning hot sledgehammers wielded by a legion of angry gods.

"Ahhh!" she screamed in terrible, genuine pain as what remained of her clothing immolated, followed by her human skin, and the top layers of muscle beneath that. The heat—the raw, destructive power of the blast— was destroying her more fragile human form.

What is this? Not just fire... Must... shift... she struggled to maintain a single strand of thought in the wake of the obliterating energy eating its way into her belly and neck from beneath. She'd never—NEVER, not in a string of countless millennia—experienced such pain. A part of her mind—an old part, one that controlled the essential dragon she was—triggered, and forced her metamorphosis into full dragon form.

She too exploded—her transformation releasing gigawatts of energy her body had absorbed moments earlier — releasing a shockwave of force that tossed the nearby humvee on its roof, and cast away the touring van several yards. The windows that hadn't shattered in the initial explosion had no choice but to yield to her release, and what didn't break from the concussive wave of heat and light warped, bent, or melted. Streetlamps toppled over like sticks of taffy and bricks charred black and crumbled into so much carbon dust.

Two apartment buildings covered in debris plus a ramen restaurant caught fire as her wings flapped down to the street. Unable to fight off the pain, Zeud's head fell to the ground near the two energy-terrorists. She closed her eyes, and succumbed to exhaustion.

*****

"Z," she heard a hoarse Henry call to her.
He's close.
"Z, you gotta wake up," he pleaded.
He's frantic. She opened her eyes with great effort.
The small human who she had a relationship with stood near her head, one hand resting on the bony, scaled brow above the eye she'd just opened. His eyes were filled with tears that he clearly waged a war to keep from flowing down his cheeks.
"I am okay," she lied. "Are you and Abe okay?"
"Abe's a little shaken up by it all, but he's lying about it, like a trooper. I'm fine. What the fuck happened? We had to look away when the chick went supernova," he asked her. "She's gone, so is the guy."
"Where did they go?"
"I don't know. When she blew, we had to duck, and when you blew up, we had to run. You see the buildings on fire all around us? Abe is trying to track them with a spell, but he says the whole area is fried. Too much magic, too much fire and too much radiation," Henry said. "Can you catch their scent?"

She sniffed the air, but caught nothing beyond the smells of destroyed construction. "Nothing. And radiation? What? I thought the radiation here was gone?"

"Yeah well, it fucking came back," he said and wiped the unrealized tears from his eyes. "When they went all Mount Vesuvius, it was like a little dirty nuke. All the Geiger counters around here are going off like STD detectors at a fraternity house. The Japanese people are tripping balls."

"You're quite colorful," Zeud said, hiding a sudden surge in agony coming from the raw scales and muscles at her belly.

"You're in a lot of pain," Henry said to her.

"I am. I thought I'd concealed that little fact just now."

"You're in a puddle of blood the size of an Olympic swimming pool. If you weren't in a lot of pain, I'd be worried about that. What can I do? Can you shift down? We need to get out of this radiation and get showers, and take all these damn precautions to hopefully stop the cancer from setting in within the decade. They're worried we're going to contaminate the rest of this fucking island. Do you need to worry about radiation?"

"I do worry about it. It won't kill me, but it will make me very ill," Zeud answered. "I already feel it affecting me. Like a…. like a fever, I think you'd say. Nausea."

"Shit. Alright. Well, we gotta get out if you can change, or walk out like this. The local fire departments aren't coming and these buildings are gonna come down. They're gonna put the fires out with helicopters and planes I think. Want me to get a flatbed truck? Ride out like Cleopatra with me driving? I'll wave a fig leaf and feed you grapes."

"I knew Cleopatra, albeit briefly. Not the nicest lady. Though I was sad when she killed herself. With more guidance, she could've improved humanity's lot a great deal."

"You must've been real pissed about the dinosaurs."

"I wasn't that attached. Too ponderous, no passion beyond hunger or intellect beyond the cunning needed to hunt. Tesser was pretty damaged by the whole affair."

"Yeah I bet. He's emotional like that," Henry joked. "Now can you walk, can I carry you? You shift? Need one of those red potions that heals your wounds?"

"If you have one, I'll take it after I return to human form. Can you fetch my luggage from the van?"

"Z, babe, the van is a block of Swiss Cheese that's been set on fire. Unless your shirt is some next-level flame retardant shit, we're gonna need to hit a Walmart for more clothes for ya."

"I'd rather go naked then. Give me your suit coat," she said, and eased into the shift down to the much smaller human form as she got to her feet.

Henry slipped out of the ash-covered leather bomber jacket, revealing his side arm in the leather shoulder holster, as well as a handful of pouches for magazines, and at least two of Mr. Doyle's little metal cylinders filled with rejuvenation red liquid. He put the jacket over her shoulder, and started to walk with her towards the rear of the convoy they'd been at the tip of. Far in the distance she heard the rumbling of trucks, and faint human voices.

"Where is everyone?" she asked him. *This jacket feels good on my skin.*

"About a half mile away, outside the radiation."

"That localized? Crazy," she said

"Yeah, pretty nuts. We gotta find those two, and figure out what happened. They're beyond dangerous. Human nukes."

"Yes. We definitely need to find them and contain them. I hope Abe is able to catch their trail."

Chapter Eleven

Tapper Special Agent Abraham "Abe" Fellows

Abe's breathing wavered as he jogged past the burning building whose fire ripped towards becoming a raging, consuming inferno. Black smoke poured upwards into the ski from every busted window, and the concrete exterior was breaking apart and crumbling to the street as he watched. He coughed, and the sweaty hand he lifted to cover his mouth trembled.

Abe's lungs weren't struggling because he was out of shape. They weren't pitching in and out because of the dense, chemical smoke that threatened to suffocate the neighborhood either. His breathing was ragged because he was barely keeping his shit together.

His lower jaw alternated between a vice-tight clench and a quivering tremble depending on how close he was to the corner of a building, or a place where the man or woman who exploded and didn't die could be crouching, waiting to disintegrate him with their insanity-inducing power.

The fear of almost dying — pending doom at the hands of agonizing flame — reduced a massive portion of the man inside Abe's head to gelatinous, useless pudding.

"Sack up," he whispered aloud, dropping his hand from his mouth. In the other hand he held his antique Enfield revolver, and for whatever reason, that hand wasn't trembling. *Maybe it's the magic in the gun. Maybe it's just holding a fucking enchanted hand cannon.*

Abe dropped down behind a tipped-over vending machine and closed his eyes. He took a deep breath, counted to five, and steadied his breathing. Like the therapist in England taught him after the terrible incident on the Isle of Lundy, he put his mind in a quiet, calm place, and let a seed of serenity take root. He watered the seed, let the sun shine down on it, and let his breathing give it sustenance. He settled a bit, and dared to stand. With the moment of peace he had from the monsters of the past, he summoned magic from within.

Show me the way. "Ostende mihi viam," he said in Latin, begging for raw magic to pave a way for him to follow the terrorists who nearly killed him, and truly hurt Zeud.

He caught flickers of ethereal, multi-colored light at the edges of his vision, and narrowed his eyes without looking at them; he could ruin the chance the magic would bind into an effect if he scared it off.

At least, that's what he believed, and so much of using magic came back to whether or not you believed something would work. So, he brought his lids close to each other, and let the iridescent light mingle towards the center of his vision where he hoped it'd cling to the retreating footsteps of his prey.

The light fizzled out and blew away like a unicorn fart in a stiff breeze.

"Fuck," Abe spat, and shoved his pistol into the shoulder holster beneath his left arm. "This place is fucking baked to shit!" he screamed loud enough to hurt his vocal cords. He sat down on the horizontal vending machine and kicked it with his heel. "I came here to see something amazing, not get blown up and set on fire."

After a few seconds of closed-eyed meditation, he looked back towards the apartment building.

Straight out of a B-Grade apocalypse movie, he thought as the flames grew, and the smoke continued to thicken. *And to imagine, Zeud did that when she vented the blast she absorbed. I wonder if it was worse because she was the source? She's got to be a battery of godlike energy, being the dragon of fire, and all.* He paused and watched a chunk of concrete the size of a basketball break free and fall to the pavement. It exploded into dust and smoke.

"Yeah I get that feeling some days too."

He looked over his shoulder in the direction he felt sure the two... exploding terrorists ran in, and looked for some kind of evidence—a clue, a marking, anything—that'd give him a shred to follow. No blood smears on walls, no obviously kicked garbage or debris, no footprints on the sidewalk, no-

"Wait a second," Abe said as he got to his feet. He walked away from the burning buildings and towards the brick exterior of the building in the narrow street he sat in. At the base of the wall, on the ground, was a thin coating of sand and dirt that had been disturbed. Footprints—rough, partial sole patterns—tore at the loose material and cast it in the direction of the ambush. The feet were perpendicular to the wall.

"Someone was standing here, then ran away. Ha, bastards. Wait, that means there are more than two of them," Abe said, and drew his Enfield from beneath his arm. He cocked the hammer and stepped forward. The pace of his breathing picked up, but he paused on a deep breath and kept it in check.

Abe kept walking with a steady pace, looking at the faint traces of sand and dirt tossed wildly by whoever ran from the explosion. The special agent controlled his breathing with dedicated, focused effort, but he couldn't stop the trembling in his hands. He steeled his arms and wrists, keeping the barrel's nervous wobble to a minimum, but still… it was unsafe. Too risky to carry a weapon with such weak, afraid hands.

He kept on, damning the risk his weakness was putting himself in.

"Quit being a bitch," he whispered. "Be the hero Mr. Doyle thinks you are. Step up for Spoon."

He rounded the corner of back end of the block that had been set aflame and saw a small subsection of buildings that stood out; industrial warehouses and a garage, then some kind of workshop hidden behind the apartments and businesses now falling apart under the wasting fires and gene-caustic radiation. They'd set where the people lived on fire, now he would search where they worked.

"All this radiation is gonna make my fucking kid's three arms glow in the dark," he said to himself. "If Alexis ever lets me touch her again." The mere mention — the thought — of his fiancé and how he hadn't talked to her since cancelling their plans did worse things to his stomach than any of the fear he was experienced could've. He could die, sure, but knowing that he was hurting her….

He pushed forward. Better that he die than deal with her being disappointed.

Abe searched the street opposite first. He looked at each door, each window, each low, single or two-story building roof-edge for signs of life. Signs of someone fleeing, or hiding, or preparing a dangerous ambush.

Behind every door he imagined a multi-faced monstrosity, mouths drooling acidic slime, and eyes running with tears made of pus, and he fought those battles of the mind and memory as they flamed up. He won many, but not all.

He saw nothing. Well, not nothing, but no clues. No scuff marks in the dirt, no tire tracks, no smoking guns. Or in this case, smoldering Caucasian woman and Middle Eastern man. Two of the group that hopped off the tour van and sauntered into one of the most poisonous environments on Earth.

And apparently… fixed the destruction but damned themselves in the process. Or maybe they did it on purpose… to empower themselves with latent energy in the destroyed Japanese countryside.

So Abe pushed on, with his eyes held open, his gun held up, and his heart smashing its way out of his chest or up his throat, or both if he didn't try to stay calm.

Behind him, the raging inferno grew.

He reached a building with a pair of low warehouse dock doors—suitable for loading vans, or small box trucks, not tractor-trailer trucks—and he jumped when he felt a buzzing sensation in his back pants pocket.

"It's your fucking phone, Abe," he whispered to himself. He fished the device out of his back pocket and looked at the screen. "I'm shocked this thing still works. Tapper phones must have some next-level magical shielding to survive this." He read the name on the screen.

Shit. The incoming call came from Alexis. He went to answer it, paused, looked around for danger—realized nothing was more dangerous than not answering this call—then braced for impact and thumbed the slider to answer.

"I'm sorry."

"You better be. What's going on? Did I see you on television in an airport? Are you in Japan? What's going on? Was your phone broken?"

"I'm in Fukushima, yeah. Something amazing caused by magic happened, and all the radiation disappeared. I volunteered to come help figure out what happened. I'm sorry I didn't call, I'm an asshole."

"I was getting ready to come meet you in Europe. We had a plan."

"I know."

"It's challenging for a COO to get time off, you know that right? Lots of moving parts for me to just pick up and leave for a week."

"I know," he said, trying to hide his shame as he tried to keep watch on his surroundings.

"I'm sure you know how hard it is, but I'm not sure you know how much it hurts me when the man I am planning on marrying doesn't return my phone calls after apparently bailing on an overdue vacation with me."

"I'm sorry."

"Look, babe, I know England was bad for you. I know you were hurt there. Body, mind, and soul, and you know I love you, but you cannot be an empty body for me all the time. I need you to be present at least a little. I at least need to know that you're trying to be present for me again. That you're planning on coming home soon, and that I am still your future. We need to spend time together. I miss being with you. I miss being with the man you were before London happened."

"You are my future, and I miss you too."

"Make me believe it, Abe."

"How do I do that? What do I need to say?"

"If you can't figure out how to convince me you still love me, and that I am the most important thing in the world to you, that's another problem we need to talk about. Abe, you aren't well, still. I don't think so, at least. You should be back in Greece, or here with me. I need a man that leans into me when he has a problem, not one who runs away. Decide which you are. Look, I love you, be safe, and when you're ready to deal with our relationship, come home, or at least fucking call me. I can't say where we go from here, but we have to figure it out."

"I love you," was all Abe could manage before she ended the call, and even that felt like a lie.

When Abe put the phone back into his pocket he looked at the pistol in his hand. The cold steel barrel didn't look dangerous to him. It looked like an answer to the problem that he felt like he was. A better band aid for the wounds he had than any pills, or therapy, or time with friends.

He took a deep breath, and lowered the pistol.

"Vocare sanitatum."

He took his pills, and put the gun back in its holster. The man with the cracked mind cried the entire way back to where the Japanese authorities had setup a crisis center. He blamed the smoke for how his eyes looked when he reconnected with Zeud, and Spoon.

Chapter Twelve
Seamus Drake

"Stop, don't," Seamus said to Hamza as he reached out to grab the man's clenched fist. He slipped his hand from the knuckles to the man's wrist. *It's red hot still. He's like a fire poker pulled from the stove. Lord.*

"He's with Tapper. Look at him," Hamza said with wide, crazy eyes as he pointed out the warehouse's lone office window into the street where the young, suited man stood holding a phone to his ear. "He'll bring the dragon here. We cannot hope to defeat her if she tries to kill us."

"Look at him," Seamus said. "He's crying. He's fucked up. He has no idea where we are."

"I saw him do magic," Hamza said as Fiona cradled Laurie on the floor behind them. "He tried a spell as he chased us. It failed, but still. We must kill him, or he will see to it we are killed."

"Hamza," Seamus said, moving his hand from Hamza's fist to his upper forearm. He leaned in, lowering his voice and using his full level of genuine charm. "We are *not* the bad guys. We are not murderers. Listen to yourself."

"I killed men and women just now," Hamza said,

losing his vitriol of fear and anger and exchanging it for the slump of shame. "I have memories of watching their lives disappear in a flash of light, and ash. I am a murderer."

"That was an accident. The spell went awry. It's not okay, and we need to make amends for it, but you are not a bad person, Hamza. We came here with good intentions and pure hearts, and the world will recognize that in time."

"They're going to kill us,' Fiona said. "Unless we can somehow get someone really important to listen to us. Maybe we appeal to the fire dragon? Before it's too late."

"No," Hamza barked, then ducked from the window. "I hurt her. Laurie hurt her. We must walk away from that hope."

"Then who?" Fiona asked as she brushed a lock of Laurie's hair from her sweaty forehead and cheek. "We need to find some proper mates and do it quick or they really will hurt us."

"We must prove we aren't a threat," Seamus said as he watched the Tapper agent outside hang up the phone call.

Is he about to... shoot himself? He watched the man lower the gun, mutter some words with half a heart, then put his palm to his mouth as if he were taking pills. He dry swallowed whatever he put in his mouth, and turned away, his search for Hamza and Laurie abandoned. The man headed towards the now raging inferno caused by Hamza's and Laurie's twin explosions. *He really has given up on us. Helluva phone call.*

He turned back to the group. "Who can help us? We need to prove we aren't a threat and we need a reputable organization or person to vouch for us."

"Turn ourselves into to Tapper? The United Nations?" Fiona offered.

"Tapper, no. Maybe the U.N., but they'd just kick us to the Atomic Energy Commission," Seamus said as he took a knee beside Fiona and his unconscious wife. "Worst case they'd just give us over to Interpol or worse."

"That's it," Fiona said with a desperate smile. "The Atomic Energy Commission. Remember that woman in Europe we read about last year? She works for the Commission in like, Vienna, right? Doctor... Tidwell? She was sympathetic to the idea of trying to manage atomic issues with magic. If we could get in touch with her...."

"Fiona that's genius, you're so right," Seamus said, giving her his trademark smile. He fought the smile through a surge of white-hot pain in his chest. *I'm gonna need to vent this energy soon or I'll blow up like Hamza did... Maybe that's the lesson here. Controlled burns.*

"So do we make our way to a phone and call? By now they'll have our cell phones and can track us if we try to use them," Hamza said. "We'd have to find a landline."

"And everyone in Japan by now knows what we look like, and who we are. A phone is a non-starter. We need to just leave the country. Get out as fast as we can and don't look back."

"We're on an island, my friend," Hamza said. "If we try to steal a plane they'll track it without doubt. A boat?"

"A boat. Maybe we can steal one, or somehow get passage," Seamus said. "Either way, we need to get the hell out of here, because we're about to be burnt to a crisp by the fires that were set, or arrested by the sudden surge of officials."

"Do you think there's any way we can harness the power we absorbed?" Fiona asked, her voice meek.

"Like how?" Seamus asked her. "We know teleportation magic is basically impossible. Well, impossible if you want to arrive the same way you departed."

"Sane, you mean," Hamza added.

"Right."

"I mean, what if we can... change ourselves?" Fiona

offered. "We're creatures of almost pure energy now, right? We can all feel what's happening inside us, you know. Why can't we just dissolve into that pure energy, leaving the flesh behind, and then travel through time and space as like, lightning bolts or something, then reform elsewhere?"

"That's some impossible physics," Seamus said. "Turning matter into energy and back? Einstein would roll over in his grave."

"Relatively speaking," Fiona said. Fiona and the two men shared a laugh. "Look, physics is the rule of science, right? To hell with it. Magic isn't science. We just absorbed countless jules, or watts, or degrees of power from the world, and there's nothing stopping us from using our magic to harness that power. Hamza's spell backfired, but that doesn't mean we can't try to do something else special with this."

"This sudden confidence is amazing, Fiona," Seamus said. "I like it. What's your gut tell you we should do?"

She thought for a minute, then smiled. "We transmit ourselves, like data. That's what we're becoming, right? Sentient energy? Instead of disappearing and trying to reappear, we break ourselves down into just the energy portion, and blast along like a high-powered email to someplace else."

"On a phone line?" Seamus asked.

"Fiber optic line, if we can find it," she replied. "I figure if we become intelligent light, and zip through to someplace else, then we can reassess after we materialize."

"How do we do this, my friends?" Hamza asked. "We have no spell."

"Hamza," Seamus said, "We have Fiona, and I think she'll be able to figure something out. I have a good feeling about it. Do you think you can work something up in the next ten minutes for us to try?"

"Not much choice in the matter. I'll figure it out," she

said back, showing true confidence to Seamus.

"I know you can do this. I chose you to be a part of my family, Fiona. You came to Idaho all the way from Australia and there was a reason it all happened. How we connected, and now are here. You're proving me more right than ever before."

Fiona beamed, and Seamus watched her mind kick into gear as she comforted his still unconscious wife.

"Hamza, let's try and find a junction box on the block for phones and internet. If we can do that now while Fiona works her magic, we'll be better for it."

The two men departed the office, bolstered by a tiny bit of hope.

*****

"This is reckless," Fiona said as the four human batteries stood in front of the opened fiber optic ground box.

Inside the torn open steel case was a vertical plate of wires that could've been squid-ink spaghetti. The bottoms of the wires appeared out of several large tubes that pierced down into the ground of Fukushima, connecting the data of this place to all others.

"And I need you all to understand that if we melt into a puddle of goo, or get lost as energy in the grid forever, I'm sorry," she continued. "But I think this'll work."

"What could happen that is bad?" Hamza asked her.

He's worried we'll hurt more people. Or break shit. Poor guy, Seamus realized.

"We turn into goo," Fiona started. "We could torch the lines, ruining phone and internet for… who knows how many people. We could set more fires. I don't know. There's the chance we can't materialize after entering the cables. We could trigger a thermonuclear detonation and *really* ruin Fukushima. But trying this is no more risky that the spell we tried earlier."

89

Hamza looked away in shame.

"We can turn ourselves into the coppers too, if that sounds safer or more appealing," Fiona suggested.

I think she's ragging on him. You go, girl. "No, there will be no handcuffs on my people's wrists. What do we do, Fiona?"

"Join hands, like we always do," she instructed.

Seamus stood on one side of her and Laurie—still shaken by the events triggered by Hamza's spell—groggily stood on the other. The married couple took Fiona's hands, then Hamza's, and they turned their attention to Fiona.

"I think we failed earlier with the ritual because there were too many voices," the quiet girl began, still whispering as the inferno raged a few streets over. "Too many words that could be said wrong, or thought wrong. Too many ideas. And with Hamza's spell, I think he had too much power. Sort of… two spots of bad luck in a row, I think."

"So…?" Seamus posed.

"I'll do the talking. You three just have to concentrate on the sound of my voice, and the sensations inside your body. Focus on our inner heat, and as you do; imagine it turning to light. Imagine if your bodies were filled with light, like a million candles all lit for love," she said, and Seamus didn't miss her glance at him out of the corner of his eye. "Imagine that you are becoming that light."

"I've begun," Hamza said with his eyes fastened shut, and his chin pointed to the sky.

Seamus watched Fiona smile at Hamza, then he closed his eyes to focus as she instructed.

She spoke, but in what language, Seamus didn't know. *It sounds… like, Swedish? Or like, Finnish maybe? Could be German I guess. I didn't know she spoke more than Japanese and English. Go Fiona. Smart girl.*

Her words—whatever language they were from—soothed and built an inner focus for Seamus. She strung soft syllables next to harder ones at a melodic pacing, and as her sounds assembled words, and as her words assembled sentences, Seamus could feel the roiling fires within his body begin to dance to her, like she had a flute, and he was a snake in a wicker basket on the streets of Cairo. He even began to sway as he envisioned the growing conflagration of power inside his body turning into a pure, white light.

She spoke, the fires — within, and without — burned, the light grew, and then, without any warning or build-up, his consciousness shifted, and opened.

As if he'd opened his eyes he could see the presence of the wires and cords in the junction box they stood in front of. Outside of his body — several feet away — he could sense them as if they were wrapped around his body like ropes, or pressed against his skin like the tines of hard comb. He could feel their proximity, and perhaps more importantly, their gravity.

He — his body, his mind, and perhaps his soul — felt drawn to the nest of crossed fibers and wires as if they were a churning whirlpool, seeking out the energy he and his friends were becoming. He disassociated, breaking his conscious thoughts away from ideas and words — feelings — and become one with the moment.

He no longer heard Fiona. He could feel her, and her guiding light as if she were a lighthouse on the shore of the sea.

Then, in an instant, he was no longer Seamus, and he no longer stood in Japan.

That part hurt.

Chapter Thirteen
Zeud

"How are you feeling?" Spoon asked her as she sat down on a bench and he draped a blanket over her shoulders.

"I'm fine. You know it's ninety degrees right now? I don't need a blanket," she said, then coughed. *My insides feel... rotten. Radiation is so awful.*

"It's not to keep you warm," the agent replied.

"Ahh, modesty. Cute."

"Well, I don't want to sound possessive, but I dislike the idea of a hundred Japanese men and women ogling the woman that takes me to bed at night," he said with a wink. "Half of 'em are thinking of tentacle porn too, I bet. The young half, of course. Makes my trigger finger itchy."

"Well we wouldn't want a shooting on the heels of a small-scale thermonuclear detonation, would we?" she said, and coughed again.

"That'd be a fucking tragedy," Abraham said from nearby. "And if you could never say 'tentacle porn' again, that'd be swell."

The young man sat on the bumper of a small, dirt-covered car with his elbows planted on top of his thighs.

His head hung lower than she'd seen it hang in days (unless the subject of Alexis came up) and he was filthy. Smears of grease or soot covered his face and hands, and his previously sharp, clean suit was now a mess.

"Abe, are you well?" Zeud asked the agent as her insides twisted into a Gordian knot of epic proportions. She fought a wince off before it turned into a gasp of discomfort.

"I'm fine," he said without looking at her.

"Now, now," Zeud said. "Your body language disagrees with you. The only time you've looked like this lately is when the subject of Alexis, or your relationship with her has come up. Did you speak to her?"

"Are you fucking psychic?" he asked her, almost like it was an insult.

"No, just observant. Dare I say caring as well. You are important to me."

"Yeah well fucking why?" the young man said, exasperated.

"First, it was because others I care for, cared about you. My brother Tesser loves you dearly, and my dearest Henry here considers you family. That's enough for anyone to find you important. But now, you are important to me because I know you. I see who you are, and I consider you a kindred soul. A friend and ally. Someone who is, as I said; important to me."

"Sick of being important to people. All I do is fuck it up for them."

"Dude, shut up with that shit," Henry said from her side. "Crisis of confidence. Shake it off. We got shit to do, and you're the man."

"Thanks, G.I. Joe," Abe said. "But that pep talk isn't helpful right now."

"She called you, didn't she?" Zeud asked. "Alexis?"

Abe nodded.

"Didn't go that well, did it?"

He shook his head.

"I'm sorry."

"Not as sorry as I am. Not as sorry as she was."

"Did you… break up?"

"I'm not sure," he said to Zeud. "I did damage. Not sure if we'll heal. I mean… I think we're over. Just got to say the final words. Split up the DVD collection."

"We all heal over," Zeud said. "It's lingering on the scars you have to worry about."

"I don't know if I agree with you about that. Some wounds are fatal."

"And like many relationships, some things should die," Henry inserted as the commotion of Japanese workers grew.

Multiple red fire trucks were surging up from the rear of the sprawling assembly of first responders, scientists, and military service members. The group of duty-filled, frightened men and women parted to allow the trucks through to the fires started by the two-person explosion that happened earlier.

The dragon and her Tapper agent friends watched the trucks pass, then head towards the churning column of smoke coming up from the still-raging fires.

"They're brave," Henry said. "Hey, can't you put the fires out?"

"Normally, I would say yes, but I do not feel well enough to try," Zeud said back to him. "My presence is actually making the fires worse. I'm like oxygen for flames. We should leave."

"Why do you not feel well enough? The burns?" Henry asked her.

"Radiation. An enormous amount was shot into me when the woman exploded. I can easily shake off fires, and heat, but the poison… it hurt me. It's cancerous in a different way for me."

"How do we get rid of it?" the agent pressed. "I'm betting the answer isn't, 'take a shower,' is it?"

"I don't know," the dragon whispered. "I've often

been able to sleep for a few decades when hit with this kind of radiation. There used to be a kind of creature that lived in what's now southeast Asia that could eat the radiation. Many lived here in Japan. They call them baku, now, but I haven't had the need of one for thousands of years."

"How often has this happened to you?" Abraham asked.

He's perked up a bit. Caught his interest with a mention of the past. "Ten, maybe fifteen times."

"Are you shitting me?" both men said in perfect chorus.

"How?" Abe asked.

"Solar flares, you call them," Zeud said. "Crushing extraterrestrial energies from… the stars. Other things."

Abe's face drained of what color he had below the soot, and he returned his gaze to the dirty street between his feet.

A pulsating vibration rumbled through the ground beneath their feet, persisting and growing stronger with tremendous rapidity.

"What the hell is-?" Henry said, but was interrupted by the ground nearby jolting several inches upward, then cracking open.

Zeud, Henry and Abe jumped out of the way as the fissure in the ground erupted in a blinding burst of light. Faster than their consciousness could comprehend, the white explosion passed from their right to left, ripping more pavement and street away before it disappeared around the corner at a modest intersection several hundred yards away.

The passing of the light left an open wound in the city suburbs, and a faint vibration in the ground. The sensation below grew faint as the light and energy presumably traveled farther away.

"What in the shit was that?" Henry blurted, looking around like he was about to get hit in the head by someone wielding a baseball bat.

"You ever see those old Warner Brothers cartoon? Looney Tunes?" Abe said. "You remember the one where Bugs goes underground? And as he tunnels, he leaves this like, tube of piled up dirt as he goes?"

"I do recall that, Abe. I do," Henry replied to him.

"What are you talking about?" Zeud asked.

"Old cartoons, Z. Abe's thinking the people just shot through the ground here, making their great escape."

"How?"

"Fucked if I know," Henry said. "I am not the smart one in this class, but it sure does look like they left a trail for us." He pointed at the crack in the ground that disappeared into the distance. "Start making some calls and see how far the crack goes."

"What are dealing with?" Abe asked.

"I wish I knew," the dragon said. "But as soon as I feel better, I'm going to find out."

"Speaking of which, we can't wait for you to shower away like, a bazillion units of radiation. So I'm making a call, and seeing what magic can do for you."

"Who are you calling?" she asked Abe, then coughed.

"The man, the myth, the Methuselah; Mycroft Rupert Doyle," Abe said, and fished his phone out of his rear pants pocket.

Chapter Fourteen
Mr. Doyle

Mycroft Rupert Doyle wiped a thin layer of green slime off his wrinkled chin with a handkerchief older than the Tapper agent who'd ruined his impromptu office-cafeteria experiment with a poorly timed cough.

The British ex-pat, archmage and scholar, turned head of Tapper's training facility took a deep breath and steeled his patience to not respond to the failure of the potion-brewing. He folded his handkerchief into a small, sticky square and sat it on the smooth plastic table in the tiled floor eating area he sat in with the trainee, and pushed the glass beaker away.

"I'm really sorry," the recent Quantico graduate said, then scratched his head through the short trainee haircut he had.

"Failures are a part of experimentation," Mr. Doyle said. "It was folly of me to try and illustrate the process of a current pet project here in the cafeteria. A controlled environment would have been far more beneficial than this...." He slid his fingertips over the fabricated school table's surface and then rubbed them as if touching the clean parts of the table made him dirty.

"I'm so sorry," the trainee repeated. "I shouldn't have

touched the beaker while you were reciting the spell. I know better than that. I'm sorry."

"I am aware that you are sorry, young Mr. Wabun. Your miniscule slight against me is forgiven. Please do fetch us some napkins to wipe this up. I suspect given enough time it will make acquaintances with the invisible filth here and spawn a bastard child of dark, dark magic. And spirit the rubbish off to the magical incinerator with haste."

"This potion was only supposed to be a protein shake."

"Never underestimate the power of magical proteins," Mr. Doyle said. "You cannot imagine how far they can turn on you when the magic goes astray. Think of the nightmares that could grow in a trash bin. Teeth, tentacles, and eyes. So many eyes. Now please, run and fetch some napkins."

Mr. Doyle's cell phone rang.

The aged—deceptively older than he looked, due to a potion recipe he'd perfected a very long time ago—man reached into the pocket on the breast of his shirt, and fished the phone out.

Ah, Young Abraham. "It is good to hear from you," Mr. Doyle said into the device.

"Sorry I've been so out of touch," Abraham said to him. His tone said more than the message the words gave.

"You have nothing to fret about. I have kept my tabs on my protégé. I know you are in good, caring, and capable hands."

"How's your neck doing?"

"It is fine. The strike to the head, fall, and subsequent injury in Las Vegas has not kept me down. Magical restorations coupled with the finest healthcare available in New England has made me more or less whole again, minus brief occasions of numbness in my feet at the end of a long day. For a man my age, my health is miraculous.

Now, what brings your phone to your ear today? What crazy buffoonery have you and Henry entered into?"

"You seen anything on the television the last couple of hours?"

"You know I do not enjoy television. It rots your ability to think for yourself. Also, I have not received any memorandums from anyone here regarding any urgent happenings."

As he said that a young Tapper staffer left a sheet of paper on a clean spot on the table he sat at. He looked at the memo's header and saw that the message regarded Abraham's recent exploits. He didn't read it.

"Ah, well then. A memo was just handed to me. Perhaps I shall hear the news from the horses's mouth rather than read a transcribed version. Do tell me what you have been up to in Japan."

"We encountered the group we believe drained the radiation away. They ambushed us in the streets as we headed into the former quarantine zone. Adult Middle Eastern male with an adult Caucasian female. Adult male did some kind of crazy spell, and literally turned into the fucking Death Star."

"Two items I would like to address; One; I do not know what the Death Star is, and two; mind your language. It is unbecoming of a Tapper agent to use profanity as you do."

"Sorry. I'm sorry that you've never watched Star Wars."

Stubborn. But that is one of his greatest strengths. "Elaborate on your story."

"Dude exploded into a massive ball of light and energy. Shot these lasers out that toasted our cars, killed a bunch of people. Made a helluva mess. Then whatever he did seemed to trigger the woman, and she did the same, but Zeud jumped on top of her, containing it and kinda saving us from the brunt of a second blast."

"She 'kinda' saved you?"

"Yeah, kinda," Abraham said. "She like... sort of exploded too. Absorbed too much power and had to vent it off, or something. Set a ton of buildings on fire. It's a shit show."

"I see. That sounds like a show I would not like to attend. I will be reading your reports as soon as they are filed."

"Gonna be a bit. I've got an issue I need some guidance from you on."

"What can I help with?" the old mage asked as he left the cafeteria to head up to the surface levels of the facility where his office was.

"How do we get rid of massive amounts of human and dragon absorbed radiation in a very short amount of time?"

"Please repeat that. With some context."

"When Dudebro and Dudette blew up, they belched about a bazillion units of radiation into the area. Zeud sucked it up like a sponge, and is now sick, and says she has no way to purge it. Also, Spoon and I are now infertile, and our hair is chartreuse."

"You will have radiation sickness soon," Mr. Doyle said. "If that is the case."

"I feel fine for now, but yeah, we're gonna die young of some ugly fucking cancer. And by young, I mean in the next few weeks. The locals here don't even want us to leave the vicinity we're so hot."

"Abraham... I... am very unhappy about this."

"Probably not as unhappy as we are about it. Look, Zeud said some old creature called a baku can eat her radiation, but she hasn't seen one in a long-ass time. You have any idea what a baku is, or where we can find one?"

"The Japanese mythological creature? I am sure they are quite real, though I know little."

"Yeah. Wikipedia says they can eat nightmares. Zeud says they ate radiation too. I imagine with the ugliness of Hiroshima and Nagasaki here, there ought to be some fat bastard baku around we can track down."

"I am unfamiliar with the Japanese lore, sadly, but I can commence research with all due haste. If what Zeud says is true, and if they were to have survived the magical diaspora of Kaula's incarceration, then I would imagine that any baku in Japan would have made their way to Fukushima. You might have one of the creatures very, very near."

"I hadn't thought of that," the young agent said. "Boy wouldn't that be nice."

"Two heads are better than one, yes? Have you asked any of the men and women who are helping you from the area? Perhaps they have seen one of these creatures? Or signs of one?"

"Spoon and I could ask around. They're pretty tight lipped about that stuff here, at least, that's what I've been able to glean off the internet. Tied into their Shinto beliefs about nature spirits and stuff. They might think we're going to hurt the Baku. On purpose, or accidentally."

"You must convince them otherwise," Mr. Doyle said as he entered the elevator that would take him to the surface or the above levels. He hit the button for the 2nd floor and the doors closed.

"I can be persuasive," Abraham said.

"No, you generally cannot be persuasive. Most of the time you show frustration, or scathing sarcasm that becomes untenable, and then people give you what you want to make you stop talking."

"That's about as harsh as it can get, Mr. Doyle. Damn."

"Ribbing," the old man said. "I am giving you a ribbing."

"Ah, sarcasm, right. Didn't think you did that. Doesn't feel like you do it well."

"Sarcasm is a weapon that must be wielded with great care and precision, my young friend. Used too much, and it loses what impact it could have."

"Or use it so infrequently, you just seem like a dick when you do," Abraham said. "I'm dying of cancer, Mr. Doyle. I'm liquefying."

"Plenty of time to spare for dying later. Right now focus on the things you must attain and the tasks you much finish to remain alive."

"You got it. In the meantime, can you try and dig up some ideas on how we can either remove, deflect or absorb radiation? I think if they let us leave we're gonna try and track down these nuclear bomb people and we're just gonna get sick again if we can't bring a baku with us."

"This issue, and your health has my full attention, Abraham."

"Thank you."

"It is my pleasure. Is there anything else you need assistance with? Any Tapper resources that can be allocated to you?

"Japan needs one of our great SUVs, and a Tokyo office, but other than that, we're good enough right now. I can always call if I need something else."

"That you can. Do be careful, Abraham. And I am glad you called. I miss hearing from you. If you have not assembled it, am terribly fond of you."

"Really? No shit?"

"No shit. I will be in touch with you regarding my radiation purge and protection findings. I have a feeling I know exactly who to talk to."

"I knew I could count on you."

"And you always can. Goodbye, and do be careful."

"Later tater."

The call ended as Mr. Doyle walked around his massive, rune-covered cherry desk. He sat in the leather high-backed chair and pulled the antique phone on the desk's surface close to his face. The century-old device was a perfect match for the one he had in his Back Bay Brownstone.

"Now, the two countries on this world with the most robust nuclear research programs are the United States and the former Soviet Union. The United States program avoided magic as if it were the Bubonic Plague. Who might I know that still resides in Russia that would have some idea if the Soviets used any kind of magic in their nuclear program?"

Doyle smiled, and from memory he dialed the number for his friend Belyakov. It took him quite awhile to spin the numbers on the rotary dial of the enchanted relic, but the feeling of the cold metal ring gave him assurance that the call would be protected by the magic he'd placed on the device.

Now my broken friend… tell me how you are faring.

"Da, Doyle? Why do you bother me?"

Mr. Doyle smiled, and had a good conversation with his old friend.

Chapter Fifteen
Tapper Special Agent Henry "Spoon" Spooner

"Doyle thinks there might be a baku near here," Abe said. "Could eat our radiation and give us a clean bill of health if he's right."

"What the fuck is a baku?" Spoon asked Abe after his younger counterpart hung up the phone. "Is it dangerous?"

"Ask her," Abe said, pointing to the ill dragon masquerading as a woman, sitting on a Fukushima bench, draped in a blanket on a hot day.

Spoon pivoted to her. "So what's a baku?"

"Tesser could describe them easier than I could. Call him," she said with great effort. "Another one of his pet projects."

"I'm not making any more phone calls. Tell me what you can, please. Use small words."

"They're magical, not mundane," Zeud began. "So

they don't follow the same rules as a lion might, or a komodo. They are part... uh... part imagination? I guess you could say. Not all real."

"Make-believe monsters? Is that what you mean?"

"I don't know how to describe it," she said. "Conceptually. I can tell you that they appear different to several viewers looking at the same animal even at the same time. When I saw something that looked like an elephant, my servant Kumiho saw a much smaller creature. Like a... mongoose, but with horns and tusks."

"So we have no idea what to look for?" Spoon said. "Great. Are they dangerous?"

"Ask the people what they've seen. Baku were good luck, mostly safe. They protected people form nightmares. For a long time, they were beloved here. Someone might know where it is," Zeud suggested.

"That's what Doyle said," Abe added.

"Still need clarification on what 'mostly safe' means. Mostly safe is still kinda dangerous," Spoon said.

"Some baku would get addicted to eating nightmares," the dragon said. "If they got addicted to yours, they'd eat more of what was inside your head."

"Like... thoughts and prayers?" the agent clarified.

"Hopes and dreams. Memories. Personality. Rare, but it happened to a few."

"Fantastic. Sounds awesome. Look, I'll go ask the people in white suits over there. Hopefully someone speaks English in the crowd," Spoon said before trotting off towards the mass of emergency workers clad in head to toe sealed hazmat suits who were avoiding them like the plague.

They backed up several steps as he slowed his jog to approach them. Spoon towered over them, despite being under six feet.

"Anyone speak English? Sprachen de... English? Habla Ingles?"

A frail little woman wearing a hazmat suit three sizes

too big for her raised a plastic sleeve covered arm and looked up at him.

"Fucking perfect," Spoon said. "I'm Tapper Special Agent Henry Spooner. Most of my friends call me Spoon. You can call me Spoon if you like. We can be friends. I need to find a baku."

The Japanese scientists arrayed around him turned to one another and exchanged expressions that varied from humorous disbelief, to flat-out rolls of the eyes and even anger. An elder man with hair as white as Elmer's glue and smaller than the woman who raised her tiny, plastic-encased hand gave Spoon a look that damn near turned his hair white too.

The fuck is this guy's problem? "What's up?" Spoon challenged him.

The grumpy man looked away and made gestures indicating he had no ability to converse, or interest thereof.

"I know you speak English, you reacted to what I first said. Talk to me, please. Lives are at stake."

"No."

"I'm asking for help," Spoon said, softening a bit. "Big Z is sick, Abe and I were dosed with lethal levels of radiation, and we just found out that a creature called a baku can help. Baku are from this area, and we're betting there's one near here. If we don't find one, there's no way we'll be able to catch who did this. Please help us if you can."

The old man shook his head behind the clear plastic faceplate of his oversized suit.

"You all in agreement with this?" Spoon asked. "No one wants to lend a hand?"

"I am very sorry," the woman added. "But none of us know about any baku. To our knowledge, they are myths."

"Zeud says otherwise, and I'll take her knowledge over yours any day. Look, do any of you know about any areas that have seen a sudden drop in radiation? Places where people are sleeping better? Or where they might go to sleep better? Any places where that Venn fucking diagram has some overlap?"

"There is a place-"

"Yameru," the old man barked at the middle aged scientist who dared let something slip. The glasses-wearing, slight young man pointed his face and plastic face shield at the ground, and took a step away from the conversation.

"Go on," Spoon said to him. "Please." *Talk motherfucker or I swear I'll tear your head off, and jam it up the old dude's tiny little butthole.*

The man looked at his elder leader and sighed in frustration. He then looked back to Spoon.

Nose first. "Please, please. Just point us in the right direction. We'll figure it out. We know what we're doing." *Shit or get off the pot, kid.*

"Lies," the old man snapped. "This would not have happened if you knew what you were doing."

"Look, Mr. Miyagi; I came here to help figure out what happened, and we got blindsided by an ambush. Things haven't gone well thus far, but now, *this* is what I get paid for. I don't cash a paycheck for swimming in the shallow water. I fix problems of a troubling, magical nature, and right now, I need your help to do my damn job. So with all due respect, if you know where one of these baku creatures is, or might be, it'll be the difference between whether or not we find the people who just exploded and killed a bunch of folks, or whether or not they're left to wander your precious fucking island loaded up with enough power and radiation to ruin it like teeny-tiny fucking Godzillas. Wax on, or wax off. Be a team player and save lives. My life, for example."

They stepped back after his leash slipped off, but to their credit, they didn't stray far.

"We are only now learning of the treasure the baku

are. We cannot risk you being in the presence of such a precious animal. You are reckless," the man grumbled, matching Spoon's intense stare.

"We got hit by a fucking ambush," Spoon nearly screamed, drawing the attention of everyone in the area. "Look over my shoulder, sir. See those fires? We were there when they the two living bombs blew up. I watched people die. We stepped into harm's way to help Japanese citizens, you want to talk to reckless people? Let's find these idiots who sucked up all the radiation here, and now can't control it, or are seeking to use that energy as a weapon. That's reckless."

The man's eyes screwed down into narrow pips of pure distrust. Spoon watched through the shield of the man's suit as he debated Spoon's statement, and then with a look up and down, Spoon's presence, and character.

"What is your plan?"

"Cleanse our bodies of radiation while we track down where the tear in the ground went. We all know they left that way, and we're hoping we can follow them straight to where they surfaced. But before we can contain them, or kill them if need be, we have to get Zeud up and running."

"What will prevent them from poisoning her again?" the old man pressed. "You will be begging to bring the baku with you, no doubt."

"We have other assets working that issue," Spoon said, his voice as soft as he could make it. "We have Tapper working on that as we speak."

"I don't trust you. I don't trust any of you. Especially the young man over there. He's not well."

"He isn't well, but beyond his radiation poisoning, his health is not your concern; it's mine. He's my family. Just know he's a good agent, who you already owe a tremendous debt to for work done elsewhere. Now he's here, in person, damaged, trying to save lives again even if it costs him every last bit of health he has left."

The old man grumbled again.

The younger scientist pleaded to him in Japanese, his hands swaying back and forth from the Tapper agent to the fires beyond, to the bench where Zeud and Abe sat and back again. The elder tolerated the case the younger scientist made for a minute, then shut it down with a dismissive wave of the hand.

"We control the time and place. You will be escorted to the baku one at a time, starting with the dragon. If at any point in time we decide it is too dangerous, or have any objections, you will be brought to isolation and cleansed as best as possible."

"Agreed. When do we leave?"

"We must ask the baku when it wants visitors," he answered, and turned away. "I will let you know."

The other scientists followed suit.

"Asshole," Spoon whispered.

The youngest scientist—the last to turn and leave—turned back to Spoon and flashed a thumbs-up with a paired grin.

"You, I like."

The Tapper agent returned to Zeud and Abe.

"What's that facial expression mean?" Abe asked him.

"Partial victory."

"How so?"

"They know where a baku is."

"That's fucking great," Abe said, then coughed. "We're in business. How's that a partial win?"

"They said they ask the baku if it wanted to see us, and, the little pricks said if they think anything is going wrong with a meeting with the baku, they're shipping us to isolation. Zeud goes first, then you and I after."

"You agreed to that?" Abe said, confused.

"If it gets one of us into the presence of the baku, I'll agree to eat a bag of vegemite covered dicks."

"Jesus man, vegemite?" Abe said, then gagged.

"Yeah, vegemite. I'm serious about this."

"You two are something else," Zeud muttered from under her blanket. "When can we meet the baku?"

"Soon, I hope. I think they're figuring that out right now."

"I hope it's soon," Zeud said, and looked at Spoon with yellowed, runny eyes.

Her eyes are... She's real sick.

Spoon swallowed, and forgot for a moment how shitty his body felt.

Chapter Sixteen
Laurie Drake

Fiona's spell worked. The four mages winked out of existence as forms made of flesh, and boiled down to nothing but consciousness, and the power they had absorbed.

Divine, cleansing fire cascaded over them at a speed that bewildered Laurie's mind. Like a rushing river of light, heat, and sound she and the three souls she held the hands of thundered through time and space along the thin lines of fiber-optic cable buried beneath the ground. For a fleeting instant the crushing fatigue and pain she felt from exploding in the street at Hamza's doing faded, replaced by a complete, orgasmic joy of transcendent fulfillment.

That ended.

Her ears—she had none at the time—ruptured and drowned in the chaos of whirling energy. Dimly she sensed the claustrophobic presence of Hamza, Fiona, and her husband Seamus. Like individual beams of sunlight streaming through a window against her skin, she felt where their absence was like cooler shadows cast by intervening, warmth negating walls. Somewhere, she imagined feeling the grip of their frightened hands.

Frightened save for the confident, nonexistent fingers of Fiona, their leader in the pipeline of pure energy.

They passed from the greased, frictionless fiber optic lines to slower, painful wires and cables that felt deep underground, and damp. Laurie felt grinding, miserable pain for a time that felt like forever, but just as fast as they'd disappeared the pain ended, and they passed through a massive nexus of even more lines.

Almost like a Dyson sphere of energy and threads — a spider's web in all dimensions — she felt as Fiona slowed their transit, orbited in the nexus and search until she selected a path for them to travel. That next portion of the journey caused even more pain than the wet, dark part.

She lost her sense of balance as they torrented through the information infrastructure of somewhere in the real world. Off-balance, and nauseous without a brain or a stomach, she felt violently ill as the heat, dizziness and pain brought on by their laser-fast transit grew. Made of energy, she had the sensation of drowning in even more power as their speed slowed, and slowed, and slowed, and the residual power they created and drew upon built like a wave on their heels.

They exploded back into being, as naked as the day they were born.

Showers of flame, sparks, rivers of bitter black smoke coupled with a thunderclap of noise triggered when they erupted into physical existence. Tossed out of an older version of the junction box they'd entered in Fukushima, the four spellcasters spilled out into the street of a strange land.

Fiona and Laurie landed and rolled into the rough pavement as Hamza and Seamus tumbled diagonal to them into a grassy wedge running alongside the road. Laurie's elbows and knees — naked as jaybird — scrambled into blotches of bloody red pulp as they banged and smeared on the rough road surface. She yelped in pain — finally able to speak — and tried to arrest her wild spill forward before she lost even more flesh to the hard surface.

As the world around her tumbled around and around she caught a glimpse of Fiona cart wheeling end over end further out into the same road. Laurie heard the throaty hum and whine of giant engines just like the truck her dad used to drive for a living nearby.

Not just nearby, but feet from her head, nearby and getting closer, fast.

Laurie's tumble ended with her head five feet from the oncoming, crushing wheel of a giant truck. She heard the driver slam on the brakes but the vehicle was going too fast; the tired stopped spinning but they instead vibrated and skipped on the road, allowing the giant transport vehicle to shake forward to its murderous end.

She screamed.

Nearby she heard her husband belt out a holler of panic. Coinciding with his scream, and her scream, she heard and felt a concussive snap of energy pass over her head. Her hair blew like a hurricane's gust struck her.

Unable to turn to see him, eyes frozen on the massive, filth-crusted grill of the truck about to obliterate her, she went silent, accepting her fate.

The grill dented inward, crushed by a translucent fist that manifested just in front of her. The entire semi buckled on the immovable object made of magic, and Laurie stole a glance up at the driver as he shattered the windshield and soared over his truck's hood. The man flew out over her, screaming. The sound of the vehicle dying drowned out the sound of him smacking into the pavement, and meeting his own awful end.

They had taken another life.

Truck stopped, Laurie looked back at her husband, and two friends. As she took that scene in, screaming and hollering in a language she didn't understand broke out in every direction.

Seamus was manic with fear as Hamza picked him up

from the grass. She saw every ounce of love the man had for her in the pain he showed. Hamza too, judging by how he was frantic.

In the road, ten feet from her, safe on the other side away from the truck lay Fiona. She had a single fist up, pointed at the truck.

"You saved me," Laurie said with what little air she had in her lungs.

Fiona nodded in disbelief, then looked at her balled up fist.

"Why?"

The spent, naked, sweaty, wisp of a girl unclenched her fist and looked at Fiona. "Why would I do anything different?"

She could've had Seamus all to herself.... "I um... thanks."

"My friends, come, we must go," Hamza belched at them, interrupting the awkwardness.

He had Seamus in one hand, and used his other big hand to pick Laurie up by the arm around her bicep. He put her on her bare feet and went to Fiona to do the same, all while never letting go of his beloved leader, Seamus. Once he had her upright and mobile he dragged Seamus towards the sidewalk of the dirty, wide road they crashed into.

Cars were stopping, people were approaching, and nearby, the junction box they arrived at caught fire, and cackled a terrible electrical sound.

All that happened twelve hours ago, give or take.

Now, the beleaguered crew of misfit sorcerers hid again, this time in the basement of a concrete slab of a post-Soviet apartment building. Clothes tucked away in storage covered their bodies, a size too large here, or too small there. They hadn't run far from their crash landing site. Seamus thought it best to stay close. Any radiation they'd let off when they burst back into the real world would cover any radiation they gave off while in hiding.

At least, that was the theory.

So far, despite the threatening sound of foot patrols and military vehicles shaking the ground, they were safe behind the steel door they'd welded shut with a touch from Seamus' glowing finger.

"Not Russia, but close," Hamza said. "Kazakhstan, for certain. I saw a sign for the Cosmodrome before we disappeared. Baikonur."

"Is that like the Thunderdome?" Seamus quipped from yet another uncomfortable resting place in a concrete room. He pulled his wife tight to his side, and shared their copious warmth.

If anything, I'll never be cold again, Laurie thought, and pressed back into his presence.

"No, it is not like the Mel Gibson movie. Cosmodrome. Where Russia shoots rockets into space. They are renting a large piece of land from Kazakhstan for the place. Like your NASA, but with Russians," the Iranian explained.

"Do they speak Russian here?" Fiona asked him. "You can speak Russian, right?"

"Very basic Russian," Hamza answered. "But I wouldn't trust it if we really had to converse. English or Persian would be best for me. Most of the astronauts speak English, which means many more people here who work at the Cosmodrome should speak it too. But there will be many men from the Army here. And many policemen. Moving around will be... very challenging."

"All we really need to do is buy enough time for us to find a junction box that can take the heat of us going long distance again," Seamus said. "We don't want to fight anyone, or cause trouble. We just need to get to Austria and try our hand with the Atomic Energy Commission."

"That might not be that easy," Fiona said, her voice exhausted. "A lot of the wires and cables I felt as we moved closer to here were in terrible shape. I had to eject us or we'd burn up under the ground. I should've taken us in a different direction, but I had no idea how the road would be. I knew we'd probably die if I kept pushing us forward, but I was just as worried about the damage we'd do when we went. We still don't know what'll happen if one of us dies."

"All that energy let out at once?" Laurie said. "With no containment vessel? Are you kidding? We'd go nuclear."

"I had that thought," Fiona said. "And didn't want that weight on my shoulders. Better naked and lost than guilty of ruining a country. I think we need to assume that if one of us dies... we're gonna go off like a nuclear bomb."

"I think you made the perfect choice," Seamus said, giving her that same patented smile. "And you're right, our lives must be protected at all costs. More so now than ever." He added another smile.

God he makes me sick sometimes. One of these days I'm gonna slap that expression straight off his chops.

"Someone still died. That truck driver... he didn't make it," Fiona said.

"But you saved Laurie," Seamus said, leaning forward off the pile of blankets they'd tossed in the corner. "And if she'd died, we'd be talking about a much larger loss of life. Personally to me," he paused and looked into Laurie's eyes, "and also to the world. This city might've been wiped off the planet, maybe worse. Who knows?"

"I'm still quite shook by it all," Fiona whispered as if that was the loudest sound she was capable of.

"I bear a similar burden, my friend," Hamza said, sitting forward on a pile of clothes he'd taken from a damp wooden crate nearby. "I have taken the lives of innocents today. Or yesterday, however long ago the day of my worst shame will be. I didn't set out to hurt anyone, yet here I am; a murderer, and fugitive. I will bear that weight for the rest of my days."

"Do you think we can ask some of the Russians to help? Or Kazakhs?" Seamus posed. "They might be more sympathetic to our situation."

"I'll die first. The Soviets must never be allowed to have access to what we are," Hamza said to him. "Look at their history, Seamus. They are monsters of the worst kind. Just look at the buildings we are hiding in. Cold, hard, without art or grace, and spread out like a pox on the land. People just like these buildings had them built."

"Okay, okay, I get it. Sorry I brought the idea up."

"I am not angry at you. I am angry at a century of their policies and politics. Almost as angry at America for the same. Some days, I change my mind on who I am more angry at."

"I hear you."

"So what do we do?" Laurie asked. "We need food and water, and we have to find a place where a real phone line or internet line can take us to Austria, right?"

"I can slip out and get us food and something to drink," her husband volunteered. "I have a spell that changes my appearance slightly. Copied those women in London. I won't talk to anyone, just mumble like I'm drunk."

That's creepy. I didn't know he had gotten good enough with that spell to risk his life on it.

"I think I know where I can find us a strong enough line out of here," Fiona said. Everyone turned their attention to her. "You said there's a Cosmodrome here? A place where they launch ships into space?"

"Rockets, yes. Russian rockets," Hamza clarified.

"Well then they must have good lines of communication to Moscow from there, then. And from Moscow, we can get to Europe."

"In the fast lane. You're a genius," Seamus said, clapping his hands in excitement.

"All we need to do is get past whatever police or army people they've got looking for us, and then past the security into the Cosmodrome."

"Is that it? No problem," Seamus said. "I'll get the food and scout the area. Laurie, hand me the money you found."

She handed over the pile of used but colorful paper money and put her head back flat on the blankets. Seamus leaned over her and kissed her forehead, lingering his lips on her skin for an extra second. *That feels good.*

"Don't get caught."

He flashed her that damn smile, and stood up to leave.

Chapter Seventeen
Zeud

The scientist Henry had complained about for hours returned, flocked by a small herd of similarly white-suited junior scientists. Arranged in a V formation like ducks in flight, the elderly scholar arrived at the bench she sat on, then stood silent until she regarded him with a weary nod.

"You are the dragon of fire?"

"I am," she replied. "Weak as my flames might be." She stole a sideways glance at the two agents sitting together on a bench across the street. Zeud sent them there to commiserate away from her. She was sick of their whining. *At least now they're getting good calls from authorities about where the people who escaped went. I just overheard them talking about how the lines from Japan to South Korean under the ocean were ruptured.*

"It is unfortunate that you are not feeling well. You claim a baku spirit can cleanse you of radiation."

"Yes, they can. Radiation is a strange energy. It's more than just what science explains. It can become a taint on the spirit of a place or being, and baku can cleanse that soul. I've enjoyed the restorative attentions of many baku in my lifetime. They are wondrous creatures."

"We are aware of a place where one of these creatures lives, and we have reached out to it. It has agreed to meet you and your friends."

"That is wondrous news. Is it far?"

"Forty kilometers. Half an hour by vehicle."

"Do you have a transport that can bring us? Something that'll contain the radiation we're giving off?"

"There is a special truck we can bring you there in. You will be locked in the airtight back, and must remain inside until we arrive. I am sorry, but we must protect what has been cleansed by these strange people."

"Good. That's fine. Henry and Abraham will cope."

"Good. I am glad you find this agreeable. The truck will be brought closer to here to alleviate the distance of your walk. It will be here in ten minutes."

"That's very kind. Your generosity will not be forgotten," Zeud said, and coughed. *My lungs are thick with the poison. Worst I've ever suffered.*

"Japan has many questions we would like to ask of a dragon, if you would entertain the idea of talking to us."

"I'll have my aide Kemala purchase a house in the prefecture that is most advantageous, and once this debacle is sorted, I'd be happy to talk as much as I am able."

"Japan and its people appreciate your willingness."

"Where is the baku? Where is it living?"

"There is a hot spring retreat that has long advertised its medicinal benefits, especially in regards to trying to recapture your quality of sleep. Up until the magical resurgence several years ago, there has been no reason to suspect anything other than good beds, food, and warm baths, but since the taint of the tsunami and reactor meltdown, the small resort area has notably not suffered any measurable increase in radiation. We were drawn to it to discover why readings were so low."

"Baku eat nightmares, and radiation. What a perfect pairing in this human world. Old, and new as one. Very good. I'll speak to the boys and make sure they're on their best behavior for the ride."

"That would be good. The older man seems to have a desire for aggression."

"Yes," she purred. "He does have a habit of that, from time to time."

*****

"This place skipped at least five hundred years, probably more like nine hundred," Abe said as they were let down the ramp of the large repurposed cargo van they had been transported in. They were in the middle of a small convoy of white government vehicles that trailed off behind them on a driveway made of flagstones, then over a wooden bridge and past hedges that surrounded the resort. Cedar and cherry trees clung to the road, casting cool shadows, and giving the place an aura of magic that even the mundane could sense. "Look at that roof. Look at the little moat and bridge surrounding the place. Straight out of the Kamakura and Muromachi periods. Gorgeous cinnabar colors on the timbers. Look at that rock garden over there past those trees. It's perfect. Every grain of sand is where it is by design. God, that's beautiful."

"Kamakura period?" Spoon teased. "Where in the hell did you learn about the Kamakura period?"

"I watch a lot of anime."

"You need to get out more," Spoon replied.

"I feel like I've been out quite a bit, of late," he replied after turning his eyes back to the dated, sweeping architecture of the sprawling complex of large and small buildings that made up the resort. "Magic tourneys aside."

"He has," Zeud said as Henry took her arm to steady her. *My insides feel like moldy gelatin. This is unpleasant, and I hate it. This baku had best be hungry.*

125

The tiny scientist that led them to the baku's resting place appeared from around the back of a smaller van just behind them. He wore the same white suit that protected him from the invisible taint of radiation, but he approached at a rate that seemed unafraid. He produced a small Geiger counter from a hip pouch and held it aloft. The tiny measuring device remained silent as he swept it from side to side, and only began to tick off the presence of radiation when it grew near to the dragon and her two friends.

"Yes, yes. Even here your level of radiation has diminished. Such power this creature has."

"They are wondrous, no doubt," Zeud said to him as they reached the driveway of the secluded getaway. "Are we close to it? I need to rest if the walk is far."

"I am not sure. The owners of this establishment have been sent for. We will know soon. Rest until then."

She leaned on Henry's strong arm as Abe circled them, gawking at the perfectly manicured gardens, trees, hedges, and the immaculate buildings that dated back hundreds of years. Time seemed to pass slow, but in this place, Zeud didn't mind it. In fact, the longer she stood there, leaning on Henry, the better her churning insides felt, and the better the fog obscuring her thoughts became. *I can feel the baku's effect already. There is joy to be had.*

One of the junior scientists trotted down a series of stone steps that connected the driveway and the largest central house of the sprawling bed and breakfast. When his white booted foot landed on the driveway, he was met by the leader of their cadre. They exchanged at length in Japanese, and both men couldn't hide their excitement.

The moment someone realizes they are on the eve of amazement. Humans are such wonderful things. I'm glad they've survived this long.

"The baku is large, and has a central lair beneath us,"

the elder scientist said. "The ancestors of the current owners built extensive passageways it could traverse to attend to the sleep of any and all guests. The owners are glad to give us access to the creature's passages, and it will meet us where it chooses to."

"Where's the closest access?" the dragon asked him. "Though I feel well enough now to walk a fair distance. The baku heals as we speak."

"I *do* feel better," Abe said. "I don't think I realized before how shitty I was feeling."

The small man shuffled around, looking at the ground near his feet. "There is an access hatch somewhere near here, hidden beneath a stone slab that can be lifted."

Zeud closed her eyes and leaned over. She inhaled deep, and slow as she drew her face left to right. She caught the faint trail of air with more dampness in it, and she stepped forward. She sniffed again, then walked forward again, then again, and once more until she had pulled Henry ten steps around to the side of the car parked behind theirs. Beneath the exhaust smells, and greasy oils, and plastics and manmade stinks, she knew the passage lay beneath. The lair of the baku smelled like fresh earth, cloying incense, and the musk of a large animal.

"Right here. Move this van."

"Your sense of smell is that good?" the scientist asked her.

"Right now my nostrils feel plugged by slime, and ruin, but it's good enough to find a hole in the ground. My senses are even better when I'm feeling well. Have the van pulled back. We'll get down after the flagstone is pulled away."

The scientist called out to have the white vehicle backed away, and within a minute, the stone had been pried up, and pulled to the side. A black hole opened where it had been.

*****

The ceiling of the tunnel was tall enough that she didn't have to duck to walk. Zeud leaned on the tiny arm of the old man in the plastic suit, alleviating the soreness in her body. Taller than most women, she was heavier than most, but the man's small arm remained strong, and kept her steady.

"You're quite capable. Very strong," Zeud said as they turned to face down a perfectly straight passageway with an arched ceiling that set free a fat drop of water every few seconds. They hit with muted plops. Ahead Zeud saw faint firelight curving as the passage turned to the left.

"Pursuits of the mind are aided when the body is taken care of," he answered her, then started leading her down the way to the central lair of the baku.

"This is true."

"Tell me of the baku," he asked of her.

"Spirit creatures. Half animal, half magic. Some are small, others large. Judging by these tunnels, this particular baku will be no larger than a horse. Based on my encounters with the creatures, that would be on the larger side."

"Our history is deep with their lore. We fear them as much as love them. Why?"

"Like anything that can be consumed, addiction to what they eat can occur," she explained. *How many times will I have to explain this to people?*

"Elaborate, please."

"They eat the nightmares that plague the living. It sustains them, and does them no harm. But, if they get greedy—too hungry, or if they eat a particularly delicious nightmare, and lose their self control—then they can eat more than just the nightmares. They can continue their feast until they've dug down into the good dreams, and hopes, and memories. They've been known to erase a person whole, making them comatose forever."

"Can they be controlled?"

Zeud shrugged. "For what purpose? You can't even control your fellow humans. Why would you be so arrogant to think that you can control a creature that's been overwhelmingly noble, and good for most of its existence?"

"To help people," he answered as they came to the bend in the brightening passage. "Think of the troubles they could free people from."

Troubles like those that plague Abraham....

"But we would need assurances that those who were attended to by the baku were safe from any excesses that could cause harm," the scientist added.

"Do people die from chemotherapy?"

"A small number."

"And yet people get that treatment. We are aware of the deaths from prescription drugs, yes?"

"An epidemic, yes."

"And yet people still take their pills. If those two truths remain, then baku therapy is fine, as is, were it to happen."

They rounded the corner, and the scientist froze as they saw the center of the monster's lair, and the monster itself.

"I am not sure people would be that close to... this."

"I think I might agree," the baku whispered in reply.

Chapter Eighteen

Zeud

Bigger than a hippopotamus, covered in a leathery, tiger-striped hide that was pebbled and rough like the skin of a rhinocerous, and topped at the shoulders with a bony crest around its neck that surrounded a tiger's head, the baku laying on the thick rug crossed its front paws like a business person starting a corporate meeting.

"I thank you for meeting me on my terms," the baku hissed in a luxurious, accented English. A reptile's tongue spilled out of a mouth filled with nightmarish teeth. "Very respectful of an old lady like myself."

"Where did you learn such good English?" the dragon asked her.

"In the wake of the human's biggest war. The Americans dropped their atomic bombs, and I grew fat, sipping and feasting in the shadows. I spent many years eating the bad dreams of the soldiers who fought. I learned to speak the tongue then."

"You are much larger than any baku I've ever had the pleasure of meeting," Zeud said, addressing the massive beast that lay atop a small mountain of pillows in the room lit by yellow paper lanterns. The soft light illuminated dozens of narrow, tall tapestries showing

Japanese life from centuries ago. Life that had bakus depicted in it, at least. Zeud's eyes lingered on a painting of a mongoose-sized spirit creature beside a sleeping child. A thin ribbon of smoke wafted from the child's ear to the inhaling mouth of the animal. The little girl looked at peace.

"I am well fed here," the baku gloated, rolling to its side to reveal an ample belly. "There's a human saying about how disasters breed opportunity."

"You are right in that. I am Zeud. Do you have a name?"

"I ask the humans I speak with to call me Moriko," the creature said.

"You are of the forest?" the scientist asked the strange creature.

"For a time I was, yes. But I go where I can survive. And now, for a long time, here is where I survive," she answered and added a wave of an articulate paw in the subterranean chamber she called home.

"Well, Moriko, I am unwell. Sick with the scourge of radiation, and I know baku feast upon it. I have come to ask if you would have a meal, and release me from the fetters that bind me," Zeud asked. "I would also ask if you would do the same for two who are near and dear to me."

The baku tilted its head in a human way, assessing the weakened dragon and her request. She turned her alien attention to the man behind the clear plastic facemask, and then back to Zeud.

"You are a powerful creature, are you not? I sense that the skin you wear is not exactly your own."

"I am," the dragon answered. "But even creatures such as I can be laid low."

"The thorn in the lion's paw?"

"I don't understand," Zeud said, confused.

"A fable," her scientist/cane interjected. "A dangerous lion asks a meek mouse for assistance. The prey helps the predator."

"I see," Zeud said. "Well, I have never wanted to eat a baku, and I still do not. I appreciate the powers of the baku, and I know that in this moment, we are friends. Or least, we can be friends."

"What will you do for me?" the baku asked her.

"What?"

"Let us suppose that I agree to feast on your sickness, relieving you of the pain and discomfort you are in. What will you then do for me?" the monster rolled over on its mound of pillows until it came to a rest on its back. It looked at the dragon, upside down.

"The meal isn't enough? You need other compensation?"

"I do. The owners of this establishment offer me shelter and protection in addition to the meals I consume, for example. A fair trade for services rendered, and benefit obtained."

"You seek wealth? I have money enough to make you rich," the dragon offered.

The bulky frame of the creature rolled back onto its prodigious stomach, then waved a clawed paw to dismiss the offer.

"Property? You wish land to be yours for time eternal?"

"No, I rather like it here in my little cave by the river. It's quiet, the food is good and the locals are pleasant. This is a lush life."

"Material wealth doesn't interest you, so perhaps a service? Is there something I can do for you? A forest fire set? A volcano to erupt? A volcano to be made dormant?"

"You have magic?"

"I have some."

"I seek a spell done for me. I need to try and find my family," the baku said in a somber tone that seemed jarringly different from its previous discourse. It looked Zeud in the eyes.

"You're telling the truth," the dragon said, knowing that without any magic. "And I have good news; my friend above us, waiting for your help has such magic. I will ask him to do this for you. Have we a deal then?"

"He will be able to find my family for me?"

"Once you have eaten away his sickness, his magic will allow him to put you and whoever you seek to contact in touch, if they are... able to be spoken with. As far as finding them in the world, he can explain more." *I hope that spell he does to talk to people all over the world can do that, otherwise, I've just screwed over the only baku in the world I know, and put Abe on the spot with a monster that could trigger more nightmares for him. Not my finest moment. I'll owe Abe a steep debt for this.*

"I see. I guess one way or the other I'll have my answer. Come then," the baku bid to her, rearing up like a lion statue in front of a library. "Sit at my feet, creature who wears the skin of another, and allow me to alleviate your suffering."

"Certainly."

The dragon smiled and walked into the center of the baku's lair.

I already feel better.

Chapter Nineteen
Hamza Totah

"Alright, my friends. The car is running, and we must get out of this basement and up to it before anyone steals it," Hamza said in the middle of the metal doorway that led to the concrete cellar he and his friends had taken shelter in.

Quiet and powerful Fiona, fierce and wise Laurie, and his inspiring leader Seamus all got to their feet and pressed forward. As they approached him they adjusted the inappropriate heavy winter clothes they'd stolen from an empty apartment a few floors above them. A heavy coat here, a hat and scarf there, all designed to obscure their faces.

We are just as suspicious wearing these clothes as if we were running around in circles yelling of our deeds and guilt, Hamza thought as he adjusted the sit of a winter cap on his bald head. *We should scare up some AK-47s to complete the terrorist look and really stand out.* Once his friends got to him, he turned and jogged down the hall to the concrete stairs that led up to the alley. There, he'd parked the small sedan freshly stolen from a dusty parking lot several streets over.

He burst into the street and held the door open for the

small train of friends on his heels. *We must move quickly. Into the car and down the road before the soldiers see us acting or looking strange.*

He went to the driver's door and pulled it open. After ensuring no one at either end of the narrow alley was watching them, he got in, then Fiona, Laurie and Seamus followed suit. Fiona sat in the front beside him, as they had planned. The moment all four doors of the rickety, post-Soviet era vehicle creaked shut on rusty hinges, Hamza put the car into first gear, released the parking brake, and pulled the car forward to the edge of the street they needed to enter.

"Bang a right," Fiona said after consulting a small paper map they'd traced the fastest route on top of. "Then bang a left at the next intersection. Hundred yards, no more."

"Okay."

Hamza waited for a car to pass, then pulled out into the sparse traffic. When they had breached out of the junction box on arrival, this area had been filled with pedestrians and cars, but now, all had left except for a scant few willing to risk an area that might have very strange and dangerous people in it.

Us. We are the dangerous people. They fear us. I must say this aloud to myself; I like that they fear me. Not the Kazakhs... but the Russians who are no doubt here.

"Right there," Fiona said, pointing at the turn he had to make.

Hamza waited for the crossing traffic to clear and made the turn.

"Wait, you just took a left on a red," Seamus said from the backseat.

"No, I didn't see a light," Hamza said. "You're mistaken, my friend."

Somewhere behind them, a police siren flared to life. Unlike the western sirens Hamza had grown accustomed to hearing in Boise, near the Drake ranch he called home, this electronic wail sounded more like a robot trying to not tip over as it was shaken back and forth by an even larger robot. The siren sounded tinny, timid, and more like the screech of a bird than a deep alarm by the authorities.

Fiona looked over her shoulder. "They're coming for us. Do we pull over?"

"No," Seamus said. "We can't even talk to them. As soon as they see us in this car, we're fucked. Floor it. Punch it for the Cosmodrome. We'll have to race them to a junction box Fiona can port us into."

"Grrr," Hamza grumbled, and punched it, down shifting the car and shoving the accelerator into the floorboard.

The vehicle jerked and sputtered as he aimed it around a slower moving car ahead of them. What their car didn't do, was pick up a real amount of speed. It accelerated at a pace that could've been made faster if they rolled down the windows and started flapping their arms. The small Baikonur police cruiser closing in on them closed the gap fast.

"We cannot race anything in this *piece of shit*," Hamza said as he pushed down on the pedal with more force. The car failed to respond.

"Can we make it go faster?" Laurie asked as she looked over her shoulder through the dirty rear window at the closing red and blue lights of the police car. "With our energy?"

In the rear view mirror Hamza watched as she looked at Seamus, then at Fiona.

"I don't know," Seamus answered her.

"Fukushima high-test fuel?" Fiona joked. "A tiny trickle into the engine might super charge it."

"How?" Seamus asked her.

"Who cares?" Fiona answered him. "Will it to happen. Use our powers with confidence. It's magic, not science. We're only ruled by our creativity." She grinned at

Hamza and rolled down her window.

The woman — timid, almost frail a week prior — leaned out the window like a crazy person, hiding any fear she had behind an infectious grin. The girl's short red hair whipped back in the wind as she waved at the police car now just a few feet off their bumper. Fiona turned, and with the same hand she waved with, she focused, palm out at the hood of their rickety, awful vehicle.

A multi-colored, swirling pulse of light released from the flat of her hand, shooting downward through the metal covering the engine. Fiona belched a sound of pure joy, and did it again, then a third time.

On the third pulse of... energy, Hamza felt the car respond. The shifter in his hand began vibrating — singing almost — and the pedal beneath his right foot shook, and somehow sank deeper into the car's floorboard. The feeling of acceleration kicked in, and Hamza struggled to cling to the steering wheel as his body was shoved into the seat.

Their boxy, non-aerodynamic sedan from the 80s took off like a rocket, careening around the car in front of the and cutting back, putting steel between them and the police. Not a trained pursuit driver in the least, the mage did his best to steer their magic-powered missile through the light traffic in the Kazakh city.

"Yee haw!" Seamus hollered in the back.

Hamza weaved in and out, side to side, driving past the bland concrete buildings of the downtown area, avoiding the pursuing police vehicles — now three — with a glee.

Fiona pulsed another shot of Fukushima juice through the hood of the car and slid back inside. "Take that right after the big blue building."

"Down the ramp?"

"Yeah. Right there," she pointed.

Hamza let off the gas to try and decelerate and turned the wheel towards the downward sloping right hand turn. The road tested his strength, and the car's ability to turn, but he screamed and fought, clutching the wheel with everything he had — his body overheating in the process, searing the outline of his back into the cracked, cheap vinyl — and made the turn.

They burst into the two lane highway like a cannonball, and Hamza pushed the gas pedal down again. The car and its occupants picked up more speed, and by the time the trio of police cars, and their tinny sirens joined them on the highway, Hamza had put a hundred yards between them.

"We're gonna make it!" Laurie exclaimed, leaning around to see their pursuers falling behind.

"Follow this road," Fiona instructed after picking up the map from the floor of the car. "It'll stay mostly straight, heading north until it hits the gates. What do we do when we get there? Surely they'll have the place guarded."

"Now that we're on this road, they'll know where we're headed," Laurie said, jubilation replaced with worry.

"Shit," Seamus added. "They are going to scramble a helicopter to shoot at us before we get there. I guarantee it. They don't give a shit about anything but stopping us."

Shit. "What do we do?"

"Drive real fast, and when we see something that looks like a box for wires, we'll stop at it, and port into the network," Seamus decided.

"Don't we need to get into the base itself?" Laurie asked.

"All the communication lines coming out of it are probably enough for us. We can ride the local wires in, and then go into the heavier, faster cables from there," Fiona said.

The god of thunder appeared, crashing their world with a barrage of ear-splitting explosions. On every side of the speeding car plumes of evaporated pavement shot up into the air, accompanied by tremendous shocks of noise. Every window in the car shattered as the rapid-fire barrage of…something plummeted down and tore up the road around them.

I hear… it is the helicopter Seamus predicted. "Above us, the helicopter is here! They know we are coming to the Cosmodrome!"

"No shit," Seamus screamed as the world exploded over and over just a few feet outside the cracked windows of the rocketing, magically fueled hunk of eastern European metal and rubber they were in. He covered his head and ducked down.

"Hamza," Fiona yelled in his ear. "You have to hit the helicopter with your energy!"

He looked at her as he swerved side to side, trying to dodge the powerful machine gun fire coming from the aircraft above. Futile as it might be, it felt better to try that, than simply drive forward like a fattened pig heading to slaughter.

"You want me to shoot at them with my power?" he asked her. "Shoot them down? Why me?"

"I think you're the best at that kind of thing. Shoot them or build a shield out of your energy," she yelled, leaning to look up at the belly of the tan colored helicopter. "When they want to kill us, they will. These are just warning shots," she cautioned. "They want us to surrender to them."

She's right. We can't be taken prisoner, and we can't die. Fuck these Russians. "Take the wheel," he said to her, and smashed out the window with his left arm. He felt the hot slashing of glass on his skin and the paired sting a moment later. He leaned away, out that window and pivoted his torso to look upwards.

A scant hundred feet above the road, and perhaps a hundred yards behind them was a Russian military attack helicopter. Long, and cigar-shaped with two stubby wings and a bulbous glass cockpit, the alien-looking aircraft pointed its nose-mounted machine gun down at the car hurtling beneath on the road.

The barrels do not move from our heads, even when the helicopter drifts up, or down, or left or right. Fiona is right. They can kill us at any moment. And if we die... we could kill everyone here. Easy choice.

"Prosti moi druz'ya," he yelled up at the menacing, insectoid aircraft, and held his palm at it, much like how Fiona had to the hood of the car prior to energizing it with their newfound magic.

Hamza felt a surge of rushing heat move from his chest out his shoulder and down his arm to his hand, tearing at the nerves and muscles as it went.

The flesh of the palm of his hand blasted open as if he'd taken one of the helicopter's massive bullets straight to the base of it. The hole burst outward as the magic and radiation released from his core, harnessed and focused with his will into a spreading cone of white-hot light.

The blast issued upwards like a geyser of raw power, and its force shook his hand like the end of a spraying fire hose. With great effort he muscled his tattered and wrecked hand in the direction of the slowing, and peeling off helicopter then watched as the tremendous power flowing from inside him worked its magic.

Above, the tip of the machine gun's barrel blossomed with its own energy, as the pilot or gunner made the decision to try and kill them. Hamza watched as the projectiles it rained down burnt up in the stream of energy he shot up. Meteors melting in the atmosphere.

Then his beam finished its ascent, and hit the chopper. Marshmallows.

One of the things Seamus liked to do with his friends and fellow spellcasters back at his ranch in Idaho was roast marshmallows over the fire pit he and Laurie built in their massive backyard. Hamza had never roasted the sweet treats like that before, and he had been mesmerized by the way the white foamy cylinders bubbled, burst, then turned brown and black in hypnotic wave.

Here in Kazakhstan, he was the fire, and the chopper was a marshmallow.

Except this marshmallow exploded into a fireball that lit the early twilight sky when too much of it turned black.

The beam of power leaving Hamza's hand ceased when he recoiled from the explosion and slid back into the driver's seat of the piece of crap they were making their great assault on the Cosmodrome in. The flesh of his hand was still ruined from the release of power, but he felt no pain, just euphoria. In the back seat Laurie and Seamus hooted and hollered in joy, embracing one another, drowning in relief that they had survived the calamitous moment.

The helicopter wreckage crashed to the ground, releasing a tremendous fireball that cracked the windows of their car further.

"Right there," Fiona said, pointing at a large, gun metal gray box mounted on a short, flat cement platform. "That's a junction box. I can hear the wires talking from here." She grinned. "It's fast stuff too. Super fast."

"I'll pull over."

A sudden burst of round holes stitched their way across the shattered windshield, cracking it into further oblivion as a dozen high velocity rifle rounds penetrated the vehicle. In the backseat Hamza heard Laurie and Seamus call out in agony as the bullets crashed into their flesh, rending and tearing their fragile bodies. A wave of warmth crested over the back of his seat as the energy contained in his friends escaped out.

"Oh shit," Fiona said, looking over her shoulder and ducking as more loud smacks of bullets from somewhere ahead hit the car. "They're hurt bad. They're frigging glowing on the inside too. They're gonna blow."

"We will fight," Hamza said, and pushed more of his inner core to his reddening, glowing hands.

"No. They'll die and take everything around us with it. Drive straight into the box. Hit it and bust it open."

"What?!"

"I can transfer us at high speed. Straight to energy. Trust me. Bullet wounds won't matter!"

Another peppering of rounds hit the car, and Hamza's upper left chest caught a round. It didn't hurt. *I have been hit by a large hammer. It should hurt, but doesn't. Is this shock?*

"Ram the fucking box!" a delirious, petrified Fiona screamed at him. "I can do it!"

So he did.

At eighty five miles an hour their beat-up and shot-up Opel hit the metal, gray junction box, and obliterated both in an explosion of magic, gasoline, radiation and more that eclipsed the disaster of the helicopter's demise tenfold.

Chapter Twenty
Tapper Special Agent Abraham "Abe" Fellows

Abe sat on the bumper of the white van that brought them to the lair of the baku. His palms sweat. His legs shook like bamboo in a strong breeze. He felt sick.

Mom's spaghetti.

"Tell me it wasn't that bad," Abe said to Spoon as the older agent exited the hole in the driveway that led to the baku's tunnel.

"It wasn't that bad, man," Spoon said with far more energy and positivity than he'd had since the terrorists blew themselves up back in the city proper. He sat on the back bumper of the van beside Abe and patted him on the shoulder. "Get going, cancer-boy. I'm getting sick again just being near you."

"I uh... not gonna lie, I am scared shitless. Does it look like a fucking weird monster?"

"Yeah, kinda, but it's real nice. Like going to a zoo,

but the animal there makes you feel better, and can talk to you."

Abe took a smooth, deep breath, but when he exhaled, it came out uneven, in hitches that seemed to sync up with his erratic heartbeat. He nodded.

"What are you most afraid of?" Spoon asked him.

"Seeing the same monsters I saw in England," he answered without pause. "Or at least, being so reminded of them that I'll have a panic attack. Dangerous people I can deal with, but anything with horns, a shell, tentacles, or teeth larger than a dog's and I just lock up. It's bad. My dreams, man. I wouldn't wish my dreams on the Devil."

"She can help with those dreams, you know. Just ask her. I bet the shit inside your head would be like a Chinese buffet to her. Could take a lot of weight off your narrow shoulders."

"I've put weight on since Quantico."

"Fat doesn't count."

"It's muscle, ya jelly dong."

"We'll agree to disagree. Look, you want me to be there with you? I'll stand right there with my gun in my hand in you need me to."

"Maybe."

"Zeud's already down there. There's that as well."

Abe sighed. "I'll be okay. I just… I needed to talk for a minute. Thank you."

"Of course. Go get fixed. Not neutered. Similar but actually quite different," Spoon counseled.

"Help me to the hole," Abe asked of him.

"That's what I always say."

*****

Abe pressed forward at a snail's pace down the tunnel towards the baku. He controlled his breathing and measured his steps with his eyes fixed at the smooth, worn stones just ahead of his feet. Trying to lift his eyes to look ahead at the monstrosity he neared was too herculean a task.

"Take my hand," Zeud said, and Abe did.

Pace quickened, they entered the larger, better lit central room of the baku's tunnel complex.

"I smell incense," he whispered.

"I enjoy a pleasant aroma when I sit down for a meal," an alien, hissing voice said.

Abe's whole body froze solid, and he felt his nervous system go apeshit. He started sweating as his mouth went dry, and his hands started to quake.

"Oh dear," the voice whispered. "I'm sorry I frightened you. I didn't mean to."

"It's... it's okay. I'm just dealing with some issues," Abe stammered out.

"That much is apparent, my guest. If it pleases you, keep your eyes lowered. I will remain still, here on my bed of pillows while your friend the dragon brings you to me. I will not touch you. My name is Moriko."

Somehow, her words stilled his heart a tiny bit. "Okay, thank you."

"It is my pleasure. I wish your visit to me didn't cause you such dismay. Perhaps once you are well, you can tell me what happened to you that gives you such fear about creatures such as I."

"I had to fight monsters. Real bad ones."

"I see. I am glad that you came out of your battle with the monsters. At least, came out in the condition that you are in, and not worse," the baku said.

"Just because the outside looks good, doesn't mean the inside is alright. I'm a grainy apple on two feet."

"Abe, you're strong. You'll be okay," Zeud said, guiding him to a spot on the floor just in front of a bed of red pillows.

He almost looked up at her to thank her.

"I enjoy the smells of western food," Baku said. "Most

especially, baked foods."

"And? What does that have to do with us getting radiation sickness? Or your incense? Clearly by the way, not biscotti scented."

"Banana bread," it said.

That managed to get Abe's eyes up off the floor. He took in the majestic, terrifying form of the baku and felt... fine. No shaking, no fear, no violent retching. All he felt was curiosity in the presence of the strange beast, and a pervasive intelligence behind the creature's human eyes.

"Yes, banana bread. Did you know that banana bread is made with bananas that are bad? Old? Passed their prime for regular consumption. Did you know that?" it asked him with a mouth that didn't look capable of such mundane human speech.

"I knew that."

"You remind me of banana bread. On the inside you seem useless, and yet there are things that can be done with you still. Great things, judging by the measure of your character, at least how your friends speak of you."

He blushed and the corner of the creature's feline mouth cracked a smile.

"If it pleases Abraham, Zeud, I would ask you to remain at his side while I cleanse him of the taint."

"Stay," he said to the dragon still holding his hand. "Are you going to touch me?" He asked the baku. "I don't know how that'd go."

"There is no need for my paws or mouth to touch you. Simply remain close, and relax. It is painless, and quick."

Abraham looked the baku straight in its human-eyed tiger-face and nodded before he had any chance to think about it. He closed his eyes, and let his chin slip downward to his chest. *I don't have to watch. I don't have to watch. Please don't sound like wet slurping, and crunching, and swallowing. I'll fucking kill myself.*

Humming. The creature started humming. A soft melody not unlike the sound that his mother would make in the living room on the weekends when she did her cross stitch projects. Or was it embroidery? Memories of warm summer days in Framingham Massachusetts, and baked goods on the eve of Christmas flooded into his consciousness, obscuring the real world around him. As the soft humming kept on, Abe couldn't help but smile.

"Feeling better yet?" Zeud asked.

Her speech broke the illusion of being back at home. "Uh, yeah, actually. I feel much better. My chest doesn't hurt, and my skin doesn't feel like it's trying to walk off without me."

"The baku is a wondrous creature. Thank Tesser for whatever hand he had in guiding evolution to give them to the world."

"More dragon fingerprints on the world," Abe whispered in a laugh.

"Yes, well, given our tenure here it stands to reason there would be quite a few."

The humming continued for several minutes, and Abe's body felt more and more his again with each passing second. The illness he'd received due to the radiation exposure faded away, up and into the baku's mouth like smoke off a fire.

The humming ceased, and Abe took a deep breath. He almost expected a cloth to be whisked away from his chest and neck as if he'd just gotten the best haircut of his life.

"My belly is overfull, and you are now well, Abraham," it said, then purred like a tiger. "Well enough for now, at least. When you have time, you should return to me and dream. I can help you with the troubles that plague your mind."

"Thank you, Moriko."

"You are welcome. Now, if I may ask something of you…"

149

He looked up. The baku wore a pleading expression on it's very not-human face. A sudden dose of sympathy shot into him, and he knew whatever the baku was about to ask of him, was very important to it.

"I seek to contact my family. We have been disconnected for decades. I wish to know if they are alive. Zeud believes you are able to put us together using powerful magic."

"I can try a defero spell. Do you know what a telephone is?"

"I live in a cave, but I know much of what lies beyond it. I don't have my family's phone numbers," Moriko said.

"All I really need is a strong memory of them, a name, and a few minutes to prepare the spell's circle." Abe looked around the room at the decorations and shelves, seeing jars of strange substances with labels in Japanese. "I think you might have the raw materials I need. I can also fetch the case from... shit. My case of goodies was trashed in the tour van," he said, giving Zeud a frown.

"I'll replace it. Talk to Mr. Doyle and get a list," she said.

"Whatever. Look, tell me what's in your jars, and I'll do everything I can for you," he said to the baku. "It won't take long to get answers. I... can't tell you whether or not they'll be the ones you want, though."

"I'm not asking for reassurances from you. I'm seeking truth. Even a baku has trouble sleeping at night."

*****

Abe gathered sufficient materials off the baku's shelves for the defero spell his mentor Mr. Doyle taught him, drew his circle of salt on the floor, and cast the spell with the magical Moriko at his side.

No one from her family answered Abe's call, but the spell did connect them with other surviving baku, though not many.

He stayed with her until Spoon came down with news that the men and women who attacked them had surfaced in Kazakhstan, and it hadn't gone well there either.

Abe promised Moriko he would help her if he could, and he meant it.

Chapter Twenty-One

Tapper Special Agent Henry "Spoon" Spooner

Sixteen hours later Zeud's private jet touched down on the single runway at the tiny Krayniy airport to the west of Baikonur in the old Soviet republic of Kazakhstan. Just prior to the jet's final approach Spoon saw a pair of Russian Mil Mi-24 attack helicopters moving in predatory circles between them and the distant Cosmodrome. One had taken up residence over the city of Baikonur proper and the other moved in the space between the city and the launch area for the rockets headed to space.

"Two choppers. Russian markings," Spoon said to his two travel companions. *I wonder how much damage these assholes did to the spaceport. Not too many people launching rockets into space anymore. Would be a shame if these assholes we're chasing screwed stuff up.*

"Should we be worried about those helicopters?" Abe

153

asked.

"I am not worried," the dragon answered. "Nothing flies in the skies that will push me away from finding the people who incited the events in Japan."

"That's all well and good, Zeud," Abe said. "But I am considerably more vulnerable to air to ground rockets than you are."

"I wouldn't worry," Spoon said. "They're here to protect the Cosmodrome. Without doubt they know Zeud's a dragon, and they know this is her plane. They know we're here to investigate, and help. The fallout of attacking Tapper agents and a dragon would be real bad for them. They have no reason to shoot at us."

"We're protected by potential fallout. Irony," Abe said. "Who do you think that plane belongs to over there?"

Abe pointed to a similar sized private jet sitting near a rusting hangar that leaned just enough to the side to make it look entirely unsafe.

"Probably Doyle's Russian buddy," Spoon said. "Belyakov."

"Doyle said he'd meet us here. How do you know it's his plane?"

"My powerful detective skills have revealed a small man standing at the front wheel of the plane who resembled the picture Doyle once showed me of Belyakov," Spoon explained with a sigh.

"Oh no shit, yeah."

"Let's go say hi," Spoon said. "Dude is one of Doyle's inner circle of trusted friends. He's got to be the real deal."

"You know Mr. Doyle can be a bonafide asshole right? I love the guy, he's done amazing things for me, but he can be abrasive. Anyone he calls friend could be just as much of an asshole as he is. Belyakov has his own agenda as well, I might add."

"Doyle calls us his friends," Spoon countered.

"You need more proof than that to be on guard around this Belyakov dude?"

Ah shit.

*****

"Your prey eludes you," the bent Russian said in accented English before anyone exchanged greetings on the tarmac. "They have already gone into the thin air."

"Hi, I'm Spoon," Spoon said.

"Da, I know of who you are," the Russian answered. "All of you. You are the card player, and you lady, are the dragon of fire."

"And you're Belyakov," Zeud purred. "I've heard so many things about you."

Belyakov lifted his wrinkled chin up to look at the tall woman with the crimson curls. His gray-blue eyes lit up when he truly took her in.

"You are as pretty as the stories tell."

"I'm more than just a pretty human skin."

"Da, so much more," he blurted, then collected himself. He gave her a tiny bow over the cane he leaned on.

"You're healing well," Abe said to Belyakov. "Mr. Doyle has been worried sick about what the varcolac did to you in Romania."

"Artur," the Russian mused. "A man who lost himself, nearly killed me, and somehow found his way back to civility. He is a treasured resource to those of us who stand between the darkness and the light. I call him friend."

"He was badass," Spoon said. "I fought the vampires with him in Vegas. He did fucking *work*."

"Killing vampires is what he was born to do," the Russian said.

"I heard he got married," Abe said.

"Yes, and is expecting twins in the autumn," Belyakov

added with a wry smile. "More Cojocaru varcolacs, if the world is lucky. If there will always be vampires, there will always be a need for hunters of them. I wonder if the father of vampires will take a dislike to the werewolves who hunt the children he has suddenly embraced as his progeny."

"Ambryn isn't that fickle," Spoon said. "He understands the predator and prey relationship."

"Werewolves," Zeud whispered with a smile. "You know in all my years I've never met one. I would like to, one day. Meet another creature that can shift between skins. There aren't many, and they're reclusive. One foot in two worlds, a member of neither. I feel as if they are kin to me, in a way."

"Once we nab these walking bombs we can book a flight to Romania and you and Artur can kick it. Leave your booze in the mini bar though. He's clean and sober now," Spoon said to her.

"I would like that."

"What happened here?" Spoon asked the Russian. "They tell you anything? Are you up to date with the events?"

"I am," Belyakov said, nodding and leaning harder on his cane. "Your… prey erupted out of the ground in the middle of Baikonur. Caused a traffic accident resulting in the death of a truck driver. They used magic that triggered radiation sensors all over the city. Very unusual."

"They cleaned up all the pollution in Fukushima using some unknown spell," Abe volunteered. "Stored the radiation inside their bodies, then attacked us with it. When they popped, it dumped a ton of radiation out, but in a small area."

"Their mark has faded a bit already," Belyakov said. "But they have done more damage since. The city will suffer great disruption. Measures must be undertaken to cleanse the area, I fear."

"What?" Spoon asked. *I hope they didn't kill anyone else.*

"They attempted to flee north towards the Cosmodrome in a stolen vehicle, and when a helicopter fired warning shots to get them to stop, they used more magic, and shot it out of the sky. All crew dead. The helicopter crashed into a small business, killing more there."

Shit. "Russian Mi-24 like those?" Spoon asked, pointing out towards the two attack helicopters circling the nearby skies.

The Russian man replied with a somber nod.

Mixed bag. Fucking Russians. "Where are our peeps now?"

"They drove their car into a communications junction box on the side of the road several kilometers short of the launch facility. Large explosion."

"Did you collect bodies? How many?" Zeud asked.

"Nyet. After the fires went out, we searched their vehicle. There were signs of blood in the back seat. A lot of blood. Yet we found no bodies."

"So they went into the wires again," Abe said. "Same as Japan. I wonder where they're heading now. Was there any damage to wires heading in any direction? We can track them straight from Fukushima to here based on damage done to fiber optic cables, and ground lines. Like the fuse lit on dynamite. They did so much damage to the communication systems in South Korea and China. Damn near an act of war."

"Nyet, just kaboom," he said, blossoming his free hand's fingers into a gesture of explosion. "And goodbye. And China will recover. They always do. Resilient and hardy."

"Fuck," Spoon said. "Now what? If we lost the trail, we're screwed. They could pop up like the Devil's gophers anywhere. Go off like a dirty nuke then be gone."

"I do not believe your people came to Kazakhstan

intentionally. If they travel on the wires why would they head to here through China, and Mongolia? Would it not make more sense to go another way?" the Russian said.

"Unless they wanted to leave Earth on a rocket?" Abe supposed. "Do you think they're stranded aliens?"

"It's possible," Zeud said. "However, Earth has been visited by precious few beings from other planets. None have used magic beyond what you have already experienced in England, Abe."

Spoon watched Abe's face lose its color before he turned away.

The evils that boy saw in England, man. Poor kid.

"Let us think that they are not wanting to leave Earth. Who comes to here by accident, and why?"

"Maybe they were just running blind. Maybe they had no idea what they were doing," Abe offered.

"Maybe they tried to travel in a straight line, instead of following the best lines heading where they wanted to go," Spoon added.

"If that logic holds, then we can guess that they were headed to... Europe?" Zeud said. "Larger targets to attack?"

"Running home," Abe said. "I think they bit off more than they could chew in Japan, then maybe made a few bad decisions and are trying to get to familiar ground. They're eluding us, sure, but I think they're running scared. This has soup sandwich written all over it."

"Good a theory as any," Spoon said. "So we head to Europe? Germany? Wait and see what happens there?"

"I know a very nice restaurant in Frankfurt. After World War Two it had a history of catering to... unusual clientele. Also offered a fantastic coq au vin. Best I've ever had outside of France," Zeud said.

"What's Coke-oh-veen?" Spoon asked her.

"It's food, you troglodyte," Abe said.

"Yeah your momma kisses this troglodyte," Spoon shot back at him. "I like food, and I hate Kazakhstan—no offense, Belyakov—so I say we drop a bomb in the airport shitter, stretch out for a few minutes, then push off for good eats in central Europe."

"And pray they don't pop up and annihilate Istanbul while we're in the air," Abe said.

"I'll talk to the pilot. Mr. Belyakov, it was a pleasure meeting you. I hope we have the chance to meet again," she said, extending her hand to the Russian. He took it, and bowed a tiny bit.

"Before you go in such a rush, I have come to here to lend gifts because my old friend has asked me to," Belyakov said, reaching into the small pocket on the belly of his also-small sicken vest. He fished out a piece of coal and held it aloft so they could see it. A warm breeze blew through the flat airport grounds just as it appeared. "This is black tourmaline."

"Looks like coal," Spoon said.

"And yet, it is not," the Russian said. He put the stone back in his pocket and produced a silver-chained necklace from under his vest and shirt. A silver pendant hung on it. At the pendant's center was a piece of the same stone. "This is a secret Russian development. Very old. Very effective when enchanted properly. We used almost our entire supply during the early days of the Chernobyl meltdown. Still... many died and got sick."

"What does it do?" Spoon asked.

"Absorbs radiation. Very effective. I have brought each of you two. Wear it when you feel exposed."

"Do they expire?" Spoon asked.

"Da, indeed, they do. They absorb a tremendous amount of energy first, but will then crumble to dust, and leave only the mounting behind. When that happens, run, and pray if you believe in God."

"I believe in Zeud," Spoon said. "Same thing really. Did you know people worshipped her at one point?"

"Don't," Zeud chastised. "Thank you, Belyakov. I hope that we don't need them. I'll see to it they are brought back to you when we have finished with this."

"Nyet. Bring them to Doyle. I owe him a small favor. This makes us even. Tell him to stop calling me with problems."

They laughed at the Russian.

"Thank you, really," Abe said. "These people are a real conundrum. I don't know how we're gonna track them down and either help them, or stop them."

"If you seek to catch a bird, you must clip away its ability to fly. Not just run behind it as it flits from tree to tree," Belyakov said before turning, and walking away. "That or offer the bird a better nest."

A moment later they realized a wooden case sat on the ground where Belyakov once stood. In the case were eight of the black tourmaline amulets.

Chapter Twenty-Two
Belyakov

[TRANSLATED FROM RUSSIAN]

The old Russian with the broken back and worn body leaned on the silver headed cane forged in the deep of Siberia's frozen forests as the dragon's little jet lifted its nose off the runway and took off into the warm Kazakh sky.

He reached into the pocket of his slacks and removed a small medallion not unlike the set he gave the people departing in the thundering jet. Belyakov looked at the black, roughly diamond shaped chunk of mineral, seeking out any cracks, discoloration, or flaws that any radiation their presence brought.

"Clean as whistles," the old man muttered. "Cleansed by the Japanese baku, no doubt."

He turned on sore feet and shuffled in the direction of his own small jet. A small set of metal stairs on wheels ascended from the tarmac to the open door at his chest height. As he reached out to grab the rail with his free hand, one of the pilots leaned out the nearby opening, and addressed him in Russian.

"Moscow wishes to speak with you."

"Tell Moscow I am old, and tired, and have nothing to

tell them."

"I... don't think they'll like that," the pilot said. "They are firm. You must speak to them."

He took the first step up then paused to look at the pilot and shrug.

"If you will not talk to them, what do you want me to say?"

"I say to tell them I am old, and tired, and have nothing to say."

"I have to give them some kind of news about the Tapper people or the dragon. Some intelligence they can assign value to. They didn't lend this plane to you only to get nothing in return."

"Ah, I see. Now comes the price," Belyakov said after taking another step up. "Always a cost to be paid, yeah? So, tell them the dragon is as they could've thought; perfect in every way, and capable of doing whatever she wishes, whenever she wishes it. All their fears reside in her and what she is."

"Okay... and the men?"

"They already know about Henry and Abraham. Tell them to dig into their FSB records, and search the tube online. They have left a large fingerprint on the world at large and I am sure they have large dossiers about the both of them."

"The tube?"

"YourTube."

"YouTube?"

Belyakov stopped just a few feet away from the pilot and gave him a glare that made the other man take a step backwards towards the cockpit. "Enough stupidity."

"I'll tell them the men gave up no secrets of value."

"Very good. Smart. Now, I will sit down, and then you are to take me home. I must enchant more medallions to replenish my stock now that I've given some away. Weeks of work lay ahead."

"May I... Before I report to them? I have a question."

"Yes?"

"So... I know that magic is real. I know that there were many years where it faded away and we thought it lost, and no one believed in it, and many of us have forgotten about it or don't believe in it, and I know that with the dragons being so... popular, and known, magic is being used by many more people, but I have a wonder. Something that I have always thought about...."

Now is the time he tells me about something deep and personal, and he tries to bond with me. Such awkwardness.

"Is Baba Yaga real?"

Belyakov felt a chill run up and down his body. His knees quaked a tiny bit, and he had to grab the entry to the plane to steady himself.

"She's real, isn't she?"

Belyakov moved with deliberate purpose to the couch across the center of the plane's interior. He collapsed into it before the pilot arrived to help him sit. He breathed heavily several times, coughed to clear his thought, and composed a response.

"Baba Yaga is... a story. But like all stories, there is an element of truth within. With no doubt to be had, she is real, and you should mind the warnings contained in the stories about her. Avoid the deep, old forests. Avoid the oldest magic that is alive again unless you want to attract the attention of the things that feast upon it. Things equally old. Curse the baby dragon for what she's put a meal in front of, once again."

"I will fly this plane, and never hike the mountains again," the pilot said. He rubbed at the stubble on his chin out of worry as his eyes darted around. "I thought this world was simpler than it is."

Silly child. "Boy, you are a veteran? You perhaps are still active duty?"

"I served, yes. I work for the government now."

"Then you have seen or heard of unspeakable things, yes? Watched bombs fall from the sky? Watched body parts fly into the air? I'm sure you know secrets the Russian government would kill you for, if you were to talk about them, yes?"

"I can't say."

"Wise child, perhaps not too silly after all. Now, if you have seen these things with your eyes, things that are not so simple after all, things of terrible military tragedy, then you know for certain just how dark man alone and his deeds can be, and imagine yet… there are monsters that make the darkest of men pale as ghosts before their time."

"I don't feel well," the pilot said. "I must get us into the air."

"That could be the feeling of Baba Yaga hearing us speak of her, you know," Belyakov said. "She hears her name when it is said." He leaned towards the pilot. "She *knows* of you now. More than ever before, and she'll come for you if you speak ill of her. Do you have children? Are they safe?"

The pilot ducked back into the cockpit and yanked the security door shut. After a few seconds Belyakov heard the man talking on a cell phone. He had called his wife.

The old Russian chuckled.

"Were you telling the truth?" a male voice called out from deeper in the plane.

Belyakov turned his attention to the speaker at the back of the aircraft. The man who came from Moscow to oversee it all, and see to it Belyakov didn't say more than was necessary. *Ah, my 'handler.'* "You saw many of the same things our pilot saw, yes? But much worse. You didn't watch the bombs fall from the wing of your airplane. You saw what happened right on the ground. You kicked in doors, and stared evil straight in the face, yes? On your hip under that little jacket you wear is the pistol you would use if you need it, yes? I can smell its iron and steel. More yet, I can smell the blood it has spilled. You earned the right to carry that weapon because you earned the right to carry other weapons that smelled of iron and steel and blood, at an earlier time, yes? Not that long ago. You are still young."

The taciturn man with the shaved head nodded, but his expression remained unchanged. "Were you telling the truth about the old hag? Is she real, or just a story made up to scare children into staying near home?"

"What makes you think I really know that answer?"

"Because, the people I work for, are terrified of you, your powers, and the friends you keep. And the people I work for scare everyone else in the world," he said, and his expression changed into a smile. "And when those that frighten all others are frightened of something...."

Ah yes, the viper hisses. Or perhaps that's admiration. How would a viper tell you it respects you? "Well, I am glad my years on this world were not spent in vain. I had always wanted to grow up in such a way that I would strike fear into the hearts of the men who work at the KGB, and FSB."

"Is she real?"

"Worry less about the dark tale of a creature that you have never met, and likely never will, and worry more about the man who scares the people you work for."

Belyakov leaned his head back against the top of the couch and closed his eyes. He slid a hand into his slacks pocket and removed a handful of enchanted stones. He closed his hand around the rocks, and drew power from them.

He fought a smile, and said a silent spell to ward against the prying eyes of Baba Yaga.

Chapter Twenty-Three
Fiona Gilmore

Blown on the wires of the world like a leaf in a hurricane, Fiona led her three friends towards Vienna. Unlike their first grand exit out of Japan, this time Fiona had a better sense of how to navigate. At the very least, she knew to not point herself in a physical direction and then try to force them to that point. She had to be like water, and take the path of least resistance, even it if was further to "physically" travel.

This time, she knew that the fastest point between Kazakhstan and Austria wasn't the path a crow would fly; instead it was the path that data moved fastest in. Fortunate for her, Seamus, Laurie and Hamza as soon as they got to Moscow the infrastructure heading west into Europe became far more robust, and easier to navigate.

With eyes that didn't exist, she saw the data this time, too. She watched the zeroes and ones fly by, and let the magic she was made of make sense of it for her. She saw splits in the directions they could go and in her mind's eye she saw street signs telling her where they would take her. So, she looked and watched as the languages in the streams changed back and forth between local tongues, and when she saw a prevalence of Hungarian,

167

then German, and a strange dialect of German, she reached out and sensed the great city they sought.

Like a forest made of glowing spider webs that reached up to Heaven and down to Hell the city exploded into her consciousness. She could hear, smell, and taste all the experiences every person interacting with the internet there had, and she found the threads of conversation, and information that showed her where they ultimately needed to go; The International Atomic Energy Commission.

After circling that area of the data and wiring of Vienna, she searched social media posts, blogs, and found the names of people who worked at the Commission that they might find a sympathetic ear with, specifically searching for Dr. Tidwell, the woman they knew who would be a good possibility for them. That done, she found a soft place for them to breach back into reality.

She followed the signs marking the pathways of energy and information as they became smaller and smaller, and the wires as they became thinner and thinner until she felt a pain free physical pressure squeezing them into a shape and size that had to be subatomic.

Then, with a pleasant pop, and the physical release that usually accompanied the departure from a chiropractor's office... They rematerialized. Fiona had found them an exit into an apartment with tall ceilings, white walls, and windows that looked out into the old downtown of Vienna. Sunlight streamed in, illuminating expensive paintings, and find furniture, but the brightness paled in comparison to the storm of energy they'd just exited.

"Where the-" a naked Seamus asked in a panic. He clutched at his crotch, then at his torso where just minutes before he'd been peppered with gunshot wounds.

Laurie stood a few feet to his side, touching at her own perfect body, searching for blood and gore, but finding nothing and saying an equal amount.

Hamza looked at the married couple with wide eyes. He stole a glance to Fiona, who had already started to look around the apartment to see if anyone was home.

"I should be dead," Seamus said. "You should be dead," he said to Laurie.

"I know," Laurie whispered. "You saved us," she said to Fiona.

"I did," Fiona said, then smiled. "I thought jumping might fix you. I was right."

"Spot on, Fiona," Hamza said. "You're a miracle-worker."

"Thank you," Fiona said.

Seamus stepped to Fiona and embraced her. Fiona's air slipped out of her as he held on tight.

"You saved Laurie's life. You saved my life," Seamus said into her ear. "You are an angel of light, and power. You are a prodigy."

That feels good to hear. "Thank you. From you, that means a great deal."

"Of course. Where are we?"

"Vienna," she answered. "Not far at all from the IAEC. I wanted us to land in a place that had some privacy. There should be clothes here at the very least. I brought us to a place with four bedrooms. Figured there would be a better chance at getting a wide selection of things to wear. Better than us blowing up into traffic and getting more people hurt butt-ass naked. I'm sorry. I guess I should've dropped us off right in the commission building. It would've been faster." *Shit. Shit. I screwed up again.*

"No, no," Seamus said, squeezing her shoulders. "This is perfect. We're close, it's private, no one got hurt," he paused and looked around the apartment, "I mean, no one got hurt more... Did we even leave a torch line like before? Did we leave no trail getting here?"

"I tried to go slower, take my time. Be selectful about how I steered us. I'm sure there are places that we burned lines through, but whatever it is, it's nothing compared to the mess we made leaving Japan, or arriving in Kazakhstan."

"You are amazing," Seamus said, then let go of her.

Laurie stepped in, continuing the naked embrace-session. *Our bodies are red hot. All of us. We're barely containing the power inside us. It's getting worse.* She kissed Fiona on the cheek before stepping away, and covering her more private spots on her bare body with her hands. *If she noticed the heat, she isn't saying anything.*

"Let's search the closets and dressers for clothes we can wear," Seamus started. "And then we can figure out how to approach the nuclear people."

"We should remain focused on Dr. Hillary Tidwell. From what I saw, she's still our best bet. I already dredged up a few names for alternatives, but it's a big drop from number one to number two," Fiona said. "As it pertains to quality."

"What? How? We've been together the entire time since Fukushima."

"When we were on the lines travelling."

"What?" Seamus pressed.

"I... I figured out how to read the data as we travel. It's like... It's like I can see what information is moving beside us and read it. Like sitting down at a browser, but at a hundred miles an hour and all the information is screaming by on digital billboards in every direction. It's full tilt crazy."

"You Googled something while we were tearing ass through the wires in the ground?"

"More or less, yeah. Brilliant little accident, yeah?" Fiona tried to hide her proud smile.

"Unreal. You are... just unreal. What're we looking at? Who do we need to talk to?" Seamus asked. "Tidwell?"

"Yes, the same two scientists have more posts online that made it sound like they wanted to talk to us. They know about us, who we are, what our names are, and they want to help us. Well, they at least made it sound that way. I'm thinking we start by calling or emailing them."

"Or just paying them a visit," Hamza suggested. "Calling or messaging might make them notify the authorities, and we'd be back on the run again."

"You might be right," Seamus wondered. "Yeah. Let's um, get some information about where they live, and what we need to do to intercept them somewhere, and make a plan. Fiona, do you know if anyone lives here? Should we be expecting the return of people?"

"I didn't catch any names, but I'm sure there's mail around we can read," she pointed at a large family photo portrait on the wall. "Mother and father, two kids of Uni age. Expect a return when work gets out."

"Right. Well, let's get clothes, and get some food, and see if there are some things we can grab, and then let's sail off to a quieter place where we can set up shop. Look everyone; we have no reason to rush. We're safe now. We can go as we please, and get things done without having to run like chickens with our heads cut off."

"I'm not sure," Fiona said. "When you and Laurie hugged me... you were both on fire. I feel like I'm about to erupt into flames. Like a fever that doesn't feel like I'm sick, but something else."

"She's right," Hamza said.

"She is," Laurie said. "I think we need to talk to these people sooner rather than later. If the energy inside us is growing, then we could release that energy at any point."

"We could blow up, or worse," Fiona said. "And we can't be inside a city the size of Vienna when and if it happens."

Seamus sighed a frustrated sound then nodded. "Okay, we still need to do all the things I said, but let's do it faster. If we can meet up with one of the IAEC people Fiona found tonight, or tomorrow, and have it not be a frigging kidnapping, let's make it happen."

"If I can find a computer I can log onto, I'll dig up more info on the two people," Fiona offered. *Or, I can just load myself back into the web, and absorb all the info immediately. Be faster.* "There has to be a PC here, or an internet café close."

"I'll watch the windows and doors," Laurie said.

"I'll... I'll help find clothes," Hamza said.

"And try not to blow up. Everyone try not to blow up," Seamus said.

Fiona laughed, but the heat clutched around her heart reminded her with a boil and a scald that her laughter was, at best, ill advised.

Chapter Twenty-Four
Zeud

Henry made a call to the Berlin office of Tapper while they were in the air. By the time Zeud's jet lowered its staircase, the German Tapper agent had one of the sleek black American-Made SUVs waiting at the bustling Frankfurt airport.

"I am Tapper Special Agent Daniel Chung," he said to Henry with a British accent. "I work out of the Berlin Tapper office."

"Special Agent Henry Spooner. Call me Spoon."

"It's an honor, sir." They shook. "You must be Zeud, then?"

"Were you expecting a different woman to be with them in her private jet?" she joked. They shook hands.

"No, ma'am," Chung laughed. "Wow, your hand is very warm. Guess I should've expected that, given your nature. No offense intended. You could be your assistant, Kemala. I don't know what she looks like. Could mess that up. It's a pleasure to meet a real dragon. I haven't had the chance to yet."

"I understand. Thank you for meeting us here on such short notice."

"Of course. You must be Special Agent Fellows."

"Abe is fine," he replied and shook as well. "You're originally from the UK?"

"I am, London. I was in training at the New Hampshire facility in the States when everything went down with you and the mutant virus in London, and on the Isle of Lundy. Personally; thank you for what you did. You saved countless lives and put us on the trail of rooting out some damned evil infestations. And what you went through sounded hellish."

You could say that, Zeud thought.

"You could say that," Abe echoed. "Thank you for coming with the truck. Can you stick with us to act as a guide?"

"That's what I requested."

"So," Special Agent Chung posed on the tarmac of the warm Frankfurt airport, "Do you have actionable intelligence on where the fugitives are now? I suspect you didn't come to Frankfurt Germany without some kind of an idea of what was about to happen."

"We came to Frankfurt for food," Zeud answered.

"Food?" the British agent replied.

"Yes. Coq au vin, specifically. There's a very special restaurant here in Frankfurt that I'd like you to direct us to. It's old, and well hidden from mundane eyes, but I hope you can get us to the entrance if I give you some landmarks."

"I'll do my best," Chung replied. "I can translate as well."

"The food will not disappoint, and if the place is at all like it used to be… neither will the company," the dragon said. "To our obsidian chariot, friends."

*****

"Stop right there," the dragon said to Chung. *These buildings are the right ones. That courtyard over there is the right one. There should be an alley right behind that stairwell heading up the hill.*

The agent pulled the large SUV to the side of the street and parked it. "We getting out?"

"Follow me," the dragon said, opening the rear door she sat beside.

Abe exited the passenger front and Spoon the passenger rear. The four met on the sidewalk, three men in suits, and a tall, dark-skinned redhead wearing a crimson and orange summer dress. She smiled at the men, slipped her arm into Henry's and led them down the sidewalk towards the stairs and the alley she expected to find.

Sandwiched between the rear of a long row of apartments and sheer concrete retaining wall that edged a small park a full story above the alley's floor, the narrow passage was only wide enough for transit on foot, bicycle, or moped.

"Now on the right here," Zeud explained, "these buildings housed normal humans, unaware of the quite unique location and its unique guests just opposite on the left."

"The park up there?" Henry asked her. "Park's pretty obvious."

"No, this cement wall here. There are cracks in it, you see," she said, and let go of Henry's arm. She walked closer to the retaining wall and ran her slender, strong fingertips against the stone. She traced the flaws in the manmade surface as if following the lines in the palm of a trusted lover. She stole a glance at Henry, and continued walking, leading them. Her fingers remained touching the wall.

"The last time I was here the first human world war was about to start. The engines of destruction were idling, and the soldiers moved about. Tanks to tread on the ground, planes to rule the skies above, all that. Oh, and perhaps most important were the murmurs in the shadows by assassins and spies. Such a story, truthfully.

Such a romantic notion to see nations at war on the backs of their populaces. Heroism and bravery and nobility, all hiding behind the bloody veil of savagery."

"War is hell," Henry said, flat.

"That it is," she agreed, "and yet your species loves it like no other. Perhaps they seek a world that is as good as the afterlife they'll wind up in?"

"That is Bleak. As. Fuck," Abe said. "You're on our side?"

Zeud laughed. "Ah, I'm sorry. I am on your side. I am on Earth's side. I take no sides among that which walks often though. Not my place to influence the actions of every individual that has walked the world."

"Dragons are fascinating," Chung said. "I would give everything to hear what you've seen and done over the millennia."

"Some *have* given everything," she said without looking at him. "Look where that got them. However, here *we* are."

Zeud stopped at an iron drainage grate in the ground, careful not to step on it. She waved her hand at the moss-covered wall behind it and the ground around it as if she were presenting a five course meal atop a satin-covered table. The area smelled of garbage, and the earthy scent of water run-off.

The men looked around, each seemingly hoping one of them saw the Emperor's clothes.

"You don't see it?" she asked.

"No," all three of them said.

"Oh I forget your haven't the eyes of a dragon. This grate here, it's old. Cold iron, forged by hammer by blacksmiths with troll and dwarf blood in the great Black Forest, not far from where the Seven Standing Stones are. Its underside is covered in runes and etching of terrible power."

"Earth has dwarves?" Abe asked.

"Had," Zeud answered. "They didn't survive the

pogrom of the second human world war. Died off as a result of Hitler's craving for the blood of Jews. Your media would call them 'collateral damage,' I think."

"Fucking ouch," Henry said. "Were they cool? Like Gimli, and Thorin?"

Abe looked at him as if he'd grown a third eye. "You read The Lord of the Rings?"

"I saw the movies. Tried to read the books as a teenager but they moved too slow for me."

"Good enough," Abe said, and patted him on the back. "Here's your nerd card."

"They're really good books," Chung said. "And the movies were very entertaining. I mean, there was a lot of walking in them, but thematically they were accurate to the story. I still think the eagles could've flown over the mountains into Mordor."

"I know, right?" Abe said. "I mean yeah it would've been tough with the elevation and all, but I think they could've done it."

"Gandalf was a bit of sandbagger like that," Henry said, jumping in.

"This is a portal," Zeud said. "It sends us to a pocket dimension inside the cracks of this wall where the restaurant is-but-not-is. Is any of that thematically interesting to any of you? Real life magic versus the literary kind?"

"Reading books is the purest form of magic," Abe said. "Words create thoughts, and thoughts create the world. Prove me wrong."

Zeud gave him the stink eye.

They shut up, and nodded.

"To enter, you step on the grate, crouch down low, and whisper a secret you've told *no one* to the gatekeeper that hides below. Once the entity has your secret, it will decide if what you share warrants travel to the restaurant."

"What if it doesn't?" Abe asked.

"Then you must tell the entity another secret."

"How many chances do I get before the gatekeeper swallows my soul and shits it out in the Frankfurt sewer?" Abe asked.

"What's left of your soul won't go to the sewer," Zeud answered. "Three times. If you fail by the third secret... the gatekeeper deems you unworthy of the portal and the secret it holds. Just... tell a good secret. Tell a secret that *no one* has ever heard. The subject of the secret is irrelevant, only the secret's perfection."

"Who goes first?" Henry asked.

"Henry, why don't you?"

"Should I expect danger?" he asked.

"No. The restaurant is a peaceful place, albeit strange, as is its proprietor. Equally, your weapon will be useless there, only magic, and raw physical power. The place has a way of draining danger."

"Maybe I should go first," Chung offered. "I have a few spells."

"As you wish, Special Agent Chung." *Bravery? Or heightened trust?*

"Step on the grate, crouch, and speak your secret to the gatekeeper below."

The British agent stepped forward — slow at first, then with some confidence — and guided his way to the top of the grate. He placed both feet on the iron and bent down at the knees to crouch. He looked through the iron bars into the dark depths of the German sewers. The moment he dropped low to the ground, all sound from inside the grate's perimeter voided from the world. He was present, but no longer quite... there. Agent Chung had entered the gatekeeper's realm.

She watched as his eyes widened, and he smiled at the gatekeeper below. He coughed — a silent thing in the vacuum of magic he was in — and whispered something into the grate with his mouth obscured. He listened downward, nodded in response to something said from below, then stood. He turned to them, flashed a thumbs up, and erupted into a downward splash of pure water.

The waterfall fell through the grate with eerie precision, leaving no traces that moisture had passed.

"Holy shit," Abe said. "You didn't say that was gonna happen. Is he okay?"

That'll never get old. "He's fine. Which one of you brave young men wants to go next?"

"I'll go," Abe said. He stepped forward onto the grate and dropped down without moment's hesitation. After a brief pause he whispered to the thing below, stood up, and dissolved into a downward blast of water.

"Holy crap," Henry said. "Good secret. Okay my turn." Henry stepped into the grate's void and looked back at her. His eyes lingered, locked with hers, and he smiled. Henry crouched, spoke to the gatekeeper, then stood.

Nothing happened.

Henry looked down, confused, then kneeled. He argued down into the darkness, making his case. Then he gave up, and looked at Zeud once more. He sighed, spoke again to the gatekeeper, then stood.

This time, he erupted down through the portal's grate, and disappeared, leaving everything as dry as could be.

Zeud stepped forward and crossed the invisible, yet tangible boundary of the magical portal. The fabric of her light, bright dress went still as the breeze bounced off the spell and went around her. The dragon placed her feet on the iron, and looked downward.

Two human eyes set too wide on a face that wasn't human at all looked up at her. Zeud heard the creature's light breathing in the space it lived in, and could heard the pace of that breath pick up in anticipation of her secret. She tugged the bottom of her dress closed. Modesty, and all. She dropped down to be closer to the gatekeeper's eyes and ears and smiled.

"I love Henry," she told it, then stood.

Turning to water was painless.

The monster grabbing her throat when she arrived hurt a little.

Chapter Twenty-Five
Tapper Special Agent Abraham "Abe" Fellows

Abe's body returned from the state of pure water to its normal form with a shocking snap to his nervous system. Everything tingled, and vibrated.

I don't remember the transition getting here. Holy shit, this place...

The pleasant smell of expensive tobacco wafted across his nostrils from an array of hookahs on the rug-covered floor of the low, dim, alcove-littered and warm space. The walls were made of beige stone and were covered in almost every conceivable way possible with artwork of a Middle Eastern and Greek bent. Images of deserts, minarets, djinn, ifrit and obviously Greek architecture and myths were on all the walls, and gave the place an exotic feel beyond the arcane manner with which you got there. Tables no higher than his knees were arrayed around the center of the main chamber of the dark establishment, and each had one of the hookahs.

Each table had from one to three mundane guests sitting on the floor — on pillows, or thick rugs — and they regarded Abe with a mixture of amusement, or annoyance. Sitting at the table closest to him was one of the long-nosed, green skinned goblins that Henry had gone to war against in Mexico. It smoked from a pipe then sipped on the straw buried in a traditional cup of yerba mate, casting a sideways glance in their direction. It chuckled.

Hidden behind the smell of the luxurious smoke was an indescribable aroma of food almost think enough to see. Abe's mouth began to water as his stomach rumbled in hunger.

"Don't look now, but there's a dude standing behind you that might make you shit your slacks," Spoon said at his side.

Without thinking Abe turned and looked straight into a muscled chest of a towering humanoid creature. He tilted his head up, and matched the downward stare of an enormous bull head with glowing red eyes.

"Welcome," it growled at him in deep, German-accented English, baring teeth that had been filed into sharp points, and capped with a gleaming silver metal.

"Wassup," was all Abe managed. *Holy shit it's a minotaur. For reals. Fuck me that's so cool and terrifying at the same time.*

The creature wore no shirt over its tawny covered fur, but protected some of its modesty (or the food on the plates of those eating in the restaurant) by wearing a plaid kilt that hung to its backwards-facing knees. Hanging off a belt at the monster's hip was a warhammer sporting a head the size of a loaf of bread, and a kitchen knife large enough to wage war with.

"I am Chael," the beast said. "How many in your party?"

"Um, us three plus one more."

"Human sized?" it asked as it reached to a wooden podium to grab a stack of heavy leather-bound menus.

"Usually," Spoon replied.

Then, with a gurgling rumble of bubbling water, a female form in the shape of Zeud appeared. The water-woman raised her hands with fluid grace, and snapped them down to her sides as if she were shaking water off. The effect of her action was timed perfectly with her rematerialization into physical form, and the water she flung off went in two directions, spattering the rugs, the nearby tables, and the people sitting. The goblin sipping on yerba mate took a fat drop of water straight to the eye, and he nearly toppled over. He cursed and garbled at her in a tongue Abe didn't understand.

The minotaur saw her, and lunged forward, snapping a massive hand around her neck and picking Zeud up from the floor. He pinned her against a column of stone near the podium and held her aloft, growling.

"Whoa whoa, pre-burger," Spoon said, reaching for his pistol at his hip. "Why don't you set the lady down and get us a table before you get tossed in the grinder."

The minotaur snatched a dirty look at Spoon, but didn't put the dragon down.

Okay, hammer hand is the one on her neck so the weapon is delayed to be drawn... knife is wrong to pull as well, and it's too small a turn radius for him to charge....

"Chael," the dragon said through the choke with a slight wince. "Nice to see you. Table for four, please."

"You are not welcome here until you settle your debts," the minotaur grumbled. "And your debts have accrued interest." He pressed his weight forward, pushing her hard enough into the stone that one of the blocks cracked with a loud crunch. Several of the nearby patrons got up and scampered away.

Well, it's go time. So much for the coq au vin. Abe reached into his pockets and conjured up the words for magic in his mind.

Zeud looked at him, and shook her head just enough to get him to stop.

"Are your furnaces and forges hot enough? I can stoke their flames for another decade," she offered. "Or perhaps you need money? Still trafficking in Nazi gold, Chael? I'm sure I could scare up a bar or two from a safety deposit box somewhere. After all, gold is gold, yes?"

He grumbled an angry noise, and set her down. "I hate dragons. I hate all seven of you."

"Don't be like that," Zeud said, patting him on his giant bicep. "You haven't met Astrid yet, so that's not a fair statement. She's beyond charming, and I am certain you'd love her. And to be honest, I am very sorry that I left without paying my tab last time. There were circumstances beyond my control that pulled me away."

"You could've come back sooner," he snuffled. "Carrying your tab has put me in the poor house."

Zeud laughed and looked around the restaurant. "Nothing has changed, Chael. And this oubliette you call home is no poor house. You've everything anyone in your situation could ever want for."

"I have no freedom," the monster muttered. "And my life is eternal."

"We're all slave to something," she replied. "Allow me to breathe my fire into your ovens. I would also be happy to leave this bracelet made of the finest gold with you. Worth enough to stock your larder for a decade. Surely that will put your mind at ease." She lifted her bare arm and showed him the simple bracelet.

The minotaur leaned in and sniffed the bracelet with its two massive nostrils. Abe watched as its red eyes flared wide in appreciation. A corner of its mouth curled up into a wry smile.

"That's Greek gold," Chael the minotaur said to Zeud.

"That it is," the dragon said with a wistful sigh. "I do

love that era, and those people."

"I'll take it," the minotaur said, then reached down for the four menus it'd dropped in its haste when it tried to choke Zeud out. "Let's get your friends a table, then you can start our ovens back up to an acceptable level of heat."

"Fantastic. Is my old regular booth available?"

"It is. No one dares sit in it after the time you fried that barbarian shaman, and his soul floated into the air with the ashes, and then you burnt that too," Chael said, then laughed. "I do not lament that man's business."

"So superstitious," Zeud said.

"What?" Abe asked. "You fried a dude's soul?"

"And I've spent several centuries pondering what a waste that was. Complete waste. I regret it," Zeud said. "That was one of my more impulsive years. Really a bad year. I set a lot of forest fires that didn't need to be set."

"Wait, what?" Spoon asked. "You set forest fires?"

"Of course I do. Part of what needs to be done. Fire must burn, and there are times when the forests must be reset. Without me, the phoenix cannot rise."

"No, no. Impulsive period? An impulsive year?" Spoon clarified. "Are you saying you have years where you're like... a pyro?"

She considered the question then nodded with a combined shrug. "Fire doesn't always behave as we want it to, Henry, so why should I? Nothing has ever been able to properly control fire, nor me."

She and the minotaur turned and led them into the back warrens of the strange eatery. Before they took any steps to join them, Spoon and Abe stood, with Abe looking at the confused Spoon. Abe clapped him on the shoulder.

"Ayep. That's your woman, so long as she doesn't set you on fire during one of her bad years," Abe reassured. "Or some particularly hot sex. I bet you guys have scalding sex. Pornstar sex, but in realistic positions that are actually comfortable and don't cause cramping."

"None of that is funny," Spoon said as they started following the minotaur and the dragon to the booth where the barbarian shaman met a fiery end.

"It's pretty funny," Chung said. "Not brilliant by any measure, but I got a tiny chuckle out of it."

"I need a whiskey," Spoon said. "I hope they have whiskey here. I don't want any of your magical prison wine, Fellows."

Abe busted knuckles with the new agent and followed the dragon and the minotaur as they passed a small half-circle table mounted on the wall at head height. Half a dozen fairies hovered around it, their gossamer wings beating faster than the eye could perceive, drinking something out of tiny clay mugs. He nodded at them as he passed, and they lifted their mugs to him. Abe couldn't fight the smile, and it happened.

What a life. I wonder what Alexis is up to. I want to call her. Do I get reception here? Where is here?

Chapter Twenty-Six
Hamza Totah

Hamza rubbed with nervous fingers at the shirt on his chest. The growing heat inside burned, and itched, marking the countdown they were all on as it marched towards whatever release the energy had planned. They were running out of time.

"You are sure about this?" Hamza asked Fiona as they walked hand-in-hand down the Austrian street towards a surface tram.

Fiona's eyes were sealed shut in concentration. She nodded, and Hamza felt a jump in the energy in the air surrounding her. A wave of static electricity seemed to course through the air, and he felt his skin prickle head to toe. She'd somehow managed to go "wireless," in her ability to connect to the data streaming all around them.

She's evolving. Adapting to her power faster than the rest of us. Don't get jealous. Be glad one of us is succeeding. "Where are they?"

"In their car headed towards an area called Leapoldstadt," she managed while concentrating. "Their apartment, I think. It's near there. If we grab this tram that's about to stop, it'll bring us over the river right near their place."

"How do you know they're in a car?"

"They have a mobile hotspot in it. If I close my eyes, I can see a map of the city, and their car moving along as the hotspot connects to the cellular towers. Each electronic handshake pings in my head like a tiny bell," she said then paused. "Bread crumbs. They're slowing... stopping. Not right at their address. I think they're getting something at a restaurant or store."

"Quick then, my friend," Hamza said, taking her arm and picking up their pace to the tram. "We must make contact with them before we are identified."

A few seconds later they stepped up onto the surface train, paid for their trip with Euros taken from a drawer at their apartment landing site, and were off down the old city streets towards the bridge that would take them to the two nuclear energy scientists that could shelter them, help them, even maybe redeem them.

*****

"Leapoldstadt is one of the most affluent districts in Vienna," Fiona said as they walked down the wide sidewalk near the river. They took a seat on a bench facing the street, and the buildings opposite."Lots of Jews too."

I see the wealth. It is clean. "There are no cheap cars here," Hamza said to her from their perch. Directly opposite was the small café the two married scientists ate at. They sat against a large window at a small table that struggled to contain two large cups of coffee and a plate with a pastry atop it. "Mercedes, BMW, Bugati. And look, everything is green, and clean. I can tell how wealthy the people are here. As far as whether they're Jews or not, that I can't speak to."

He gestured up at the immaculate architecture of the apartments running along the nearby river and the endless row of luxury cars parked in front of them.

Manicured shrubs and trees covered everything that wasn't clean pavement or cobblestone, bringing the entire appearance of the area back at least a hundred years, prior to the wars that ravaged the area.

"Not all Jews are rich," Fiona began. "That's a racist notion. Anyway, her name is Dr. Hillary Tidwell," Graduate of Oxford, doctorate. Former resident of the United Kingdom. By all I could find online, calling her brilliant only barely touches her gifts. Nuclear scientist. Works on policy. Very progressive. Amateur occultist. Crystal balls and the like."

"She has soft eyes," Hamza said. The short woman with the auburn-red hair in the café did indeed have soft eyes behind her thin glasses. Hamza watched as she looked at her husband with bright interest, and the narrowed eyes that came from a smile. *Their love is unmistakable.*

"That man sitting with her with the gray hair and metal framed glasses belongs to Hillary. That's Cecil, her husband. They met as co-workers in New York City at the offices of the commission there. He's from the States, and is more of a diplomat. Travels to foreign countries to support their nuclear programs. Builds support for the organization. Speaks five European languages, none of which are useful to us."

"He's much older than her."

"Yeah. Don't know that story, but I do know that they've both put up several posts on Facebook and Instagram talking about us, and Fukushima. They know our names, and know that we contained the energy, and have both hit the nail on the bloody head about us being in over our heads with an energy inside us we don't know how to control."

"You're controlling it well enough," Hamza said. "Doing new things, at least."

"In control for now, maybe. Anyways, they're our best bet. I think. If we talk to them, and tell them the truth, we have a shot of getting shelter with the agency, and not dragged into a secure facility where we'll never see the light of day. Can't have the coppers get their hands on us before we can make our case to people who can help us."

"That might still happen with them."

"Yeah," she said. "But it's better than being the pawn of a nation or a bomb getting ready to explode in a prison."

"Talk to them inside the cafe?"

"Sure, yeah. Might make them feel safer if it's in public."

The two stood, and walked across the quiet street towards the café. They were arm-in-arm again, and both managed to do it without rubbernecking back and forth looking for the police, or some interested citizen trying to arrest them. Hamza led up the three stone stairs to the wood and glass door of the café, grabbed the brass knob, turned it, and held the door open for her to entire. A rush of warm air surged out of the bakery past them both.

The smells… such delicious smells. Life itself is in the scent of cooking food. His stomach grumbled, and he unconsciously rubbed at his burning stomach.

Fiona let herself through the inner glass door and took an immediate right hand turn back towards the floor-to-ceiling window the two they sought sat beside. She came to a halt several feet from the scientists (facing Hillary), and waited as the two chatted about something in what sounded like slow German.

"Mr. and Mrs. Tidwell?" Fiona said.

Hillary looked from her husband to Fiona with an expression of genuine niceness; a warm smile, and uplifted, curious eyebrows. She held the smile for several seconds before the brain behind the eyes recognized Fiona's face. She pushed backwards several inches in her chair, setting free a pained noise as the metal legs scraped on the black and white tile floor.

"Please don't be alarmed," Hamza's friend comforted.

"We are not dangerous. We need help."

"Hillary do you know this young-OH MY-," Cecil said, then backed away into the window, doubling the awkward scraping sound.

Hillary gathered herself. "Are you emitting radiation right now?" she then asked.

"Nothing dangerous," Fiona said. "Though we haven't tested ourselves since leaving Japan. We are still able to control the power we absorbed, mostly."

"What happened?" Hillary asked in a whisper. "How did this come about?"

"We tried to fix Fukushima," Hamza answered. "We did, but our spell didn't go quite the way we'd wanted."

"The energy was supposed to go into magical receptacles—stones modeled after the seven magical obelisks in the forest not far from here, the ones that correspond to the dragons—but they failed, or we failed, and instead, the energy went into four of us," Fiona continued. "The rest of our group died. And those of us who survived, we are able to contain it, but we all feel it getting worse. It's a heat inside us. And sometimes, it escapes."

"I've heard you can do miraculous things," Cecil added. "You are both amazing, and terrifying."

"Aptly put," Fiona said. "We need help. We are going to vent this energy soon, with or without our permission, and we have to do it safely before anyone else gets hurt."

"Why not turn yourselves into the Japanese authorities?" Hillary asked. "They could've quarantined you, started the process of decontamination."

"Agents from Tapper arrived with a dragon," Hamza said. "They saw us as a threat, and when we tried to confront them... I..."

"Oh dear. You're the one who blew up? Killed those poor people. And yet you survived?" Hillary asked.

All Hamza could manage was a shameful nod, and a look out the large window into the pretty streets of

Vienna.

"It was an accident," Hillary whispered. "I see. You can't always contain it, or harness it properly. I understand."

Hamza nodded again. "Now you know why we are so afraid, and why we need such help." As he spoke, a police car pulled to the side of the street and parked. A male and female officer exited the brightly colored sedan, and started towards the café entrance, chatting as they went. *They're both armed with pistols. Shit.*

"Fiona," Hamza said, nudging her to look out the window.

"It's ok. They won't recognize us," she said. "We're just here to talk. Figure out a safe way to resolve this. Just stay calm."

"Perhaps it's best if you turn yourself in?" Cecil suggested. "Come clean to the Vienna police. Let them do the heavy lifting of clearing your name."

"No," Hamza rebutted. "They can't be trusted to be impartial. They'll want justice for what we did before helping us. They don't know how to keep everyone safe if something goes wrong with the four of us."

The two police officers entered the café just a few feet behind Hamza, and walked towards the counter, still talking. *They're ordering. Good.*

"I am not opposed to talking to the authorities as soon as we are put somewhere safe," Fiona offered after stepping forward and kneeling beside their table. "But Hamza is right, more or less. They will cuff us, and throw us in cells, and question us about what happened whether or not we tell them we are in danger, and that risks us not being put in a place where we won't harm anyone. The police won't understand what's going on. There aren't enough nuclear scientists, or magi in their number."

"Well, those points are salient," Cecil said. "Perhaps we could bring them to the vault in the offices? Store them in there to contain any trace radiation?"

"The vault is too small. It doesn't have ventilation either. We would then have to figure out how to drain it from you," Hillary said. "Aren't there two more of you? You said four, right?"

"Correct. Laurie and Seamus are in hiding. We thought we'd draw less attention if we split up," Fiona answered.

The police officers stood and milled about, just a dozen steps away as their drinks were made. The smell of fresh coffee permeated the room even more strongly, and Hamza inhaled deep of it. He kept his gaze towards the window as best he could. The heat and pressure inside him seemed to ratchet up with each passing second. A trickle of sweat built on his brow as the pain he felt in his guts and along his spine grew.

"Please," Fiona added. "My friend is too proud to beg for help, but I'm not. We've hurt people and we'll pay the price for those misdeeds gladly, but we do not want to hurt more people, or destroy more property. I'm begging you; please help us."

"Yes, of course. We'll get you two back to the Commission, and into our small sealed room," Hillary began. "You won't be able to stay there long, but it's a start. We'll organize a team to sort this right out. I'll reach out to some of my occult contacts as well. Perhaps there are some spells that can be put up to help."

"Brilliant," Fiona said, and stood. "Shall we go?"

"Indeed," Hillary said. "Cecil, we'll take our car."

"Halt," a man's voice called out behind them. "Hands raised."

Hamza looked over his shoulder with great care, keeping the rest of his body still. At the register stood both police officers with their hands on the grips of the pistols at their hip. Without a doubt, they were addressing he and Fiona.

"You are Totah?" the female cop addressed him, her

free hand bladed at them. "And you are Gilmore?"

Hamza closed his eyes, and sighed. *Well, pray this goes well. May Allah guide us to peace, without harm to others.*

Hillary stood and spoke with defiance in English. "Officers, I am Dr. Hillary Tidwell of the International Atomic Energy Commission. This man and woman are a radioactive incident and we must get them to the commission's headquarters without delay. I plead to you; bring us there. Lead us in our car so we may put them in a safe place. They can answer for any alleged crimes after they and the public are made safe."

The sounds of screeching chairs erupted as the café's patrons reacted. A dozen people all stood and either backed to the walls, or rushed out the inner and outer glass doors to the street. The commotion—the sudden lack of control—triggered both officers into drawing their weapons.

Hamza remained perfectly still, hands stiff at his sides, half facing the police.

"They will be brought into our custody based on Interpol and Tapper requests. They are accused of terrible crimes in multiple countries. We can oblige you only after the proper authorities are notified they are in custody."

"You *aren't listening,*" Hillary chided. "They are very, very dangerous unless they are brought to a radiation-sealed area."

"*You* aren't listening," the female office responded, adding a glare. "Now Hamza, Fiona, face away, and place your hands on your head. Everyone remain calm."

Fiona looked at Hamza. She sighed in defeat, and a tear ran down her cheek. *We will not be taken.* Hamza turned and faced the police officers. They readied their pistols and shouted commands at him as he lifted his hands up and to the side with great caution.

"I am going to open the door, and Fiona and I are going to leave," Hamza said just loud enough to pierce the cop's shouting. "And you are not going to hurt us, and we are not going to hurt anyone. We came in peace to get help. I will surrender to you when we are safe. I will not hurt anyone so long as I will it."

"DO NOT TOUCH THE DOOR!" the male officer screamed in heavily accepted English. "Halt!"

"I am opening the door now," Hamza explained, and put his hand on the brass knob. He pulled a tiny bit as the officer screamed at him, and into their police walkies.

A rush of warm air pushed past him and through the crack in the door. The smell of baking pastries, cinnamon and sweet, syrupy sugar crossed his nose, and gave him a rush of nostalgia. A single gunshot rang out, and his side—just below his arm, near the armpit—erupted with white hot pain. A new pain. A new agony. Something to distract him from the murderous pain in his belly and chest.

The world went quiet as his legs gave out.

The sound of Fiona screaming faded as his vision flooded with white light.

The smell of the baked goods was overrun with the smell of charred flesh as the frenzied energy inside him erupted out.

I deserve this.

Hamza died, and all the energy his body and his will had contained up to that point was released.

Chapter Twenty-Seven
Fiona Gilmore

Fiona heard the gunshot. Felt the pressure in the air as the bullet flew through time and space and tore into her friend. Felt the tremendous surge of radiation as Hamza had a bloody hole drilled into him. Her skin prickled in a wave as the magical power inside her friend spilled outward like a surge of invisible magma pushing to the Earth's surface. Her greatest—their greatest—fears realized, all in a single instant.

The unimaginable terror contained in his body would be released onto an innocent café and its innocent patrons in seconds. After that... Vienna would suffer the same catastrophic event.

As Hamza's limp body felt to the black and white tile on the floor—hand still on the brass knob of the old door—she could sense the impending doom about to happen. She saw the first moments of it as Hamza's bloody shirt caught fire at his wound.

Fiona turned to Hillary and Cecil Tidwell and without any hesitation flashed the palm of her left hand at the wall of windows. A single pulse of the energy inside her rippled down her forearm and out, shattering the window with a deafening crash.

"RUN!" she screamed at the two people who represented hope to her and her remaining friends. She turned before seeing their decision. She could feel the fires raging inside Hamza growing.

With her other hand Fiona sent a twin blast at the two police officers before they could shoot her, sending them up and over the counter like debris in a hurricane. They smashed into the coffee makers with matching grunts of pain and disappeared down behind the counter.

Please don't die. Freed from the threat of the police officers — for a few seconds, at least — she leapt on top of Hamza's body as the hellish, godlike powers contained within began to spew forth like a bubbling, roiling storm of destruction.

I can save this. I can stop this, she thought as the bakery's temperature rocketed fifty degrees from the heat escaping Hamza's corpse. She pressed her torso against his and focused every ounce of determination and will into the sensation of the energy spilling into the world. She felt the fire on the clothing scratch at her, but that pain was nothing compared to the white hot sun of the energy. Caustic, actinic, infernal, it clawed up and out, destroying the blouse she'd stolen from the apartment, and digging into her own skin at the flesh beneath.

Wait. A portal out is a portal in.

Fiona concentrated once more, but this time she aimed her will at the hole being torn in her stomach and the barrage of pain ripping that tear ever larger. She began to scream; a primordial reverse-birth bellow as a force far too powerful for anything alive to endure absorbed into her flesh, her core, her soul, her very being. She funneled the disaster inside at a rate that nothing normal could endure, storing each and every molecule and joule in all the spaces she could, between each cell, each neuron, each mote of personality that made her, her, and she screamed, and screamed as the fires raged out of control on her clothing, spreading across the scorched tiles of the floor to the walls and chairs and counters.

She screamed again as the police officer shot at her; not because the bullets wounded, because they failed to penetrate the invisible wall of the chrysalis her magic had surrounded her and the explosion in. The tiny projectiles incinerated like tiny meteors skipping off the upper atmosphere. She screamed because she was afraid she'd fail.

Afraid that Hillary and Cecil would die, afraid that the two police officers would be incinerated, afraid that the city of 1.868 million (she knew this exact number from her time travelling the world's information network) would be contaminated or worse by Hamza's death. She screamed, and tried to cry, but the tears evaporated in the storm of atomic fire that encircled her.

Then... it abated. The fires calmed, the heat drew down ever so slow, and the pain... well, the pain stayed. With the mental and magical equivalent of unclenching her teeth Fiona let the sphere of protective magic she'd made unconsciously drop, and felt a release of energy as stored up, residual power flooded out into the destroyed bakery. Fires raged everywhere in the room, and what wasn't on fire, glowed cherry-red from the hellish heat of the event. The restaurant was a total loss, and in minutes, the building would be too.

Inside her... was all the pain and destructive power contained in Hamza, and her. She was a battery for radiation, and magic gone astray before, but now she was a warhead. Her entire body—every single cell-screamed to explode, yet she fought it. She willfully maintained her own existence through the pain, and sensation that she was about to disintegrate and fly in a thousand directions at the same time.

"Fuck," she said. Fiona tilted her head down to look at where she'd placed her tummy against Hamza and realized she was naked. She gasped. Where she'd pressed against him was a massive, raw patch of pink skin, not unlike a severe burn as it mended months down the line. *Ow, bitch. Just looking at it hurts.*

She turned her attention to the street outside the café and bakery. Shattered glass covered the sidewalk and burning bits of wood blown out from the frames flickered and wavered, casting off black smoke. She saw no bodies, nor rampant, wild destruction beyond the ruined café she stood in, and the building atop it.

"I did it," she said. "I ate the worst of it." Fiona smiled through the pain.

Fiona walked to the raised window of the café and jumped down the few feet to the sidewalk. She paid no attention to the shards of glass her bare feet landed on. Something so tiny and inconsequential couldn't harm her anymore and she knew it. The power within her flesh would melt the sharp edges long before her skin suffered any injury. It also didn't register that she'd lost her shoes along with all her clothing.

Fiona looked up and down the street at the fleeing patrons. *That they are running is good. No injuries to worry about. I hope I saved some lives here.* She looked over her shoulder where the charred body of Hamza still smoked. *How did I not realize I was getting up off his corpse? My brain must be fried. I'm not even sad. Just filled with molten power. Miserable.*

Sirens approached. Louder and louder they grew. They'll be here in a minute. No more. Fiona looked around for the car that belonged to Hillary and Cecil. The black Mercedes had left the scene. If they were real about wanting to help, it was only at a distance. Fiona closed her eyes and tapped into the wireless network nearest to her. She found the car moving towards the International Atomic Energy Commission building, and then found Hillary's phone in the sea of binary, and energy. Like opening a door, she accessed Hillary's text message program and forced messages through to the woman who might be able to help.

I'm sending this message using my powers. I don't know if it'll work right.

It took a minute for the doctor to respond, but Fiona breathed a sigh of relief when she did.

I am sorry that happened. We feared that death would release what we have contained inside us, and our worst fears came true.

What would've happened if I wasn't there to absorb Hamza's death?

I hope no one was seriously hurt, and that the radiation spillage is minor. Please make sure everything is taken care of. I guarantee they'll need to evacuate Leapoldstadt. I'm so sorry, the doctor wrote.

I'll message you again in a few hours after this calms down.

Fiona looked about for the closest phone junction box, or manhole cover. She walked to the round iron lid in the center of the street. With a casual flip of her hand and matching release of raw magical power she lifted the lid and set it aside. It clanged loudly on the stones of the street. She peered into the dark depths, and saw the thick tubes made of iron, and plastic that contained the cables she could travel through.

Message me. I'm figuring something out now to help you. For now, you must leave the city. You and your friends are far too dangerous to be anywhere near this kind of population center.

"You're right," Fiona said, then erupted into bright flash of energy, and disappeared into Vienna's grid. She had to get back to Laurie and Seamus, then take them both out of the city before she lost control of the monstrous power inside her.

Chapter Twenty-Eight
Zeud

Zeud crouched in front of one of the 1800s era wood stoves Chael used to cook his many delights in. She had the bottom cast iron door open, and looked in at the pile of petrified wood the minotaur had collected to power the rudimentary cooking appliances. Along the lengths of each log of stony wood were carved letters and symbols in old languages. Zeud read the Greek portions, and felt a pang of nostalgia.

"You need three stoves lit?"

"I do," the massive creature replied. "These three. That larger stove back there I don't use anymore. No one wants soups, it seems. Been cooking with just two of my six stoves for years now. Changed the whole menu. I've had to offer tartare far more often than I should have to. And so much hummus. So much. It's a versatile food, but it has its limits with my rather exclusive clientele. I'll soon lose business."

"I can imagine the struggle has been frustrating. The logs are suitable for firing then?"

"Been sitting in the bottom of cold stoves for far too long, but yeah, they'll burn. Just need a proper magical fire to get them lit. I've yet to find anything that cooks better than magically lit petrified wood. And the flavor it imparts… there's no comparison," the bull-headed chef said, then licked his bovine lips with a prodigious tongue.

"Well, I've yet to find many dishes that can hold a culinary candle to the food you've made on these stoves, so I think, perhaps, you're on to something. Now, if you'll take a step back, I'll get this stove going for you."

"And the other two?"

Zeud didn't respond with words. Instead, she took a sharp inhalation, and coughed out a laser-thin stream of her molten fire breath. The line of godlike fire hit and splashed on the petrified logs and set them aflame instantly, just as if they were dried firewood. They flared into a warm hearth-fire, and the first log lit crackled with the lines of coals-to-be. She watched the ignition for a few seconds, and felt the heat emanating off the logs. Coupled with that heat was the enchantment in the writing, and that had its own kind of warmth, too. She shut the enameled iron door, twisted the locking handle until it clocked into place, and then stood.

"Two to go."

Chael clapped his massive paws together, and let loose a grumbling laugh of pure creative joy. "Sous chefs, break out our finest ingredients. We shall offer a special menu for the rest of the day!"

Three goblin chefs and a fat-nosed gnome burst into action at the minotaur's command.

When she finished lighting the stoves, she handed a very happy cook a very expensive bracelet, and left to rejoin her friends in the dining area of the minotaur's prison-turned business.

The kitchen buzzed.

*****

"That was quick," Abe said to Zeud as she returned to

the circular booth set in the rear corner of the minotaur's restaurant.

"Setting fires is kind of my thing," she said, and slid around on the plush velvet cushions until she saddled up next to Henry. He gave her a half-hearted smile, then allowed himself to relax into her. *He's put off by that impulsivity comment I made earlier. I'll have to talk to him about it. I don't want him feeling lost.*

"We waited to order," Special Agent Chung said. "Though the menu looks terrific. Very Mediterranean."

"Lots of hummus, I'm led to believe," she said, and picked up her own menu. *Let's see... tartare, tabouleh, hummus three times... no coq au vin?* "Looks like the signature dish isn't on the current menu. I'm sorry to have brought you here for nothing. I think it's because he's been running a few stoves short of a kitchen recently."

"Ha," Abe laughed. "Nice metaphor. Is he bat shit crazy?"

"No, he literally had a few stoves unlit and needed my help."

"Oh, well. Nice of you to help," Abe said.

"I owed him. Plus, I like fire. I would recommend anything else on the menu," she said, then looked back down at it. "You know what, let's do tapas style. I'll just order one of everything. I can eat and drink you all under the table anyway, so leftovers aren't going to be an issue."

"That's something I like about you," Henry said. "A woman who can drink me under the table is always welcome at my table."

"Thank you, Henry," she purred. "Now, let's order." She flagged down one of the human waiters. Wearing an outfit with a distinct Greek-robed style, he stood patiently, and memorized the order as she gave it to him. "One of everything, and have the bartender work up a dozen cocktails for the table."

"Chael is now referring to the barkeep as a, 'mixologist,' miss," the waiter explained. "I'll put this right in."

Under the table, an electronic chime rang out. They exchanged glances until each of the men reached into their slack's pockets to get their phones. Chung shook his head and put his device away, and Abe shrugged and did the same.

"It's me," Henry said, reading an email. "Info passed on from Manchester about Vienna. Two police confronted Hamza and Fiona. Shooting resulted, Hamza died at the scene. Fiona is unaccounted for. No signs of Laurie or Seamus. Manhole cover in the street moved with scorch marks on the phone line pipes. She could be anywhere by now. No others dead. We have to get moving."

"We eat and drink first. Vienna is very close," Zeud said as Henry put his phone away.

"I think we should go," Henry urged.

She patted his hand and shook her head. "We eat. We drink. We recharge. Then we head to Vienna. As you said, they could be anywhere by now, and if they show up in Greenland in thirty minutes, we're in no worse a place."

"Speaking of which," Henry shot back at her, "where the hell is this place? You said it was in the cracks in that retaining wall in the alley, but we popped through a magical portal to get here. My phone just rang, so there's a tower nearby... but there are no windows, and no outside. There's a minotaur running the joint... which leads me to believe we might just be in a Labyrinth, but I don't see Jennifer Connelly or David Bowie anywhere."

"It's hard to explain. My sister Kaula could make more sense of it than I can."

"Try. I'm curious," Abe added.

"We are inside the wall. The stones the wall is made of were sent there from the Mediterranean a long time ago, and they contained the residual spirit of Chael, a minotaur. Chael is a descendent of Asterion, the original minotaur from Greek legend."

"So we're in a ghost-realm?" Abe supposed.

"What are ghosts?" Zeud replied. "Energies we cannot understand with the science you've developed. And your science has done a lot of thinking about the spaces between of late, yes? So here, we are in a space between. Here and not here. A realm that is coterminous with reality, yet apart at the same time. Built by Daedalus and Icarus using great magic and power, and here, repurposed to a great degree."

"What does coterminous mean?" Henry asked.

"Overlapping?" the dragon guessed. "Kaula used that word a lot when we talked about places like this. You see, dragons cannot normally leave this plane of existence. The seven dragons are tied to the Earth in a way that anchors us to its time and place, but a coterminous realm is fine for us to travel into. We haven't actually gone anywhere. We've simply... let's say we've taken a step to the side, behind the curtain, into the... I guess it's into where your physicists would say the dark matter is."

"We're with Oz now. No shit," Abe said, looking around. "Very cool. So the cell tower signals can slip in, does that mean we can send signals out?"

"I think so, though this realm is harder to leave than it is to enter. Almost impossible to leave, in fact. The oubliette spaces can be like prisons to some. Chael, for example, can never leave. As he is from Asterion's blood, his form can not sustain itself in an unconditioned reality. He is... cursed to remain, yet he has made the best of his predicament. He has turned his family's prison into a small slice of heaven."

"We can leave though, right?" Chung asked.

"Of course. Like all of Chael's guests, I know where the realm meets reality. Stepping through back into the real world is a mundane task, if you know the way through his maze."

"I fucking *knew* it," Henry said, slapping the table. "We *are* in the minotaur's maze."

"And we know the way out," the dragon said. "Look, our drinks are coming. Let's be merry, yes?"

The robed waiter sat down a golden tray filled with glasses of archaic, ornamented designs. Etched sides, gold and silver edging, goblets and the such. Zeud grabbed a plump tumbler filled with something crystalline red and raised her hand in a toast.

"Can we drink on duty?" Chung asked.

"You don't yet?" Henry said. "That's some rookie shit right there. Watch, I'm gonna be a bad example." He then picked up one of the taller glasses filled with a ruby-brown drink that fizzed. "Chung, you are now one of my ride or die bitches. You're with us until we leave Europe. I am sorry, and you are welcome."

"Ha, brilliant," he said with a laugh.

The other men grabbed drinks to their liking and held them aloft as the dragon did.

"To those with the bravery to stand before that which causes the greatest fears in us, and to those things for having the courage to stand before those with such bravery," she toasted.

The glasses clinked, the drinks were drank, and the food was eaten. After that, and the laughs that came after, Zeud showed the men the way through the minotaur's maze. When they exited, they appeared in the alley, just to the side of the grate with its gatekeeper, and all the secrets it held.

The trip to Vienna was fast, as promised.

Chapter Twenty-Nine
Seamus Drake

His eye wouldn't stop twitching. Try as he might to control the flutter of the misbehaving lid, it would not stop bubbling, shaking his vision over and over as he and his wife sat in the apartment Fiona landed them in. Shaking eyes and all, he sat in a low-backed chair covered with velvet fabric with a paisley pattern facing the door, waiting for the home's inhabitants to return. If they came in that door, he would do his best to restrain them. Returning residents couldn't be allowed to leave, and reveal their borrowed sanctum to the authorities.

"Seamus honey, listen. I'm telling you, you'd be better off coming all the way into the apartment," Laurie said to him for the twentieth time. "Sit in the living room. Let them shut the door and walk in before they see you."

Leave me be. I have it handled. "Look, I got this. They aren't coming home anyway. There's no luggage in the closet."

"That doesn't mean they're gone. It could just mean they don't own luggage."

"I got this," Seamus reiterated. "Go relax. Take a cool bath or something. You're high strung right now."

"I am? You're sitting in the hallway, staring at a door

that might never open, sweating like you just got done biking up and down the nearby Alps, and you're telling *me* I'm high strung? Check yourself, husband. You're losing it. I'm gonna take that bath. You kiss my ass." Laurie left the hallway and returned to the living room with all its tall, bright windows.

Bitch. Seamus sighed. "I'm sorry," he hollered out to her, but she didn't reply. *Frigging bitch, enjoy your bath.*

A crackling snap that threatened to break the windows came from the living room where Laurie headed. The sound broke the relative silence and shot Seamus' heart up into his throat. The restless, agitated mage jumped up so fast to rush into the room he toppled over the velvet chair. He didn't notice the charred marks on the fabric from his body's scorching heat. Seamus ran down the short hall and into the room. Laurie stood centered, near the hutch with the fine china, and distant he saw a naked, flushed Fiona. Just above her naval was a puckered pink scar as big around as the base of a water glass. Fiona stood alone.

She just came in via the internet. "Where's Hamza? Did you make contact with the two scientists?"

"We tracked them to a café, but had a problem. Hamza didn't make it," the Australian woman answered. She sat on the couch, uncaring about her naked state.

Seamus' blood boiled—literally. His internal temperature spiked so hard, so fast his vision went crimson and he smelled the strange odor of plastic burning. His polyester shirt smoked up from his collar.

"Seamus, calm down," Laurie said, taking a cautious step towards him. "You are… losing it. You're catching fire."

He stared at her, his breathing having become ragged at some point. He alternated his angry stares between Fiona and Laurie—both frightened at his growing intensity—and then tried to simmer down. *Jesus they're really afraid of me. I have to slow down. Calm. Stay calm.* His efforts—his attempt at a meditative mantra—mostly worked. His shirt stopped smoking, and his bloody vision cleared a bit. Seeing their expressions didn't make him feel better.

"What happened?" he asked.

"Random cops showed up as we were talking to Hillary and Cecil. They recognized us. Drew guns. We tried to peacefully exit the café we were in, but one of them shot Hamza before he got the door open. He died, and then... well, he vented out his energy."

"Oh no," Laurie said.

"What happened? How bad was it?"

"I uh... I jumped on him. And as all the magic and radiation hit me-," she paused, and put her hand on the fresh scar on her stomach, "it ripped into me here, and I was able to absorb it. Most of it, at least. There were fires, and I know some people got at least a little hurt, but I prevented what I think would've been an awful incident. Something much worse."

"They *shot* Hamza?" Seamus said, his voice and feelings brittle. The heat in his chest and head threatened to grow again, consuming his rationality. "He was our friend. All he ever wanted to do was help. To make the world a better place. There were no souls more gentle."

"You're right. He was one of the good ones, and yes, they shot him. They were scared. Hamza didn't quite listen to them either," Fiona explained. "We tried to leave, and they-"

"Do they know where we are? What about the two commission people? The married couple?" Laurie asked.

"Sympathetic to helping. When the cops were trying to get us to surrender, they were pleading to bring Hamza and I to a safe house to contain us. The lady, Hillary, was brilliant. Her husband I'm not so sure about, but the wife rules the roost I think. But I was able to get a message to her after it wound down, before the police and fire people came. She's going to help, but she wants us to leave the city. I can reach out to her using my mind. Like… mental text messages."

He lost most of what she said. "They killed Hamza," Seamus muttered as his emotions boiled again. *My insides are on fire. Pure fire.* "They shot and killed him in cold blood."

"They were sure he and I were dangerous," Fiona clarified. "I don't know if it's cold blood."

"Did he try to hurt them? Did he threaten them?"

"Anything but," Fiona answered, covering her naked body up suddenly.

"Then they shot him in cold blood. They murdered him," he said. "Pretty simple."

"It isn't. It's complicated. They shot him, yes, but they thought they had good reason."

"THEY FUCKING DIDN'T!" Seamus' shout set free two ribbons of white-yellow flame from his eyes that soared over Fiona's head, slamming into the white painted wall of the apartment. The burst of power set the drywall aflame, and within a second, it threatened to take over the entire wall from floor to tall ceiling.

Fiona jumped up off the couch she sat on, and backed away, giving Seamus a shocked look.

Shit, fuck, shit. "Ahhh!" he yelled, making fists over and over as he walked in circles, doing everything he could to contain his out of control emotions, and the power they threatened to shake free of him. He'd no ability to think about containing the fire.

A loud whoosh of fire extinguisher interrupted his upended thoughts. Several feet away his wife held a large red extinguisher, and was spraying the wall from floor up, putting out the fire he'd started. Somehow, watching her take control of the situation allowed him a moment of repose. He didn't calm down completely, but the scorching heat of his anger abated enough for him to control his breathing.

He stared at the wall and its blackened, charred edges

and the gentle wafts of smoke. *Don't hit the fire alarms...
don't hit the fire alarms.*

"Blow, gentle winds," Fiona whispered, and the
magic inside her responded.

A tiny wind—one gust as powerful as a hundred
lover's exhalations—kicked through the room, pushing
the smoke away from the circular fire alarm in the ceiling
towards the open windows nearby. She held a thin but
strong hand up, and waved it about, controlling the tiny
breeze as if it were a fan in her hand. Within seconds, the
room was clear, and the fire put out.

That's good. Good one, Fiona. "Thank you both. I'm
sorry. I'm... I can't believe they killed him."

"It's okay. He died a hero," Laurie said, moving to her
husband's side. "You cannot destroy his legacy letting
your anger get the best of you. Hamza wouldn't approve,
you know that."

"I do."

"Hillary wanted us out of the city, and I don't think
she's wrong," Fiona said to them. "We're growing more
and more dangerous, less in control, and with what
happened at the café, we're just as apt to get shot before
getting arrested now. We have to go to a place where if
we do die, or blow up, the fallout won't be too bad."

"Back to Fukushima?" Seamus asked.

"No, we cleaned that place," Fiona said. "We need a
large area that's already tainted with radiation, and is
uninhabited. I was thinking-"

"Chernobyl," Laurie finished.

"Chernobyl," Fiona said, nodding. "It's still dirty, and
if we blow up, all the proper safeguards are still in place
there. It's also not far, and unlikely that anyone will come
into the quarantine zone to find us. Too dangerous for
them, but fine for us. We wanted to clean that area
eventually, if Fukushima worked, so going there early
makes some sense."

"I don't know," Seamus said. "How do we know it's

safe for us? What's to say the additional radiation won't set us off? It's too dangerous."

"Seamus, our goal right now is to protect people from the power we've absorbed, yeah?" Fiona posed. "And in the middle of a city with almost two million people in it, we're putting all their lives in the firing line. We can't control the fallout, or the blast well enough to guarantee their safety."

"You guaranteed their safety, when Hamza died. You protected the city for him, you can do it for Laurie and I."

"Seamus, what if she's the one who dies? What's to say we'll be able to do what she did?" his wife asked him. "We should leave. Now."

"No," he said, and turned from them. "I'm done running. We're gonna stay right here until we figure this out. Right here until we get an answer from the commission."

"That's not safe," Fiona said.

"I don't care. We've done nothing but good for the world since we learned real magic. We learned how to heal, how to mend the world, how to boost fertility. We did so much good back near the ranch. What we did in Japan will ultimately save countless lives in Fukushima, and they repay us by killing one of us?"

"Seamus, forget about the good we've done. We have killed people. *Hamza* killed people. He was one of the good ones, remember? And he murdered people by accident. We shot down a helicopter. We might as well be terrorists in their eyes," Fiona said. "No amount of pleading on our part will convince them otherwise now. You know Tapper people will be heading here soon. I bet they're already on the plane, or riding a dragon that's headed here to eat us. We need to leave for this to end on anything remotely like our terms, and we need to do it before one of us gets killed."

"*Another* one of us," he corrected. "Before *another* one of us gets killed, you mean. Because we lost a lot of friends back in Japan to the accident already, and my best friend is dead now too."

"Yeah, sure, you're right. Another one of us," Fiona said. "And I don't want to lose you, or Laurie, so let's go. Take my hand, and let's get to Chernobyl before it's too late."

"Not yet. I'm not sure it's in our best interests," Seamus said, and walked away. He pulled his shirt off, and tossed the burnt fabric on the back of a chair. *Maybe I'll stay right here, where it's too dangerous for anyone to hurt me. Try and fuck with me and my people.*

"Seamus?" his wife called to him, but he didn't reply. He wanted a shower. No… a cold bath. Ice cold. He had to cool off.

Fuck you, Vienna. Fuck you, Tapper. I'm the fucking hero, and you'll see that. And if I have to be, I'll be a martyr to prove it.

Chapter Thirty
Tapper Special Agent Henry "Spoon" Spooner

Without a black Tapper SUV to ride in, Henry, Abe, Chung, and the dragon of fire rode through the streets of Austria in a rented Mercedes passenger van. Chung drove; he had driven in the city earlier in the year when a brief but intense investigation brought him there.

"So what were you here for?" Spoon asked him.

"Ever heard of the 'Sorcerer of Sistrans?' It's an Austrian legend?" he said while driving them through the fringe of the city towards the nondescript Austrian Federal Police facility they'd been directed to.

"No," Spoon answered.

"I have, please continue," Zeud said.

"Well, in Austria they have a story about this sorcerer. Pretty old story. This bloke had a clear penchant for magic, and was well known in the area for a few parlor tricks, and a few talents of notorious value. Chief amongst which, was a book that could compel thieves to return stolen goods. If he read from this tome long enough, with the victim in his presence, the thief would be geased to pick up the stolen goods, and walk straight to him and the victim to return them, and face the judge, so to speak."

"Jesus that's awesome. Can we get that book and bring it to Wall Street?" Spoon laughed.

"You'll have to ask Mr. Doyle what his plans are for the book," Chung said as they turned into the parking lot of a rather mundane business park. Behind it, the steep mountains rose to the clouds.

"Say what?" Abe said.

"We recovered the book from one of the cathedrals in the vicinity. Took some doing, as a pair of hags in league with a local priest had it, but we got it. It was sent back to Manchester for Mr. Doyle to put into Tapper storage. All on he and Director Fisher's orders."

"Man he never tells us *everything*, does he?" Spoon said, shaking his head and smiling. "Shady as balls."

"What's your saying?" Zeud asked. "Wise men keep their own counsel?"

"Bah," Spoon said. "He's just hoarding all the goodies for himself. I bet someone stole something from him a long time ago, and he's been looking for that book just to get it back."

"Wouldn't put it beyond him," Abe said as the van came to a stop.

Uniformed police officers wearing armored vests and carrying military grade weaponry were everywhere. Some were on the flat roof of the warehouse-like building holding binoculars to their eyes, others were in the parking lot, on the road, or at the glass doors to the building. Were it not for their armed presence, and the peculiar number of unmarked police sedans parked all about, the Tapper crew might've been stopping to pick up an order of pamphlets they had printed, or some other suitably boring task people did in the suburbs at a business in a business park.

Chung parked the van where an officer pointed, and soon they were disembarked, and headed inside to meet with the two scientists the Federal Police had taken into custody at the Atomic Energy Commission.

*****

Henry went into the interrogation chamber alone. He slipped off his leather bomber jacket and rested it on the back of the folding metal chair closest to the door before sitting with his back facing the two way mirror. Around his neck hung one of the black and silver pendants they'd retrieved from Belyakov in Kazakhstan.

She was shorter, with reddish hair, and designer frames. He was taller, hair almost white. Both looked like they cycled, or ran half marathons. Both looked exhausted, but defiance was in their eyes.

I don't think I'm going to like these people.

"Mr. and Mrs. Tidwell; Cecil, Hillary, thank you for coming into the custody of the Austrian Federal Police. My name is Special Agent Henry Spooner of The International Agency for Paranormal Response. Many people call me Spoon, and many call my organization 'Tapper.' It's a pleasure to meet you. May I call you Cecil and Hillary?"

"You may, Agent Spooner," Cecil greeted him from his chair across the cold, metal table.

"Call me *Doctor* Tidwell. What is your plan with them?" Hillary challenged.

She's already irritated and pissed. Damn it. "I'll be frank, Mrs. — sorry, Dr. Tidwell. We don't have a plan. Up to this point, we've been chasing them across the world, just trying to catch up to see what the hell is going on. We understand that they are dangerous, and we think that they are in over their heads. Right now, we'd just like to make contact with them to figure out what a plan might look like."

"Will you hurt them?" Hillary asked.

"I fucking hope not, Doctor, pardon my French."

"Pardoned. I want to help them," Hillary continued. "They were trying to help in Japan, and without any doubt, got in over their heads. They are not criminals."

"Doctor, with all due respect, they might've not started out as criminals, but by any measure of the law, they most certainly are now due to their actions. Look; I am not the police anymore. I am not here to arrest and incarcerate. I don't carry a badge, I carry a Tapper identification. Tapper responds to paranormal incidents with the idea that we are going to try and protect lives, and make things safe, and just as importantly; learn. Whatever legal ramifications they face for their actions will come long after Tapper has their say."

She sat back in the folding metal chair and eyed him.

She isn't sure to believe or not. Okay... with street scum I'd get a drink, and talk about family, but that won't play with her. Let's try something different. "I was there in Boston when Tesser woke up. I hunted him. I was a BPD cop. I was gonna try and put him in jail. But I didn't. I learned. I adapted. I joined. I was the first special agent in the organization, and I've helped shape its culture alongside other men and women who want the same things I do; they want to make the world safer, make the world more knowable, and build trust amongst the things that are magical, and the things that are not. If you could see what I've seen, and know what threats there are in this world beyond what the nightly news tries to cover, you'd know all I want to do is help."

"That's a nice sales line, Agent Spooner, but how do I know the local authorities—or any authorities for that matter—will respect your wishes. What's to stop them from stepping in, with their guns and their badges and their ignorance, and simply doing the insane? Nicking them off to a cave for experimentation, say?"

"Mostly it's the dragons," Spoon answered.

"I'm sorry, what did you say?" Cecil asked.

"The dragons?" Hillary asked.

"Yeah, the seven dragons. We work with them regularly to help maintain the balance, and protect humanity. They lean on the side of protecting Earth over humanity, but for the most part, protecting humanity and life on the world protects the world. So yeah, the dragons. Right now this debacle has the attention of Zeud, the dragon of fire."

"The red one, with the wings like a phoenix?" Hillary asked.

"That's her. She's here. Now. In the building."

"She fits in the building?" the doctor asked, shocked.

"She's one of the dragons that can change shape. She enjoys being in human form. Zeud wants these people protected, and she wants to protect the world from what could go wrong with them. Now, if anyone steps in our way, they are stepping in her way, and that would be a real bad idea for anyone. For any police force, for any army, and for any country. Dragons don't take shit from anyone."

"I've heard how powerful they are. I would love to study her breath. It could contain unbelievable power. We could replace fossil fuels if we were to harness it."

"I'm gonna warn you to be careful about harnessing things as it pertains to dragons. You remember what happened to The Fitzgerald Group? They're the last gathering of idiots that harnessed anything from a dragon and they almost killed Kaula, the first dragon of magic sucking her dry. Guy who ran that company wound up dead in a real awful way, and they got taken over by Tesser. They're now Tapper's chief source of financing. I would think that the dragons are a bit hesitant to enjoy any kind of union where something is taken from them."

"Not taken, no, sorry. I don't want to take anything from the fire dragon," she backpedaled. "We could learn. Study her, see how the breath is made and synthesize the process. Test it in every way conceivable. With her permission, of course. Even something just 25% as powerful might be a boon to the world."

The door opened to the room. Spoon looked over his shoulder as Zeud stepped in, floral summer dress and all. She wore one of the Russian pendants as well and somehow, the way the necklace draped itself made her look even taller than she was. *God she's pretty. Owns the room in every way.*

"I'm open to playing with fire. For science, of course," she said to the doctor.

"Are you...?" Hillary asked as she stood. Cecil followed suit.

"Zeud, dragon of fire. Keeper of the flames, burner of what must be burnt, yada yada," she said, extending a hand for a shake to each member of the married couple. After shaking both their hands, she sat. They did as well. "I thought it pertinent that if I were being discussed, I should be present."

"Very kind of you, Zeud. Can you assure me that they won't be harmed? That they'll be placed in a safe facility, or location so we can somehow contain what's inside them?" Hillary asked her.

"I will do everything I can to ensure that."

"Why?" Cecil asked. "What's in it for you? What investment do the dragons have in this? What could eternal creatures of such great power stand to gain by helping such lowly denizens of the Earth?"

"Such a selfish notion, Cecil," Zeud said. "That a creature would only do something good if it had something to gain. But, alas, you have a point. What might a dragon stand to gain by helping here? I'll answer you; a better world to exist in. A world without the taint of excess radiation, in this instance at least. It's poison, you know. Natural as it might be, it ruins much, and it should be contained wherever possible."

"I see," Cecil replied. "All for a better home?"

"Something like that, yes."

"What will you do for them?" Hillary asked Spoon and Zeud. "What medical processes are available?"

"I don't know," Zeud answered. "I am no scientist, or doctor. But I do know that there is great magic that can be brought into the mix, and I fear that no solution will come to them without that magic."

"It's all Greek to me," Spoon shot. "I carry magical gear, because I have to, but I can't understand the stuff. I do know we have a lot of people who know a lot about it, and we'll get every single one of them out to pitch in. Mr. Doyle, one of our founding fathers is a boss at making potions. I bet you anything he can cook something up. That or the Russians already got something. They're sandbagging."

"I see. I would love to hear why you think that," Hillary said. "What's the next step?"

"You said you can contact them?" Spoon asked her.

"Sort of. Fiona sent me a message right after the café incident. She said she'd message me. They took my phone. I can reply back to her, I think. I know she said she'd message me again."

"Great. Let's get you your phone back, and see where they are. See if we can steer them to a safe place where they won't be hassled by police or military, and if something does happen to them, it won't ruin a city," Spoon said.

"Do you think it could happen?" Cecil asked the room. "How close were we to dying when the young man was killed?"

"You know I can't say," Hillary said to her husband. "They haven't told either of us anything."

"We saw the café, it wasn't that bad. But the people with your own commission came out and tested the place for radiation, and it's very localized, but the numbers are lethal doses. Also, almost every single bit of electronics within a half mile seems to have been fried by what looks like an EMP. They quarantined the entire neighborhood, and shut it down until they can somehow cleanse it," the agent explained. "The whole city is messed up. We put them in touch with our contacts in Japan. There is a way to get the radiation out relatively quickly, we think."

"My phone was working strangely, now that you say it. Had she not been there to absorb his death... the entire city might've been flooded with radiation," Hillary concluded. "And if his death released a pulse of energy like an EMP, a full blast could've crippled everything for a hundred kilometers. More perhaps, depending on the power released."

"Like a dirty nuke," Spoon wondered. "A death nova."

"We have to get them to safety, and sort this out," the dragon said, "and we have to do it immediately. If this Fiona girl trusts you, let's capitalize on that, and have her get the others moving. Once to a safe distance, we will be able to enjoy some time to make this work."

"I'll get you that phone," Spoon said, and stood up.

Chapter Thirty-One
Doctor Hillary Tidwell

Her hands shook, and they never shook. Nervousness was a state that Dr. Tidwell rarely entered. The thin black phone rattled against the cold, hard table in the interrogation room as she picked it up.

"Go ahead. Just relax, and start a conversation," the American Tapper agent urged. "Touch base with her. Don't let her know you're with anyone in Tapper yet. We need to ascertain what their feelings are towards us before we announce our presence. Don't want to scare them away from the people most able to help them."

Hilary looked at the man, then the dragon masquerading as a powerful Greek goddess, then the two other Tapper agents—another American, and the other an Asian man from the UK—then unlocked her phone. They watched her, and they looked almost as nervous as she was.

"Go ahead," Cecil encouraged.

Shite. Okay.

Hillary opened her text messaging app and went to

the message from Fiona. It even had her name, despite having been sent with magic. *All this magic nonsense is ruining my sense of the world as I understand it. I'll never recover.*

"May I?" Zeud asked her, pointing at Hillary's cell.

"Yes, of course," Hillary said and handed her the phone. The dragon read the brief exchange she'd had with Fiona, and handed the phone back.

"Thank you."

Hillary nodded, took a deep breath, and sent a short message to woman she'd met earlier that day named Fiona.

Hello Fiona. Please let me know when you can talk.

"Okay, I sent her a message."

"Perfect, thank you," the older American agent said. "Now let's relax. It could be a bit before she writes you. Is there decent take out? I'd kill for a plate of spaghetti and meatballs. Do they do that in Austria?"

"Spaghetti?" the younger agent leaning against the wall said with a laugh. "I figured you'd be more of a boiled dinner kind of guy."

"Yeah well, we like what we like. Irish or not, pasta is what I want right now. Well, that and some of that magical whiskey you can make. That was pretty good stuff, especially when you consider the price."

Hillary's phone buzzed, and the men got serious.

Oh, there go my hands again. Hillary's shaking fingers picked up the still-unlocked phone and held it up. She read the message aloud.

"I can't talk much right now. We're arguing over what to do next. Can you help us? Can the Commission get us to a safe place?"

"Arguing?" the American asked. "Who is arguing over what?"

Arguing? Is everything okay? Who is arguing over what? She typed.

"Seamus is losing control," Hillary read. "He's

226

venting more and more heat and energy by accident, and his temper is unstable. I want us to travel to Chernobyl, where we can be safe if we vent, and we won't hurt anyone, but he's refusing to go."

"Whoa-ho-ho!" the agent named Abe said. "Jackpot. That's more about them then we've been able to learn since Fukushima. Nice job, Doc. This is gonna help."

"Thank you. What should I say next?"

"There *were* four of them, yes?" Zeud pondered aloud. "And the man named Hamza has passed away. Are there three?"

"That's smart," Hillary said.

Is it just the three of you now? Are you safe?

"Seamus, Laurie and I," Hillary read. "I can't say that I'm safe from another one of Seamus' outbursts. He almost set the apartment we're in on fire."

"They're in an apartment. Solid gold, Dr. Tidwell. Can't thank you enough," the main agent said. "Ask them who they've thought of approaching for help. Anyone they've already made contact with?"

Who have you considering asking for help with your problem?

It took several minutes for Fiona to reply. "No one seriously other than the Atomic Energy Commission. All other governments can't be trusted. We won't allow ourselves to be turned into weapons. We are thinking about approaching the Delphinians, but I doubt they're organized enough to provide us any real help. We could also be lied to, or misled by them. You never know."

"Ask them if they considered Tapper," the man named Abe said.

What about the people from Tapper?

"Yeah I don't know. We might've killed a posse of them in Japan, not sure they're interested in being helpful now," Hillary read. "I'm afraid of their dragon."

"They need not fear me," Zeud said. "I wish them no harm."

"Well, we gotta convince them of that. Tell them they didn't kill anyone in Japan, and we're trying to help, and that you've connected with the same team that was in Japan," the main agent said.

She typed that message, more or less, and sat back waiting. Fiona's response was immediate. "I'm so glad none of them died. Did we hurt them? Tell them I'm sorry. It was an accident. Hamza went overboard, then Laurie got triggered and vented. It wasn't supposed to go the way it went. Hamza never forgave himself. He died a broken man on the inside. He was a good person. Do you think we can trust the dragon?"

"Figured," the main agent said to Abe, and the Asian agent. "I think we can say this Fiona woman is stable, and our best chance at getting the other two to cooperate. Is that agreeable?"

All gathered agreed.

"So we make a run at her right now, and convince her to let us help them," he said. "Okay, Doctor. You're doing great. If you can let her know that we genuinely want to help them, and that we have no ill will, that'd be great."

"I'll try," Hillary said. Okay, the tipping point.

I've met some of the Tapper operatives, and they seem on the level. The dragon seems very nice as well. She's very worried about the spread of radiation. I do believe they only want to help you and your friends. They know you're in danger, they know you're in over your head, and seem only to want to assist. Can I put you in touch with them?

"Ha," Hillary laughed after reading Fiona's immediate reply. "She says, 'they're probably with you right now,' cheeky girl." *She's smart.*

I am in a Federal Police building. I'm not arrested, I don't think, but I'm with the Tapper people, yes. I'm very sorry if my conversation makes you feel misled, she typed before anyone could tell her how to respond.

"What'd you send?" the agent in charge asked her.

"Told her I was with you, and apologized for being

less than fully truthful," Hillary replied.

He sat back in his chair, and shook his head. "I'm not sure that was the play, Doctor. But whatever. We'll make it work. Let's see what she says."

Several minutes passed before Fiona replied. Hillary read it aloud again.

"Sorry, Seamus is starting to talk to himself like a loony in the bathtub. He's in growing, consistent pain. Laurie got him to take a cool bath, which seems to have helped him calm down, but his body has warmed the water up to where it's hot to the touch. Laurie has the cold tap spraying on him constantly and steam is rising off of him. He's in worsening condition."

What does his skin look like? Redness? Lesions?

Some, Fiona wrote back. *They're certainly more prevalent than they were earlier today. They seem to come and go. I can try to travel us through the lines to reset his body, but the wound I suffered from Hamza's death remained with me, so these might remain with him.*

Hillary sat her phone down and sighed. *Shite.* She read the messages to the group. "That's likely some symptom of radiation poisoning he's showing. No way to know how fast it'll creep up on him and be fatal, or cause him to go into shock, or a coma. He might lose control if that happens. We have to do something. How do we help them?"

"Ask her if she thinks they can get Seamus to leave the apartment? We could hit him with a tranquilizer dart? I mean shit, we could try that through a window too if she gives us the apartment location," the lead agent said. "Just have two shooters on a roof. One plinks the window, second fires the dart a half second later."

"That's too complicated," the man named Abe said, shaking his head. "Too many moving parts."

Hillary asked if she thought they could get Seamus out of the apartment. Fiona replied in the negative.

"If he's in pain, will he take medication?" the agent

named Abe asked. "Percocets? Vicodin? Rohypnol? Something like that? I can make a real strong version that'll put his angry ass out flat."

Will Seamus take something for his pain?

"'Beyond relief, to what end?' she's asking," Hillary read, and said.

"If we can get him to take a pill for his pain, we can knock him out long enough for her to get all three of them to Chernobyl, if that's the safest place for them to head," Abe explained. "Assuming Fiona has the guts to try and offer him pills. "Hell, I can whip up some Sizzurp for him too if he'd rather drink his medicine."

"Great idea," the lead agent said, clapping his hands.

"I see," the Doctor said. "You're saying you're offering to drug him? Is that legal? Ethical?"

"When it comes to Tapper and the law," the lead agent started, "those are muddy waters. We do what must be done to protect civilization, and we answer to no one. Benefit of working for immortal creatures like dragons. Drugging him for the purposes of getting his dangerous ass out of that tub, and into isolation where he can't hurt anyone is an action I'll defend in any court, assuming they can make me sit in that court."

"I'll testify that it was necessary," Cecil, her husband, said. "I feel like it is a reasonable, non-violent course of action."

The Tapper men are suggesting you offer pain medication to him under the guise of helping. But, you'll give him more than is needed so he will pass out. Then, you can transport him to Chernobyl safely.

"That might work. I would need the meds though," Hillary read. "How do we get the drugs to Fiona?" she asked the group. "You'll need to stop and get them from a chemist, yes?"

"I'm a chemist. Well, using magic, which I guess makes me a bit of an al-chemist," Abe said. "If she'll agree to meet me somewhere, I'll give her whatever she thinks he'll take."

"Abe, is that safe?" Zeud asked.

"Safety isn't a concern if he blows up, so meeting up with her can't be a concern either, if the aim is to get them out of the city."

He's faking it. He's scared. I can see it in his face. "Are you sure?" Hillary pressed him.

"Yeah. I've faced worse than a girl that got a tan from an atomic bomb," he said with a shrug.

"Accurate. You've definitely done that," his boss said. "Fire off the message, Doctor. Let's see if she'll play ball. Abe'll get headed to where they can meet up."

One of the Tapper agents can meet you with the drugs. Whatever you think he'll take. Just tell us where to meet you, and he'll give the stuff to you.

Can I trust him? Hillary read without saying it aloud.

He's scared to meet you, if that tells you anything. But he seems good. Experienced, but not aggressive. I would say you can trust him. He's an alchemist, he claims.

A mage? A wizard? I would be chuffed to meet more spellcasters. Okay, I'm willing. Give me a few minutes to find a location where I can meet him. I have to go on foot if I'm to bring back drugs. I can't transport anything physical through the lines.

Hillary read most of the second message to the group and they responded with enthusiasm.

"Chung, you drive?" Abe asked the British Agent, who nodded. "Let's go, call me with an address?" he asked the lead agent, who also nodded.

"I'm coming as well," the dragon said, standing up. "If anything were to happen, I should be there to accept responsibility."

"I don't tell dragons what to do," Abe said to her.

The two agents and the dragon-in-disguise left the room in a rush.

The agent I said is good is leaving with another agent, and the dragon. I think it will work out, but be careful.

Cecil, the agent named Henry and Hillary remained, waiting patiently for Fiona to answer.

"So is there any place to get decent takeout? Remember I mentioned spaghetti earlier? I'm legit starving," the agent asked said. "Meatballs would be great."

Chapter Thirty-Two
Fiona Gilmore

The connection inside her mind to the conversation with Hillary Tidwell untethered. Allowing her consciousness to connect to the invisible wi-fi in the apartment had the physical sensation of being light-headed, while someone spoke into each ear about different subjects. When no one else was in the room, the process was easier. The whole situation was exacerbated by the raging inferno of power eating away at her insides like acid poured straight into her belly. *My head too, actually.*

When she heard Seamus ranting and raving in his warm bath keeping her realities straight became harder, and when Laurie came out, ranting and raving about her husband's growing insanity, the process of managing it all became almost impossible to hide.

At least, she felt like having her awareness split in two while dealing with tremendous discomfort was obvious.

"He's going crazy, and he's taking me with him," Laurie said, exasperated. "He's an infection right now. When I'm closer to him, I can feel what's going wrong with his mind. It's like... It's like being in a drafty house in January. My skin curls and shivers as the crazy comes off of him. I can't do this much longer or I'll either go crazy, or kill everyone when I kill myself."

"He's in pain? Are those sores getting worse?"

She nodded.

"Let's give him something for the pain, at least. Maybe if he can get some real rest, it'll get better."

"Aspirin? Tylenol, what?"

"I think they use paracetamol here, but no, I'm talking about something more powerful. Something to really give him a rest. A narcotic. Just to give him, and you, a break," she suggested as gently as she could.

"I don't know," Laurie said. "Ever since he went clean in the early 2000s, he's been against any kind of hard drugs. Well, drugs and meat. If we told him we were giving him anything harder than an aspirin, he'd go into a tailspin. Could be really bad if he gets angry."

"So we lie to him," Fiona said, bluntly. "I mean, not to sound like a villain, or an ass. It's for his own good as well as ours. If he relapses because we gave him a Vicodin for this, so be it. Him needing a detox down the way is much better than him blowing up, or driving all of us batty with his ranting and raving. I can do this with a mostly clean conscience, can you?"

Laurie sat in the chair Seamus' ass had burned and put her face in her palms. Silent sobs shook her whole body, and Fiona slid to her, pressing her thigh against Laurie's side, and rubbing her friend's back.

"How did it go so wrong?"

"What part?" Fiona asked with a chuckle. "Lots of things have gone wrong. I'm so sorry. It will be okay."

"Can I ask you a question?"

"Of course."

"You love him, don't you?" Laurie stopped crying and looked up at Fiona.

I was waiting for this. One day, it was bound to happen. Of course now is the worst possible time. "When I first met you and Seamus, I freely admit, I had a crush on him. I thought he was captivating, and handsome. I stalked you both on your website for months before coming to the States to join you. Then when I met him, he was so kind and creative. But… I am not interested in him, or hurting you, or breaking up your relationship, or anything like that. My fantasy was just that; fantasy. Idol worship I suppose. I'm not a shite friend."

"He ever come onto you?"

"Not once, Laurie. You have a faithful man."

"I see the way you look at him," Laurie said. "You're in love with him. I get it, I fell for him too. Well, I fell for a different version of him."

"Laurie, Christ, let's not do this. It's not a thing, he and I. It never has been. Anything you've seen in the way I look at him is just the way my dumb face looks when I am looking at someone I care about. Someone I look up to."

"You don't look at Hamza like how you look at Seamus," Laurie said, then wiped the tears from her cheeks. "How can I trust you? How *have* I trusted you?"

"Laurie, we are not having this conversation right now, are we? We are not going to waste this time, at this precious, critical moment talking about a crush you think I have on your husband. We need to make a plan that works. A plan that saves our lives, and protects the people in this city from being hurt if something gets worse. Please trust that I want all three of us to stay head above water, and make it out alive."

"You're right. Maybe I'm just being defensive," Laurie said.

"You have *every* right to want to fight for your marriage. Right now, fighting for your marriage looks like us getting him some relief. What's going on inside him is killing him, and if he dies, the city goes. I don't know if I can contain another death inside me. If we can at least get him sleeping for a few minutes, I can transit us to the exclusion zone at Chernobyl, and we can set up shop there to sort it out without too much to worry about."

From the bathroom, Seamus started signing in a discordant pitch. The notes reverberated through the apartment—infused with his sickened magic—and made Fiona's stomach pitch and heave. *He really is infectious now. Just the sound of his voice makes me ill. I hope she agrees to this. I'm not sure what else I can try to get him asleep.*

"Yeah," Laurie said as a sigh. "Yeah okay. He'll be alright. We just need to help him right now. Easier to beg for forgiveness, right?"

"Right. Okay. We'll need something to give him. I can run out to the local chemist and get something. Are you okay here?"

"Why don't you let me run out?" Laurie offered, standing and brushing her lap off as if she'd gotten dirty. "I could use a ten minute break."

Shite. No. You have to stay. "I bet you do. Do you have any spells to get prescription meds from behind the counter without getting caught?"

"Damn, no I don't. You do? When did you practice spells like that? It wasn't back at the compound."

"No, no. But, I can do more since I absorbed Hamza's power. I think I absorbed the spells he knew as well. He had a few that I know I can use to get a few bottles from behind the chemist." *I'm going to Hell for lying to my friends. At least the heat won't bother me.*

"You mean a pharmacist?"

"Yes, whatever you call him. Let me go. Seamus will do better with you than me anyway. You want a drink or something? A snack?"

"I'd kill for a smoothie if you can find one," Laurie said. "Something with green in it."

"Consider it on the list. I'll be back as fast as I can."

"Be careful. Don't be seen."

"I'll do my best, and the same to you," Fiona said,

and headed for the door.

*****

Fiona thought she needed a public area. As if she were going to meet a strange Tinder date in the late hours. But Fiona wasn't. She was meeting an official from the Tapper organization. A fellow mage who had offered help to them. A person in authority, with a good reputation who had no ill will towards her.

Supposedly.

So instead of the place needing to be public, the meeting place needed to be where she could make a break for it. A location with a nexus of communication lines allowing her to dematerialize and transit to wherever she needed to. A place where she could be within a foot or two of a phone line, or an Ethernet cable. The smoothie would have to be a secondary mission.

After sending the message to Hillary with the address of the closest internet café she sat down at one of the decks inside the small cubicles the main room was divided by, and started to picture in her mind's eye what routes she'd take to where through the complex web of lines just a few inches from her hands.

Is Chernobyl the best place to go? Should I go to somewhere else that's just as dead? Back in Idaho where the compound is there are massive stretches of nothing. That might be a better idea. No… no. If they know who we are, then they probably have agents or whoever sitting back in the states waiting.

What about the Outback? What about the desolate plains of Australia? That could be perfect. But again… if they know who we are, then they know I'm Australian, and they might suspect that I'll run back there to get away. Maybe Chernobyl is the answer. Just commit. Chernobyl it is.

"You seem lost in thought. Good ones, I hope," a man's voice said near her.

She spun in the cheap office chair of the internet café

237

and faced the speaker. She swallowed a stone that jumped up into her neck and tried to shove the bubbling energy triggered by her fear response down. Just being slightly started almost caused her to lash out with a bolt of energy.

"Holy shit, I felt that," the suit-wearing young man whispered, taking a step back towards the center of the air-conditioned, computer-filled room. He bumped into the cubicle wall that divided one station from another. "Like a hot breeze on a hot day. Are you okay? You are about to pop, aren't you?"

"I don't feel well, and I'm the one of us that's doing well," Fiona said. "Wish I had better news." *He sensed the power surge. He's definitely a spellcaster. Cute, too. Little skinny. What's that accent? America, somewhere. What's that strange pendant around his neck? That black stone looks so soothing....*

"I'm really sorry things have turned on you like this," he said to her. "My name's Abraham Fellows, I'm a special agent with Tapper."

"Hillary said she thought you could be trusted. Can you be trusted?"

"Can you trust Hillary? How long have you know her? Six hours? Let's not play the telephone game with trust. Don't trust me because you trust her. Trust me because you trust me. So let's build that trust, and be good friends, and save some lives, and when this is all said and done, you can teach me how to teleport through phone lines. God, I bet that's awesome."

"It hurts like hell," she said to him. "It's like running bareassed through a thorn patch while someone sprays bleach at you."

"No shit?"

"It gets better. The more I do it, the easier it becomes. Speed matters, I know now. When we left Japan I was running like a bat out of hell, but we weren't really going any faster than if I'd just taken my time. Circled back on myself, took slower routes than were available."

"You torched a LOT of infrastructure," Abe said to her. "Millions of dollars in damages. Maybe a billion. Japan is ripshit over it. Southeast Asia, actually. They're gonna invoice you for every Yen of that."

"Yeah well, bollocks, eh? They can bill me," Fiona said, rolling her eyes.

Abe smiled, then laughed. "Not like they can take you to court, I guess."

"I'll just run bareass back through bleach covered thorns and piss off."

"Preach, sista," Abe said. "Look, we um, gotta get this guy knocked out for you. You head to Ukraine, and we'll rally there with a support team to get this under control. We're gonna get some serious mages on this, as well as the Atomic Energy Commission, and I think we're gonna try and get some baku from Japan to help. We're gonna mobilize like crazy."

"And then what? We get cured, the energy gets drained off, then what? We get shipped to some prison somewhere? Siberia maybe? Where we can pay the price for our crimes?" *Saved only to be condemned, right? Let's see what he says.*

"Look, I've never been good at lying. I usually just avoid the shit out of the people I need to be dishonest with, but I'm here now, and I'll say this; you're pretty fucked, but you'll have us on your side vouching for you, if this was a legitimate accident and you work with us to prevent further chaos. You'll have to pay the piper somehow, of that there's no doubt, but with the powers you have, there is bound to be a way to do it that'll be fucking awesome."

"I guess that's about as good an answer as I could've gotten. Okay, give me the pills. Something that'll knock him out, but not kill him," she said, extending her hand.

He thought for a second, then closed his eyes, took a deep breath — paused, looked at the ceiling with a thought, then closed them again—and spoke two words in Latin. "Vocare sanitatum."

In his open palm two tiny white pills appeared. They looked like any normal pills you'd take from a bottle.

"Wow," Fiona whispered. "You can make prescription pills?"

"Amongst a few other things," Abe replied. "These are for me," he said, then popped them in his mouth and dry swallowed them. "Tough day."

"You'd make a killing on the festival circuit," Fiona said with a chuckle.

"Damn right. I've got a plan B if this whole, 'suit-wearing mage,' job doesn't pan out. Just gonna follow Diplo and DeadMau5 around as they tour. Okay, your turn."

He closed his eyes again, and spoke the same two words. This time six small brown pills appeared in his hand. Round, and benign, the tiny bits of sorcery-procured medicine looked like Ibuprofen tablets.

"Meant to look like regular pills?"

"Yeah. If he's suspect at all. Give them to him like normal, and once he's out, get in the fucking pipeline and get the hell away from all population centers. Chernobyl works great, wherever you go, just get in touch with Hillary, or me, or whatever, and we'll be right with you as fast as we can," he said as he handed her the pills.

His touch... it's cooling, calming. Butterflies. Jesus not the butterflies. Though judging by his own expression he got a bit of a chub off of it too. "We're headed to Chernobyl. I've made the decision."

"Terrific. We'll get the plane headed that way as soon as we know you're off."

"Abraham Fellows, yeah?"

"That's me," he replied, taking a step back and putting on a pleased, but awkward smile.

Cute. She closed her eyes and reached out to the network. She scoured the invisible walls and mountains of data hidden in the world, looking for a phone number. She found nothing. Worse yet, when she tried to search out a phone number for Tapper, she found the edifice of information resembling it to be blacked-out, hidden behind another wall of magic she couldn't perforate with her fledgling powers.

"You're doing more magic. No invocations, or gestures. How?" he asked her. "How do you work the magic into a feasible spell effect without focusing fetters, or rituals?"

"I extend my awareness, I guess. I want things to happen, and they do. I was looking for your number."

"Traditionally, you just *ask* a guy for his number. Mostly, we're begging to give it to a nice girl. Not nice ones too. Men aren't the brightest creatures walking this planet."

"I guess I like a challenge," she shot back.

"I'm taken, sorry. Actually, I don't think it's gonna work out. It's a May-December thing, and I've been a complete piece of shit to her. I don't think we're a good fit anymore. I really need to call her," he trailed off in an even quieter whisper. His mood soured for a second, but he shook it off and put on a pained smile.

"That got real for you, didn't it?"

"Yeah. It's been weird for me since Tesser came back. Good I think, at times, but weird."

"I could very much row that boat with you. Look at me. Walking atomic bomb. Wrong time to ask you to hold my hand, eh?"

"Please don't kill us," he said to her. "Get him drugged, get your two friends to safety. If you need me to hold your hand, I'll do that for you. I'll stand at your side right to the end if need be, because that's what I do. I save the fucking world. It's in my job description, and now it's on my resume."

"By drugging my husband?" Laurie barked from the café's door. "By lying to me?"

241

Shite, fuck off. Fiona leaned to the side to look around at her friend, who had followed her. Laurie's expression was torn apart like the surface of flowing magma. Her skin had cracked apart, showing the bright red and white of pure, raw hatred brought on by perceived betrayal. Laurie's body had become the toy of her damaged emotions. *I don't even have her fucking smoothie.*

"Ah fuck, hot," Abe said, and started to move away from the heat the new arrival cast as fast as he could, reaching for a holstered weapon in his waistband.

"YOU LIED TO ME," Laurie screamed at her in a grating, mechanical voice.

"Fiona, use your magic and kindly take my friend to safety," another female voice said from behind her erupting friend.

Fiona saw the dragon pretending to be a woman. That she wasn't what she looked like was easy to see. The tall woman with dark skin and crimson hair radiated power in a way that made Fiona's mouth fall open. Around her neck hung a black stone pendant that matched the one the agent wore.

This city is fucked.

She reached for the hand of her new agent friend with one hand, and reached towards the nearest computer with the other.

Chapter Thirty-Three
Zeud

The woman spun to face Zeud, and over Laurie's shoulders the dragon watched as Fiona grabbed Abe's arm, then disappeared them both into a flash of light. A computer inside one of the café's cubicles popped and snapped with power as it was used as a conduit by the woman magic-user.

Abe's pendant, pistol, and clothes fell to the floor atop his empty shoes.

Shit. He lost the amulet.

"Who the FUCK are you?" the woman spat at her, and from several yards away her breath felt like fire on Zeud's face.

"I am Zeud, mother of fire, protector of the Earth, one of seven dragons, and *your* friend right now. You are the one we know as Laurie?"

"Dragons don't scare me anymore," she snapped back.

"Very brave of you. You have nothing to fear from me. Laurie, right?"

She nodded, her body trembling from anger. Inside the dark centers of her eyes a smoldering red light grew; coals on the fires of her betrayed soul. Her fingertips were cherry-red, and the rug around her bare feet issued a hundred tiny ribbons of acrid smoke.

She's going to set this place on fire. "Laurie, we have come in peace, to help you, and your husband. We understand —"

"SHUT UP," she snapped, her voice an erupting volcano's growl. "You and that *whore* are against my husband and I. She was always lying, wasn't she?"

"I can't speak to before we contacted her, but she seems honest. Listen, you must calm down, we must get you and your husband to safety before something terrible happens," she urged. "For the good of the planet, if not just for the people of Vienna."

"Fuck them," she grunted, her hands clenching over and over. "I'm gonna get Seamus, and we're leaving. Don't try to stop me." She started walking at Zeud to leave.

Shit. "Laurie, I'm begging you, let us help you. Let us get you to a safe place where you can be helped." She held her hands up — palms out, unthreatening — at the woman as she got closer and closer. The heat became more intense. *This whole building is going to catch fire if I don't get her out of here. Please listen, please stop.*

"You don't want to stop me," Laurie threatened. "I'll vent my energy. Hurt you. Dragon or not, you'll feel pain."

"What pain I feel means nothing. Only the protection of Earth and its species matters. I am built to suffer for her."

"So be it, bitch," Laurie said, and shoved her palms out at Zeud.

Two volcanic blasts of blue-white energy shot from the heels of both of Laurie's hands, striking the dragon directly in the sternum. Her dress was incinerated in a split second and when the force of the attack hit her skin, Zeud launched backwards through the air, through the inner glass door of the café, then the outer glass doors, destroying the front desk counter that had been evacuated when she walked in. The noise ruined the eardrums of the few frightened customers inside the café and shattered windows in the street outside.

How strange, this barely hurts, the dragon thought as she was smashed backwards into the street. She slid on her bare ass into the side of a parked car, denting it. *The amulet works. I can't even taste the radiation in the air.* She looked to her right. Two cars down stood Agent Chung. Mouth agape, he drew his enchanted service pistol.

"Get out! Evacuate everyone as fast as you can!" she screamed at him as she got to her feet. Laurie strode through the café towards the street, her skin becoming translucent and orange, like steel pulled from a furnace. Her clothes were gone, and all that remained was flesh and power.

"Everyone, run!" Chung screamed. "There's a fire!"

They listened. Chaos erupted as pedestrians within earshot reacted to the suited man drawing a handgun and screaming. Whether they were listening to him, or running from him didn't matter. They had to run.

Laurie raised her hands to blast Zeud once more, but the dragon had other plans. She crouched low, and vaulted forward at waist height, allowing the twin blasts to sail just over her red mane. With the force of a crashing car she hit the woman directly in the midsection, trying to knock the air—and the fight—from her. Laurie grunted as the wind shot out of her lungs. Together, the two women soared back into the café, through the two busted doors, over the broken desk, and back onto the burnt carpet where they first confronted each other. They landed in a twisted, molten heap.

She's scalding. Have to keep her inside. It'll contain the blast at least a little.

Laurie fought with tremendous strength. Fueled by rogue magic coupled with the absorbed potential energy of a nuclear reactor, the woman had physical power that almost rivaled the dragon's. Zeud had to grit her teeth and dig in to hold the woman's wrists and hands at bay. Blast after blast shot from Laurie's hands into the ceiling and walls of the café, lighting fires and breaking all material they touched. Each shot sounded like a thunderclap, and rattled the dragon's vision.

"Get off me! Get off me!" Laurie screamed.

"No! I will make you safe! You will not hurt anyone else!"

"They tried to kill us in Baikonur! They'll try again here. I won't let them hurt Seamus or I!" she screamed into Zeud's face, and as her fevered pitch grew, so too did the fiery innards behind Laurie's molten visage. Her breath turned into radioactive flame, and it poured upwards, scalding and burning the human flesh Zeud wore.

"Ow, dammit, stop! I'm the one who breathes fire!" she yelled down at the woman releasing power into her face, but Laurie refused to stop. She kept screaming, breathing more and more nuclear fire into the air, setting Zeud's hair aflame, and igniting the entire ceiling and all the cubicles and computer equipment. A hole bored its way into the ceiling, eating up into the floor above.

Still, no sickening radiation harmed the dragon. The amulet held firm around her neck.

That's it. Call me a bitch, then breathe fire at me? I don't think so.

Zeud's strained patience broke, and she let the dragon free. She snarled—a deep, ancient noise that came from a million years ago, that terrified anything that heard it and broke the remaining windows in the Vienna neighborhood. Laurie froze from the sound, her reddened eyes locked wide open in genetic fear. Zeud breathed deep and let her pure, inner flames free.

A roaring inferno spat downward, dropping onto the irradiated, maddened woman like the wrath of the sun itself. What wasn't on fire already immediately burst into flames, and the room exploded outward, releasing force, smoke, and fire into the street. Zeud heard as cars flipped over, crunching and shattering against other cars and mailboxes, or phone poles. Beneath Laurie the carpet disappeared, then the wooden floor, then they were falling into the basement.

The two women landed in a flaming pile on the concrete, Zeud still ravaging Laurie with her fiery breath. As she vented her own power, she abandoned the fragile, false body of the human she wore, and began the shift into her full, fiery, feathered dragon body. She crushed whatever machinery and detritus that burned around and below her as her size exploded. From the size of a tall lady to her full dragon size, she gained ten thousand pounds in ten seconds. As Laurie's tiny body went limp in her claws, she ceased her immolating breath.

The ceiling into the second floor that had mostly burnt away busted even further apart as her head reared up to assess Laurie's condition. The horns that swept back off her skull ripped apart flooring and walls two stories above the basement level, knocking down burning timbers, plastered walls and tipping furniture over into the abyss she sat at the bottom of.

She's limp. Her skull is exposed.

Zeud leaned down amongst the fires inside the space and inhaled the reeking, black chemical-infused smoke. The dragon's massive nostrils caught the dim signature of the woman's bizarre, hybrid life signs, and she breathed a sigh of relief through a mouth that was mostly burnt away.

I shouldn't have done that. I could've killed the entire city if she exploded.

Zeud's eyes caught the glimmering sight of the pendant Abe had dropped when he disappeared away with Fiona. It had landed just a few feet from Laurie, sitting atop the fires and ash as it were a crown made for the ruler of all destruction.

247

Strange.

The dragon let go of Laurie's body with one clawed hand and reached down to scoop up the enchanted jewelry. One enormous talon slipped through the silver metal chain, and she lifted it up.

"I'm dying," she heard Laurie whisper through a destroyed face.

Zeud dropped her neck down to face the woman up close. Where Laurie's skin still remained, the molten power showed through. No longer translucent and orange-red like a blacksmith's furnace, she had turned an evil shade of ash-black, and the colors twisted and bent as she heated and cooled in inconsistent waves.

She smells of… death and rotten power.

"You killed me," she whispered.

"I had to stop you," the dragon said. "I may have overreacted. I am sorry."

"Heh," Laurie laughed. "Been a bad stretch for overreactions. I'm gonna blow up. Everyone's gonna die. You killed the whole city."

Shit. "No, that's not going to happen," the massive dragon said to the dying woman. "I will remove you from this world, and contain the poison within you."

She nodded, and tried to add a shrug, but her ruined, smoking body refused the gesture. "Good luck with that." Her body twitched. Once, then twice, then in a constant stream of spasms as her death crept up to consume her, and the energy inside her threatened to explode.

Hope that baku is available. Zeud opened her massive jaws and downed the dying Laurie in a single, head raised gulp. She ignored the tainted taste of the poisoned heathen and closed her eyes to try and shut the moment out.

As her almost-corpse slid down Zeud's throat, it gave off multiple agonizing ruptures of pain, burning hot and corrosive, the sensation caused the dragon to drop down on all fours to fight back a retch. *Is she trying to claw her way back out? The pain… and my stomach is turning, she's giving me radiation. Oh no….*

Zeud's body tried to vomit the ruinous meal, and again, the dragon had to fight it back down, pain and all. She looked down at her long, slender neck and watched as the dead human mass grinded downward to her torso, and the frightened, revolted stomach below. The pain grew more intense, growing into the worst thing she'd ever experienced, bringing tears her eyes, and causing her whole body to shake and tremor. Above her, the weakened building paid the price, and began to crumble at an even faster pace. A giant chunk of stone and wood smashed into her head, knocking it down against a boiler that had softened in the heat.

Zeud's eyes caught a glimpse of something shiny at her claw tip.

Abe's necklace. Where's my necklace?

She reached up and around her massive dragon neck she found an enlarged version of the pendant. It hung there, vibrating against the conflict within its wearer, but it remained. Abe's still sat hanging from the chain wrapped around her index claw.

The dragon lifted Abe's discarded pendant, and threw it inside her fanged mouth like a dainty sweet. It dove down her gullet fast, and cooled her savaged esophagus as it went. Immediate relief spilled over her as the enchanted jewelry absorbed Laurie's radioactive death. Some of the pain—most of it, in fact—remained, but the taint of the radiation disappearing released her from the nausea, and the urges to vomit.

The heat is nothing. I am made of fire. The radiation however… this makes me ill. The two necklaces are working. Working enough. I can get out of here. Leave and go someplace safe where I can recover. They'll be trying to put these fires out soon. My presence incites them. All fires burn hotter around me.

She couldn't help but smile at that thought.

Zeud turned, and saw Abe's old revolver sitting on the remnants of the first floor. Half-covered in ashes, charred wood and wires, the gun still shined; it's nickel-blue metal as clean as the day it was made. She plucked the pistol out of the ruins with a sharp claw and continued out of the building, ripping and tearing the exit in the side larger, until she crawled out onto the Vienna street. Cars burned, buildings burned, and smoke poured up towards the clouds like rivers of black ink.

Distant crowds gathered on the streets and watched through their fear as she emerged from her chrysalis of fire, and wrath.

She smiled again, and launched herself into the air above Vienna, giving them a moment they'd never forget.

I'll find Chung later. Give Henry a call somehow once I'm safely out of the city. He must stay away. I wouldn't live down him getting hurt or sick again. At least Abe got away. He'll be fine. Tougher than he thinks he is, and I believe Fiona will take care of him. She had kindness inside her soul. Perhaps that's what tempers the fury.

She looked down into the old European sprawl as she flew over it and ascended higher. The dragon kept her mouth closed, but smiled a third time. This time, it was because she thought of her favorite human. The one she loved.

Chapter Thirty-Four
Tapper Special Agent Abraham "Abe" Fellows

He made eye contact with the dragon, and saw fear in her red eyes. Worry for him, and his safety.

Fiona grabbed his hand, and he felt a spark of pure energy pass between them. As she yanked him towards the cubicle with the computer just a few feet away, the sensation of being connected to her through more than just mere touch took over his nervous system. As she moved, he felt it no differently than if someone were moving a numb leg. Connected, yet distant, and fuzzy. They were one.

All the physical sensations changed when they turned into energy, and disappeared into the bright, scalding lights and the endless information sea of the internet.

This hurts like a motherfucker, though I have no body. What the hell?

Then he and Fiona's presence slowed a tiny bit, and at

the same time it didn't, and Abe was able to experience it in a way that didn't center around sheer torture of a physical being that didn't really exist at the moment.

Ahead of him, holding a hand that he didn't have at the moment he sensed Fiona. She guided them through the river of flashing lights, streaming numbers and images, and the cascading, crushing weight of ALL THE INFORMATION.

He tried to speak, but he had no mouth. As billboards taller than the sky, and wider than the oceans flashed by over and over, leaving ripples of energy pulsating through whatever he had for a body, he tried telepathy, but that was to no avail.

Connected to the Australian woman made of radiation, magic, and power, and yet isolated, he relaxed, and allowed his consciousness to soak in what surrounded him.

He saw databases, websites, galleries of social media photographs that created an endless collage of the human condition. He heard every single song ever put into the web, simultaneously, mixed into the strangest and most discordant of mind-changing moments. The same happened with every movie even filmed, and for some reason, only Steel Magnolias and a really weird Bollywood flick about a cop with super powers remained in his mind's eye.

I am the ultimate pirate, if only I could remember all of this.

His mind eddied and swirled around the recent media coverage of what happened in London, and on the Isle of Lundy. He saw videos — thousands of cell phone videos — of Fyelrath rampaging through the city, chasing down the harbinger's mutants. He saw more videos of himself doing battle with the mutants, and hundreds of interviews, and news clips of how much damage was done, how many lives were lost, how many people sickened, and how close the world was to being taken over by a celestial evil, and coven of witches angry about their lot in life.

Rightfully angry, no less.

It could've gone differently. I could've died, thousands more could've died. Hundreds did. I could've saved them. I could've done it differently. I might've looked at information in a different way, or been a smarter agent, or seen something I missed. I can't believe I let so many people die.

His emotions—stirred by the electronic memories he couldn't look away from, couldn't stop sensing—grew larger, and consumed him. *Where is she taking me? Where are we going? Where's my pistol? WHERE'S MY PENDANT? She can kill me right now. Fuck. Fuck. How do I contact Spoon? Or Zeud? I don't know anyone's phone numbers. Who does? Fuck, I'm not good at this. I'm in the wrong job. I want my mommy.*

Fuck magic. Fuck fighting bad guys. I should go back to accounting. My mom and dad would love that. Alexis too.

No. Not Alexis. She's done with me.

Rightfully so, no less.

Then, there was a massive, head to toe snapping of his being, and his physicality returned.

The images, videos, and audio disappeared as an overgrown suburb made of sadness and concrete appeared around him. The nightmares his visions brought to him remained. His breathing grew out of control as the memories of what happened back in the UK flooded back. Not just the recorded images he saw in the wilds of the world's wires, but his actual memories. The visions of carapace-covered monsters, venomous fangs, and a sea of eyes all staring at him with raw, seething hatred. The things he saw just feet away, hungry for his blood and soul.

He bent over at the waist and tried to gather himself as he was reduced to nothing more than panic with bare feet.

"Relax, man. Relax," Fiona said to him. "You'll get

your feet in a second or two. Walk it off."

"I'm okay. I'm okay," he lied.

"Fuck all you are. You're having a panic attack." She put her hand on the small of his back. Her warm hand felt strange there—it hurt good, like a sunburn—but it rooted him a tiny bit.

"I am. PTSD. PTSD," he muttered between ragged breaths. "It hits out of nowhere. I remember what I saw, and what happened, and I saw a lot just now wherever we were."

"Yeah, there's a lot to see when we ride the lines," she said. "I'm sorry... about whatever happened to you. Must have been real shite if it stirs you up like this."

Something in the way she said 'real shite' calmed him. Like when grandma called someone a bitch at the grocery store. You had to pause.

Succinct. "Yeah, you're right. It was real shite," Abe said, straightening out, and focusing his thoughts on his breathing. Her hand moved to his shoulder, and stayed there. The touch felt good. Felt soothing. Her presence was good. Soothing.

"I hate to rush you, but this was the best exit I could find, and we're currently naked, near a police outpost."

Jesus I am naked. So is she. Hey... she's put together nicely. Abe's hands shot down to cover his genitals, and he felt a blush hit his cheeks so hot it eclipsed the nuclear heat Fiona gave off. One hand came free, and reached up to where his Russian pendant should've been.

"Modesty is cute," she said.

"Yeah, well. What now? Do you always come out naked? Do you just start stealing clothes to wear?"

"Before I say anything further, I'd like to remind you that I just saved your life. I feel that should be brought into account if I am to face charges for everything that's happened."

"Ha. Yeah, okay. Noted. We need to figure out what's going on in Vienna. Wait. Are we in Chernobyl?"

"Pripyat, yeah. Just on the edge of their exclusion zone. In order for me to truly be safe, I need to move a few more kilometers towards the old reactor site. Won't be too safe for you, but if I explode, everyone else should be safe."

"Are you going to explode?"

"I think it's inevitable, unless we can find a way for me to either expend the energy, or harness it in a meaningful, safe manner."

"That's like, stage three or four at best. Where the fuck are we going to get clothes here?"

"Behind you," Fiona said, pointing over his shoulder.

Abe turned, moving one hand to cover the crack of his ass. Fiona had pointed at a small police or military building—a security hut, really—that had no occupants visible through its few windows.

"That'd be the police outpost I mentioned a second ago. Should be some spare clothes in there for the guards and police passing through. Well, that was my wager, at least."

"Did we come out of the lines there?" Abe asked her.

"Over here, in the ground," she said and pointed again.

On the ground was a black smudge of burnt grass, sand and soil that had been fused into a chunk of glass by tremendous heat. Heat generated by their breach back into reality.

"Nice. Good job," Abe said. "Pry that up so we can sell it on eBay."

She sighed, laughed and nodded. "We need to get someplace quiet. I don't feel well. I didn't before we left, and carrying you through the lines made it worse."

"Worse how? Why?"

"I can't say for sure, just take a guess. Your crack'd be as good as mine."

"So guess. Pick a crack and jump in."

"You aren't made of enough energy to transfer. Too

much meat inside you. Friction on the lines. Did you feel the pain when we first took off? Hurt like no tomorrow. I had to bring you onboard, into me, and slow down to make traveling with you work. I'm frankly shocked you aren't a little slow in the head for the journey."

"Like a smidge retarded?"

"That's not very politically correct word, Abe," she teased. "And yeah, a little slow."

"Sorry," he said, the blush returning, "I just got a little flustered with your relentless sexual innuendo."

"I don't hear that much anymore. I've been a good girl since learning about magic from Seamus and Laurie. The magical made me mundane. That or living in the great expanse of Idaho, with no proper suitors to draw that out of me. I guess you bring out that old quality in me."

"No complaints. Let's get some duds, and then find a safe place to shelter. If we can send a message to Spoon, or Zeud, all the better."

"Got a phone number?"

"Do you know anyone's phone number off the top of your head?"

"My home phone number when I was a kid in Kapunda. I could ring my mum up with my eyes closed."

"Well, we'll figure it out. Let's look Tapper up somehow, and ring the Manchester office. We don't know what's going on in Vienna."

Fiona closed her eyes, and Abe felt another invisible pulse of magical power release from her. She kept her lids fused for almost a minute, searching something, somewhere before she sighed hard, and opened her eyes.

"What?"

"Fires," she replied. "The café is on fire. The whole building engulfed. People took video of Zeud exiting in her full dragon form. No sign of Laurie, and that's bad for Laurie. Firey's on the way to try and put it all out. They're gonna get sick if any of the radiation slipped out."

"I think we can handle a small scale spill of radiation. She must've done something to contain your friend. I know a… a thing in Japan that could help. Plus some Russian magical tech we could put to use. Anyone hurt or killed?"

"I can't see anything yet, but the building was big, and the fires are… consuming it. There's no way someone wasn't hurt. There will be a lot of damage."

"Fuck," Abe said. "Alright. Let's get clothes, get that message to Spoon, and find out if Zeud explodes over the city like the worst possible EMP imaginable."

"Do you friends call you cheery?"

"I'm sorry, friends?"

Chapter Thirty-Five
Tapper Special Agent Henry "Spoon" Spooner

The dragon made a phone call to Spoon from a small bed and breakfast several hours away in the mountains.

Spoon hung up the phone call and dropped it into his pants pocket, just in front of his holstered pistol. He paced the hallway of the Austrian police facility, and let his mind run the numbers on what to do in the next few minutes. His hand went to the pendant hanging around his neck, just beneath his dress shirt.

Rock feels cold. Feels good. Okay, it's go time. Downtown is on fire. The drug deal went south. Abe's in the wind, already in Chernobyl, legit pants down, no gun, no pendant, no underwear, and carrying a nuclear bomb that can disappear into the fucking internet.

Several of the Federal Police officers jogged past him, trying to get out of the building to go somewhere to help. He didn't speak the language, but their faces and their urgent chatter told him they were all about to get diarrhea made mostly out of bricks.

Dangerous levels of radiation in the area, but it's highly concentrated. One building, a few streets. We've got an address for the third glow-in-the-dark douche canoe, who's supposedly a few sandwiches short of a picnic, and taking a cold bath to keep himself from blowing up. They have no solution for him. That's my problem.

Zeud's in the sky, and headed towards Chernobyl at top speed to make sure Abe is okay. That's her problem.

How the fuck do I deal with this Seamus geek? I show my face, he goes super nova, and then what? All of Vienna turns into Dresden, circa February 1945? How do I confront, and detain this guy? Or, how do I convince him to come with me peaceably?

"Sir?"

Spoon snapped back into reality.

"Where the fuck did you come from?" Spoon asked a middle aged woman wearing a suit standing just a few feet away.

"I've been standing here almost a minute," she answered in accented English. "You seem quite lost in deep, troubling thought."

"I am, sorry. Trying to plan."

"As are we. I am looking for advice, or guidance on what to do. We are out of our element with magic and radiation like this. One or the other I think we could figure out, but together... this is out of our reach."

"Can you contain a nuclear blast?"

"Our bomb unit has a towable tank for explosive devices, but a large enough nuclear explosion will tear through it. Would only contain it portionally. Robots with water cannons are the solution, truthfully."

"Shit bird," Spoon said.

"An airplane? Is that some kind of code? A Tapper resource you have access to?"

"Colorful language," Spoon explained. "No Tapper

resources in Vienna beyond Abe, Agent Chung and I right now. And actually, Abe is in the Ukraine."

"That's unfortunate. Do you have a plan?"

"I'm thinking. Wait. There *are* resources in Vienna," Spoon said, then turned and jogged back to the interview room where the doctor and her husband were. He burst in to see them sitting in the same spots, wearing worried expressions. "Does the commission have any kind of containment facility here in Vienna? A place where if one of these assholes blew up, it wouldn't wipe out the city?"

"No," Dr. Tidwell replied. "We have a small storage area in the central building that can quarantine small amounts of material. We'd planned on using it very short term to help them, but it's not that kind of facility. It would never hold back an explosion."

"Is there a place like that close to here? A place where we could transport these people? Where they could pop?"

"What happened?" she asked, her face contorting into dismay.

"The drug hand off went poorly, but not catastrophically. Fiona and Abe are fine. Answer, please."

"No. Austria is adamantly anti-nuclear energy. You could conceivably bring them to the bottom of a mine. Is Fiona alright?"

"Shit. I just said she's fine. She popped off in the internet and took Abe to Chernobyl with her. They're both butt naked, but in no immediate danger. If she pops, only he'll go, and that was a choice they made. Well, Zeud pushed for it, but we own what do."

"I see. Was it the husband then?" the doctor asked. "Did he attack?"

"No, the wife. She followed Fiona to the meet, and shit went south. Zeud ate her."

"What?"

"She's a dragon, they eat things."

"They eat people?"

"People are things, so yeah. Only done when necessary."

"The woman? The woman who sat at this table, right in that chair, has eaten someone?"

Well, she's gonna puke. "Yeah. She was in full dragon-size though, so it was more of a big gulp. Wasn't a sit-down, chewing affair. The wife was about to go kaboom, so she internalized the issue. Found a spot where the energy couldn't leak through. Smart, really."

"I'm going to be sick."

"That's probably pretty normal. Fuck. I wanted you guys to have a safe space I could lock this dude up in." *Well then, smarty pants. Looks like I need to get my ass back to Frankfurt and think of a new secret.*

*****

An hour and a half later after a trip in Zeud's plane, the agent knelt over the top of the sewer grate, and tried to think of something he'd never, ever told anyone.

For a guy who hates people, and doesn't talk much, I sure don't have many secrets.

He looked down into the depths, and saw two beady, black eyes under a thick brow peering up at him. *Feed me,* the eyes seemed to say.

"When I was in Afghanistan, I subverted the direct orders of a Lieutenant because I hated his ass. The first part is the secret."

The eyes blinked at him, and then closed, like a connoisseur enjoying a taste of a coveted morsel. Spoon stood, and before he could ready himself for the splash into the minotaur's lair, he was inside the lobby area, near the hostess podium. His collar, and the ends of his sleeves were damp.

The massive minotaur stood waiting, one menu in hand. It titled its head, examining him, then recognizing him.

"Ah, a repeat customer, my favorite. You came with the dragon before, yes?"

"I did, and I came here to ask for your help. She needs help. Vienna needs help. Frankfurt might too if I don't get this sorted out."

The customers sitting at the nearby tables paused their meals. Spoon heard spoons and forks clink down on plates.

"Please, follow me into the kitchen, where we may speak frankly. Did you know Zeud relit all my ovens for me? I am now able to offer a full menu once again," the minotaur said with pride as he led Spoon to the back of the restaurant, and into the hot kitchen.

The wave of unearthly aromas struck the agent, and his stomach rumbled in hunger.

"I wasn't hungry until I smelled your kitchen, so kudos to you."

"Magically powered ovens make meals that are impossible to refuse," the polite monster explained. "Though I would always give my customers a choice. Now, I would ask of you this; never enter a restaurant the way you just did. You alarmed my customers with your statement, made them pause from their wondrous meals, and that is rude."

"Sorry, it's just... well, things are getting out of hand upstairs," the agent explained. "And I think the only solution we have is you, and this restaurant."

"I see. What is it I can do to assist?"

"Do you know what a nuclear bomb is?"

"Oh my," the minotaur said as a tiny fairy flew on buzzing wings past, carrying a dirty drinking glass towards the sink.

"Yeah, look, we've been tracking these three people that are filled with magic, and radiation. They're about to pop, and one already did. Screwed up a whole neighborhood n the city, maybe more."

"I see," the minotaur said, setting down the menu and

crossing its' massive arms.

"One fled the city safely, with us, and is now in a safe zone. The third asshole though, is still in Vienna, and we have no way to move him to a place where he won't be a danger easily. Our best bet, is to knock the cocksucker out and get him inside your restaurant."

"Ahhh, you're a clever one. Knocking people out."

"I don't know about that, but I am begging you to let us bring him in here. If he blows up in here, I think the city will be safe."

"Blatant disregard for my safety, and the business I run," the giant monster said, shaking its head. "I have employees. What of them?"

"I'll give them a job with the organization I work for. We'll compensate you. Money, pretty jewelry, a fairy farm, whatever you want. Two dragons will owe you favors."

"Which two? Not all dragon favors are worth the same."

"Zeud, and Tesser. I work for Tesser, really."

"A Zeud favor comes fickle. It is worth little. Now the other dragon... I've only heard of since his return of late. What worth do you assign to a dragon that spent ten thousand years missing?"

"Dude are you gonna do it or not? Tell me there's a use for a man filled with endless energy here in the restaurant."

The minotaur huffed, and thought.

"Time is a factor, Lois," Spoon said.

"My name is Chael, not Lois."

"Tesser is legit. He had a daemon problem, and it took a hot minute to get sorted. If he says he'll do something, it'll get done. He just split the troll kingdom into two locations, and brought peace to them after a civil war. He can move mountains if you need it."

"I wish to be set free from my prison. I want a proper restaurant in a proper city."

"Aren't you dead? Like, isn't that your deal? You haunt this place?"

"I prefer to call myself a 'transient spirit.' One day, I could be made physical once again. Based on my research into theoretical physics, and metaphysical magic, I simply require enough energy, and a suitable mass to inhabit. An accompanying spell would allow my personality to move safely."

"This guy is filled with energy. If you can house him here in the restaurant long enough for us to find a mass, and get a spell done up, you'll be selling crepes in Paris before you know it."

"I'd rather be on the coast. When I was alive, I enjoyed the Mediterranean."

"Fucking whatever, man. I'll stick you on a boat if that's what you want."

"Intriguing. Fine then. I accept your offer. How quickly can you get him here?"

Shit yeah. "More importantly, how do I get him in here if he won't tell your sewer-dwelling friend a secret?" Spoon asked. "I might need to drag him in here like a side of beef."

"I will give you a token," the minotaur said. "A precious keepsake of mine that the gatekeeper will accept as key to re-enter."

"Bad ass."

"Like anything of mine from this prison, the key will dissolve, and return to me in just a few hour's time, so you will have to move with great effort to return via it. Any delay on your part will result in the gatekeeper resuming his role for you, and your special delivery. I cannot say if the gatekeeper will allow your unconscious bomb to pass without a secret of the utmost value."

"Wait, if the key can get in, are you sure the dude's energy won't get out?"

"Coming in, is one thing. Exiting is another. I should know," the minotaur said, morosely. He reached around to the small of his back and produced a knife that looked tiny in his massive, furred hands. He passed it to Spoon, who looked at the large kitchen blade with confusion.

"Take this," the beast offered.

"This is it?"

"What fetter to better represent someone who has made food their eternity?"

"You got me there. Hey if you get made real again... won't that mean you can die? Like for good?"

"Such a delightful notion, death," the minotaur mused. "To know that your life has finite duration, and that you must make the most out of every possible second of it? A gift, that. You know your way out of the labyrinth, yes? I would tell you the way, but despite a thousand year's wanderings, I can never quite find the exit," it said with a sigh. "One of my patrons would guide you, for a price."

What price might that be? "I remember the way, thank you."

"Wise."

Now. How the hell am I going to get him here?

Chapter Thirty-Six
Seamus Drake

She said goodbye, and Seamus finally slept in his bathtub.

Like an egg in a pot of boiling water, the sickened weaver of spells who'd absorbed too much power cooked in heat of his own making.

He dreamt of snow, and the mountains of Idaho, where he was from. He remembered the wide, clean streets of his home city, and the dome of the capital building in Boise, made seemingly to resemble Washington's.

He dreamt of the pine trees, and their distinct, Christmas-y smell, and he recalled the sound of hunters in the fall, with the distant cracks of their powerful rifles as they tried to take down their deer, or elk, or bighorn sheep. Men and women trying to recapture their hunter spirit.

His eyes blinked open, and when the raging red inferno cleared from his vision, he saw the tin ceiling and its intricate pattern above the cast iron claw foot tub.

Was that a real noise? That bang? The gun?

Seamus' heart raced faster than it had been, and he sat up in the gently bubbling water. A slow boil, a cook would call it.

He stood, and stepped over the side of the tub down to the floor. He left wet footprints on the tile as he walked towards the hall.

Laurie or Fiona would've said something out loud by now. The owners must be home. Fuck, I'll have to hurt them. I'll try not to. I'll just knock them out. Oh well, bad timing for them, he thought.

Seamus rounded the corner of the wall with a maniacal grin on his face, ready to do harm to people who didn't deserve it. Something flashed in front of his eyes, and a sudden shock of pain erupted in his face. Hot, coppery blood filled his mouth as he tumbled backwards, reeling in pain.

Too shocked by the blow to get angry, he smacked his head off the opposite wall, causing yet another ring of his bell. He slid to the floor as the hot river of blood ran down his chin, and onto his bare chest. He coughed, and several of his teeth popped out with corresponding daggers of pain. They clicked away on the hardwood floor of the upscale apartment.

Seamus blinked his trauma-addled eyes open, and saw his teeth come to a stop just past the approaching feet of a man. The man who'd hit him.

He looked up and saw the strange man—lean, military looking, wearing a buttoned-up old-school leather bomber jacket, and carrying a police baton— coming straight at him. The stranger lifted the baton up to hit him again.

"No," Seamus managed through his mashed face. He lifted an arm up to block the incoming strike, but it never landed.

"This doesn't have to go with an ass whupping. We can do this easily. Allow me to cuff you, and escort you to safety. Safety for you, and everyone else in the city. Time is a factor, and I need you to decide right now."

"Who the fuck are you?" Seamus asked him. He

looked up. Dark eyes, dark hair, strange silver necklaces with a chunk of coal hanging around his neck. In his bones, Seamus could feel cool waves of magic radiating from the man. *He's a spellcaster.*

"My friends call me Spoon. I came to help," the man said.

"You're a wizard? A mage?"

"No, but I play one on television, and my friends let me play with very cool toys. Let me help you up, and let's get the hell out of here to someplace safe. We have a place ready and waiting."

"Not without Laurie. Or Fiona. I won't leave them," he replied.

"Fiona booked it for Chernobyl already with the help of a Tapper agent. She's safe there, waiting for a solution to your collective problem, which is being worked on by smart people who care. Laurie left with her."

"They left me here?" Seamus pondered. "When did Laurie leave? I just fell asleep in the tub? That doesn't sound like them. Doesn't sound like the people they are. How long have I been sleeping?"

"I mean, when you're Fiona, and can teleport instantly across the world, distance is pretty fucking irrelevant. As for your wife, she left the apartment looking for Fiona, and went that way when she knew I was able to come here to get you," he explained, still holding the baton in a menacing fashion.

What's in his other hand? Is that... a needle? "What the fuck are you holding?"

"This is a police baton. Really good for knocking assholes out," he said, and lifted the other hand. "This here is a hypodermic needle filled with Ketamine. I got it from the zoo. Enough here to knock out a Clydesdale. I call it the 'Bill Cosby.' It's really good at knocking assholes out too. Now, please make your decision, because the window to get into the safe house will close on us real quick."

"Are you gonna Clockwork Orange me? Strap my eyes open, and reprogram my brain? Change me, turn me into a weapon?" Seamus looked at the man's face and tried to read him. As the sickened, power-infused mage scanned the baton-wielder's eyes for a tell, something that would give him a reason to either stand up and go, or fry him on the spot with the power inside him, the man shuffle d his feet, and let out a frustrated sigh.

"Malcolm McDowell was the shit in that movie, but no, I'm just trying to save lives. Let me bring you to safety. Skip the ultra-violence. Decide."

"I don't know," Seamus said. "I can't trust anyone. I don't even know you."

The man standing over him moved fast. Probably as fast he'd swung the baton into Seamus' face a minute earlier, but at least this time Seamus had the gift of seeing him coming.

Fork, or Spoon, whatever he called himself; lunged with the needle.

Seamus rolled away from the hypodermic, scrambling from the sudden attack. As he crawled away, against the hallway's wall the leather-jacket wearing attacker snapped him with the baton in the meat of the calf, and the strike triggered a pulse of agony.

"Ah, damn it!" Seamus screamed, diving forward and rolling around so he could clutch the beaten limb.

The man's baton was aflame. He stood up, shaking the weapon to get the fire to go out, but the flame held firm, and grew in fact. The price it paid for hitting Seamus' flesh.

"HA, screw you, jerk," Seamus yelled at him, forgetting he had the power of the atom inside him.

"I'm trying to help you," he yelled back, and dove forward once more with the drug-filled needle and the flaming stick.

Pinned in the corner of the floor and wall, and unable to crawl away backwards fast enough, Seamus failed to either escape or use his powers to retaliate, and the needle went into his chest. The man thumbed the plunger down, and Seamus felt the sedative course into his flesh. The sensation didn't burn, but it tingled, like how a sleeping hand, or foot felt, except this started just beside his sternum. This tingle rolled through his chest, and upper arm, and ran up his neck like a wave of suffocation.

"Let it happen," the man named Spoon said. "Just let me bring you to safety. Everything will be alright." He tossed the flaming police stick end over end into the bathroom, clanging it perfectly into the still-full bathtub. The fire extinguished with a hiss.

"You stuck me, man," Seamus managed, feeling the weird tingle cross an internal threshold where the inner power he'd absorbed was. The two feelings mixing gave him an immediate sensation of apocalyptic heartburn, and he cried out in pain. *I can't rein it in. If I pass out....*

"What? What?" his attacked asked, sitting up. "Are you fucking allergic?"

"Ahh.... God it hurts. I'm gonna lose control. We're gonna die. You killed me," Seamus managed, his ability to speak and control his body waning with each passing second. As it did, he felt that caustic burning grow larger and larger. "This is your fault. You never should've hit me. Oh, Laurie, I'm sorry," he said, and passed out.

Chapter Thirty-Seven
Fiona Gilmore

"Abe, I think Laurie is dead," Fiona said to the agent.

The two of them sat inside an abandoned apartment on the top floor of a sprawling, bland complex in the city of Pripyat. Dust and debris covered everything, and the smell of wet rot pervaded. But, they had found clothes, and were out of the slow rain that began to fall, and they felt deep enough inside the Chernobyl exclusion area that if something should happen to Fiona, there would be no new damage to the world.

They could see the reactor, and its strange metal covering in the distance.

"She fucked with Zeud. I am not shocked if that's what happened. I hope not, though. If she died, and blew up in the city, Vienna's gonna be screwed for a really long time."

"I can... kinda feel the presence of Seamus still. Like hearing someone talking in the background. In another room. I can hear him in the world, though it sounds garbled, like he's pissed drunk. I can't hear her anymore. Her radio station isn't even pushing out static. That station is black, like it was snuffed out."

"Mess with the bull, get the horns, it seems. Zeud

273

likely doesn't play around with people who do bad things. I base that on my experience with Tesser, and Fyelrath. They can be your best friend, and make your life better than you could imagine, or they could bring wrath and ruin that the stories in the Bible couldn't compare to. I'm sorry about friend. You were close to her?"

"Yeah, kinda. I mean yeah. She and Seamus led the school I studied magic at. Not much of a school, really. Just a giant ranch out in Idaho where we read books about magic and practiced rituals. Some of us had real talent. We smoked a lot of weed."

"New-Age bullshit mixed with old age magic isn't the best recipe for success, as it would appear," Abe said. He slapped the couch he sat on and a cloud of either dust of spores rose up. He waved it away and coughed for good measure.

I'm getting warmer inside. I feel a little sick.

"You ok?" he asked her. "Your facial expression just went belly up."

"I don't feel well," she said. "Well, I feel worse than when we arrived."

"Worse like you're going to blow up?"

"Like I know," she quipped. "I need to eat, I think."

"Can't you just turn energy into matter? Like a god? I mean, if you can turn yourself and others into electricity, then back again, why can't you just take some of that energy inside you, and create matter to eat?"

"Picard's tea," she said with a laugh.

"Yeah, exactly. Can you do that?"

"I haven't tried. I suppose I could give a shot."

Fiona steadied herself, and ignored the feeling of nausea, and churning heat in her belly. *What do I want to eat? Simple. Something really simple. One... item. One ingredient. Water. I'll start with water.*

She stood up and wandered into the small apartment kitchen, which took steadying herself on the walls and furniture as she went to happen. She pulled open cabinets until she saw dusty drinking glasses, and after grabbing one, she returned as she came to the living room. Fiona sat on the couch beside Abe and wiped the glass out with her fingers as best she could. *I have to catch my breath. Bloody hell.*

"What are you gonna make?" he asked.

"Water."

"Ah, easy one. Good luck," Abe said.

"Thank you," she said, and turned to the glass. As with the other applications of her power, she focused on the slow-motion crisis unfolding in her stomach.

Divert the river. Flood somewhere else.

Concentration was something Fiona had excelled at. She embroidered for fun, loved to study languages—she spoke four well—and did Sudoku puzzles, and those hobbies gave her ample opportunity to close the world down to just one thing, and keep everything else quiet. This was the same.

She stared at the empty center of the glass, and allowed the power inside her to bubble up, like a magical well filling. As the scalding heat threatened to make her choke, and vomit, she imagined the rise moving into the glass, filling it with water.

Nothing happened.

She sighed, and tried again. Then a third time.

She lifted the glass to hurl it at a wall.

"Wait," the agent said. "I can feel the magic you're putting off. It's powerful, but raw, not harnessed at all. Your will alone isn't enough to form that power into such a narrow effect."

"Thanks, that's real kind of you to say."

"Sorry. I'm saying you're powerful, and you're close. You need another tool to sculpt the energy inside you. Can I show you something?"

"Sure."

He took the glass from her with a smile, and looked at

it. "Vocare potum," he whispered, and water bubbled up from its transparent center as if it were connected to an invisible freshwater spring. He drank half the water down, and handed the cup to her. "That's a half-full cup."

"Holy shit," Fiona said. She drank the rest of it. *Clean, fresh. Wow.* "You can just do that? What else can you make? You made those meds back in Vienna, what else?"

"Fluids mostly," he said, as if he were a massive failure. "I tried a variety of solids, but I can't do much yet. Magic seems to only want to be made into things that flow, or change your state of consciousness." He added a shrug. "Try again, but say the words. Vocare potum."

"Is that Latin? Why Latin?" *Figures it's one of the languages I don't know.*

"It is. Means 'call beverage,' if you can believe that. As for why it works… well, I believe that all language has incredible power, and when I use that language to shape the magic I can access, things work better. It's part of how I was taught by Mr. Doyle too. It's about believing, Fiona. I *believe* those words will work, and with enough practice, I *made* them work."

That's the hottest thing I've ever heard a man say. "I'll try your beverage phone."

He smiled. "You do that. Ring us up a fucking beer."

"What kind?"

"I don't even drink beer, I just thought it'd be funny to say."

"Now that's something I'll remedy."

Without even a moment's focus, or attempt at clarity, Fiona surged the heat in her belly with a mental tightening of her stomach. She stared at the glass in her hand and spoke the words.

"Vocare potum," she said, and when she said it, she *believed*.

Bubbling brown ale, topped with a thin, creamy head rose to fill the glass just as if she'd held it under the tap at the pub she worked at while at university.

"Ha! I did it!"

Abe clapped his hands hard, and stood to add the full ovation. He cheered, and they both laughed together in the room that stank of mildew, and now; smelled of fresh beer. She tipped the glass and downed a gulp.

"Lordy, that is good. Tastes just like a SuperDry. It's even cold," she said. Fiona handed him the glass.

"You just drank a drink to energize yourself, made from energy you supplied. If that ain't some shit," he said and took a mouthful. "That's not bad."

"That's delicious. You'll understand that when we can drink some varieties of beer together. I'll learn you proper."

"I look forward to that. Assuming we don't go all Hiroshima here," he said, and drank a second time.

You know... "I feel better. Like I managed to get rid of some of the heat inside. Not anything big, but I can sense a small difference."

"No kidding? So maybe, just maybe we can step it up, and find a way for you to create something that can really eat up some of what you've got stored inside," Abe said. "That's what we call a 'glimmer of hope,' in the business."

"You do seem to be in the business of giving people hope," Fiona said.

"Well, it was that or a lucrative career as a rapper or gigolo. I went with my heart, not the streets or the sheets."

"I think you found your calling, but that opinion is based on only experiencing one of the professions you mentioned."

"Many days I'm not sure," he said, losing his moment of positivity.

"No, be sure. You are doing what you were meant to," Fiona said. "I believe that things happen for a reason, and that you found me when you did, and that you helped me make beer... that's a sign from... something. Someone. Proof of God."

Abe laughed, she joined, but stopped when a terrible burp triggered a wave of nausea strong enough to make her double over on the shitty couch they sat on.

"Uh oh," Abe said.

"I think the beer... Oh no. Now I think it made me worse. I shouldn't have drank it," Fiona said, clutching at her midsection. "Oh God... a fucking burp? Not indigestion... not that. Ugh... the heat is building again. Worse. Unh," she grunted, putting a hand on the old police uniform over her stomach. The agony was tremendous and growing.

"Shit, I think we poked a hole in the containment vessel," he said.

"What?" she muttered through the pulsating pain tearing her innards apart. "This is worse than it's ever been. Shite."

"When I taught you how to let the energy out to make things, it's like we cracked the can open. Can't put the tab back on to shut it. You're not a screw cap."

"What do we do?"

"Um, uh..." Abe stood, and paced, looking around the room for something that might help them, but there was nothing. He stopped. "Wait. I got it. If letting a little out helped you, then maybe letting more out will. Can you focus, and try another conjuration?"

"The water thing?" she said through teeth that wouldn't part.

"Yeah."

"I'll try."

"Come to the window," he said, taking her with care by the arm. He helped her to the broken window framed by sharp daggers of glass. He pointed out into the old, overgrown courtyard of the building complex. A rusty metal playground set erupted from the grasses and young trees like a scar that had almost been healed over.

"Say um… How would it go? Man, Doyle would be up my ass like a bike seat for not knowing this."

"Quick, Abe," she said, and fought back a wave of vomit. *That's not vomit. That's not going to be bile. Can't…*

"Sie… Um… sie flumine! Sie flumine! Conjure river! And fucking believe it when you say it," he begged her.

She took all of her power, all of her might, all of her strength, and focused.

"Sie flumine," she called out.

Chapter Thirty-Eight
Tapper Special Agent Henry "Spoon" Spooner

"Don't blow up you dick-dangling nitwit," Spoon said. "I only took three iodine pills on the way here." He yanked his Tapper phone out of his pocket and hit the speed dial for the Austrian cop he'd made friends with back at the secret interrogation building. She answered.

"Agent Spooner?"

"I got him knocked out. Had to beat him up a bit in the process. Send your men up with the stretcher. Make sure the paramedic comes too. Tell your road crews to be ready, and get the plane going. Let Frankfurt know it's on like Donkey Kong."

"Immediately."

He hung up without saying goodbye and squatted down to lift the unconscious man. "Ow, Christ, you're hot as a cast iron pan."

He stood up, shaking his hands to cool off the burnt

fingertips. *Gloves, I need gloves. Why didn't I wear gloves?* He looked around in the hallway for a pair he could grab, but saw nothing. He dashed back into the main apartment entrance hall, and saw a small side table just inside the door. Spoon leapt down the hall at it, and pulled the drawer open.

Two pristine leather driving gloves sat mixed in with a handful of papers, keys, and a small stuffed teddy bear that had seen better days. Spoon grabbed the gloves, and yanked the right hand on. *Too small. Fuck it, make it work.*

He pulled his folding knife out of his slacks pocket and snapped the blade open. He cut the wrist on the palm side to make the glove larger, and pulled it on. *Better.* He switched the knife into the gloves hand, cut the other glove, and yanked it on.

He ran back to where the man named Seamus lay, and hooked his hands under the naked, knocked out man's armpits.

"Ow, dude, what the hell?" Spoon said, ignoring the searing pain at his wrists where the leather didn't cover skin. "Hot as a frying pan."

He backed up, dragging the wet, naked man across the hardwood floor. As the bare skin slid across the polished wood, Spoon expected for it to drag, to squeak, but instead, it hissed. He looked up at the path they covered as they moved, and blackened scorch marks trailed off to where they'd scuffled, and where Spoon had stuck him with the horse tranquilizer. In the areas where Spoon's movement slowed, the wood was burnt worse. Making the whole process more surreal were fallen clumps of the man's hair.

"Shit," he said, and dragged him backwards faster, doing his best to ignore the sensation that his hands and forearms were about to catch on fire. "Need oven mitts," he joked through the heat and pain. *No really I do.*

As he rounded the corner to the central hall leading to the apartment's door he heard several people rushing in his direction. As he gassed out from the exertion and pain — sweating like he was climbing a mountain range in the Kandahar valley — he flopped back onto his ass and laid out flat.

Seamus' head banged off the wood, and left both a dent, and a burn mark. Buried in the concave depression was another smattering of the man's hair. The pendant around his neck felt silly where it brushed against the hair on his chest as the rescuers appeared in the doorway to the apartment.

He saw the steps they took to protect themselves from the poison the man on the floor was ripe with. White synthetic suits covered their entire bodies, and black gloves and boots covered their hands and feet. Clear plastic face shields gave them a window into the world, but beneath that, they wore ventilators to protect their lungs. One of them took off, looking for the kitchen while the other two dropped the stretcher to its lowest level.

Least I got this fucking Russian voodoo necklace. "He's too hot to touch! Get better gloves or go steal the damn oven mitts from the kitchen," he hollered.

"Yes," one of the responding officers, or paramedics said from inside the head to toe suits they wore to keep the radiation at bay.

"Your hands?" one of them asked, pointing a gloved finger at Spoon's stolen and customized driving gloves. "They are okay?"

He looked down at his palms and saw skin instead of leather. His fingers and palms were reddened, like his face after too much time in the sun.

"Yeah," he said. "It stings a little, but I'll smear some lotion on it tonight. Was gonna anyway."

"Very well," the cop, or medic said, then stood, posture perfect straight, betraying his nervousness.

Just then the medic returned, bearing several wet kitchen towels and a pair of oven mitts. The woman in the suit tossed him the oven mitts, and kept the wet towels for herself. Spoon got to his feet, slipped the gloves on, and he and the suited medic with the towels lifted Seamus up and got him onto the stretcher. He hit down heavy, and let out a tiny groan. The white fabric sheet instantly charred as his bare skin touched it, and a moment later, the material burst into flames. His body surrounded by a halo of fire, they backed away, shielding the plastic covering on their faces to let the sheet burn off.

"Is this...?" one of them said, startled from the scene beyond anything normal.

"Really crazy right?" Spoon said. "Strap him in and let's get moving. Our door to safety is gonna close, and maybe more important than that, this dude is gonna set us, and the ambulance on fire. Talk about fucking Hot Wheels."

"You use a lot of profanity," one of the medics commented.

*****

The medic was right about Spoon's usage of the English language, and Spoon was right about the ambulance being set on fire. Thankfully, the journey to the airport, and the flight happened before Seamus turned into a Roman candle.

As the man's body erupted into flames — actually burning like he was a log on fire — in the back of the medical transport, they produced the ambulance's small fire extinguisher, and two more they had put in just for this event.

"Back up!" he screamed, but the two German professionals in white plastic suits had already plastered themselves to the walls of the ambulance getting their own extinguishers ready. He sprayed Seamus' drugged body — still naked, because each of the three sheets they'd put on top of him had burnt away like birch bark thrown on coals. The Austrian medics had learned to leave

Seamus naked and exposed, other than the sturdy straps that held up against his furious warmth. "Open the damn door, vent this smoke!"

One of them did while the other sprayed Seamus with the fire retardant.

As soon as the van's back door swung open as they sped through the streets of Frankfurt, the wind wicked the black haze of smoke out of the van, clearing the air. The already loud noise of the ambulance's siren grew even louder, and joined in with the multitude of other sirens on the vehicles escorting them through the city. *I can breathe. Phew. We're not gonna last much longer.* Spoon looked down at his reddened, sore wrist at his watch. The timer ticked down. *Ten minutes and change at most.*

"How much longer?" he asked one of the men in the ambulance. "Our clock is running down."

"Five, maybe six minutes," one of the white-suited men said.

"Tell your driver it better be closer to five minutes," Spoon said. "Otherwise we're gonna have a wiener roast in the streets of Frankfurt."

The medic spoke to the driver in something that sounded like German and Spoon felt a slight surge in the van's speed as it swerved through the streets. Out the back, now open door he saw police cordon after cordon blocking the way for them to get to Zeud's special alley, and the special grate in the ground. He grabbed a handlebar near the ambulance's ceiling to keep from getting thrown about.

Ow, fuck, my hand burns like crazy. Never gonna be able to light a butt after this, let alone rub one out. He let go of the bar and pressed his feet into the floor and his back against the cabinet on the wall of the ambulance. *Like riding the Green Line,* he thought as he looked down at the now-bald Seamus. The man shivered, still unconscious, and his skin looked savaged by the sun, covered with lesions, blisters, and exposed tears of muscle tissue.

Where Seamus hadn't turned red like a cherry or split open, he'd turned purple like a plum. His skin had flaked, and peeled where it had developed clusters of massive, coin-sized blisters. Slick trails of pus and awfulness ran down the stretcher, sizzling, where it plopped on the floor to bubble and boil. His hands looked frostbitten—black tipped—but they were burnt from the inside out as his power escaped him, taking the quality of his body with it.

His eyes opened. Spoon rushed down to kneel near him. Not close enough to touch him, but close enough to hear him.

"Get another needle of that horse tranquilizer ready," Spoon told one of the suit-wearing people working with him. They jumped to. "Hey Seamus, me again. Don't blow up, please."

He licked his lips with a tongue as dry as sand and the color of flowing lava. He coughed, and when he did, fire belched into the air. The ceiling of the van smoldered black where the flames met it. He gagged on something in the back of his throat, then turned his head sideways, and let out a streaming shot of vomit. It hit the wall, then the floor, and sizzled where it touched anything.

"Well then," Spoon said, leaning away. *Turning into a piss-poor dragon here. Can't even fucking fly.* "Look, we are just a few minutes away from getting you to safety, and relief."

Seamus nodded, and bit his lower lip. All of the teeth he had left fell out from the slight pressure and clattered on the floor. He winced, and made a pathetic mewling noise.

"That sucks, man," Spoon said, reaching in to help him—to touch him for comfort—but he recoiled his hand away when he felt the furnace heat the man's flesh gave off. He looked for the oven mitts.

"Laurie?" he whispered.

His breath is the worst fever, like opening an oven door.

"I can't feel her. She's dead, isn't she?"

If he thinks that, he'll give up, and if he gives up.... "No, she's still around. Zeud took her." *Boy did she ever, so I understand.*

"Zeud? Oh. The dragon. She always wanted to meet a dragon. She loved them. Used to wear a tiny purple dragon pendant. She loved that baby. Had a picture of her in the mirror of her makeup vanity."

"Astrid. I've held her in my arms, you know. She's amazing. She's magical."

"She's not magical. She's *magic,*" he said with a smile that was made mostly of agony. "All we wanted to do was help."

"I know," Spoon said to him.

"We're here," the paramedic driving said, and the van slowed.

"We're here Seamus, just a minute more," Spoon said, and looked at his watch. *Eight minutes. No problem if the minotaur is right.*

The van stopped, and all three upright non-nuclear poisoned mages jumped out to the same streets Spoon and visited with his friends. Agent Chung stood at the corner of the large row of buildings with the alley at its back that led to the hidden grate by the stone wall with the restaurant hidden inside.

"Chung, get the fuck out, this dude is leaking like a cracked reactor," he hollered at the agent.

The agent backed away, and even jogged to get near the lines the police strung up. When he was far enough away, Spoon motioned for the paramedics to get Seamus out and wheels-up. As fast as the pit team on a Nascar crew they had him out, up and pointed at the alley for Spoon. Spoon grabbed the handle at the foot of the stretcher.

"Here we go, Captain Firepants," Spoon said, and started running forward with the man in front of him.

Spoon sprinted as fast as he could manage towards

the ninety degree turn of the alley. He had to slow when Seamus' body took to flame, shooting up like spouts of white and blue fire from eruptions all over his legs, and torso. The man screamed out in pain as the flares up the day even brighter. Spoon had to close his eyes, and look away, first from the light, then from the fear of having his eyes cooked straight out of his skull.

He navigated by staring at the side of the building. When the bricks changed color in a uniform line, he slowed and turned. The alley unfolded, and Spoon started running again, making the flames grow huge and hot once more. He shielded his eyes.

Do I fucking, what, run straight at the grate? Run at the wall? I can't fucking see anything, so.... Man I wish Abe was here. He'd have a spell, or have a clue. I'm getting too old for this shit. I don't wanna die in a fire. I woulda been a fireman if that was the case. I don't wanna die in a city called Frankfurt.

Spoon ran at the spot where he remembered the grate to be. The rougher surface of the alley street made it much harder to push, and his already burnt, and spent body protested with aches and pains as he tried to shove the stretcher and its torch occupant forward.

"Turn to the wall," he heard a grinding voice call out from below. The ground rumbled with a strange resonance, and without delay he obeyed the suggestion, and nearly toppled the whole affair to the ground in the process.

He dared a look straight over the fires geysering up from Seamus and saw an open passage into the stone wall opposite the back of the buildings. An entrance that had never been there before. Beyond the opening extended a dark tunnel running below the grassy green park above, and coming from it, the immediate scent of cooked food.

God I better not be smelling Seamus steaks. Fuck that. He made one last ditch rush, and shoved the stretcher forward into the manifested hall, and followed it on foot at a pace that didn't make his knees and back feel like they were riddled with shards of glass.

He crossed the threshold of the wall, and his vision blurred out for a second. When he blinked the clarity back, he was standing in the restaurant at the host's podium and the stretcher wasn't in his hands. A few steps ahead he saw the mundane body of Seamus — still riddled with the burns, and blisters, but not the flame — being pulled on the missing stretcher towards the kitchen by the massive, horned cook named Chael.

"What's going on. Where you taking him?"

"To the ovens," the minotaur explained.

"What? You're gonna fucking cook him?"

"No, silly. I'm going to put him in the largest oven I have. It's sat idle, without fuel for a long time, but I think he'll do nicely to keep it running. Perhaps I'll offer some food cooked off its surface again. Maybe a new style of coq au vin?"

"I fucking… dude? What?"

The minotaur turned, and looked at Spoon with eyes that brimmed over with sadness, and a resoluteness that made Spoon put his hand on the grip of his pistol.

"We had an agreement. I will take care of this man and prevent the evil inside him from destroying Frankfurt, or worse. And you, you will find a way to make me whole so I may live a life. Beyond that, worry about no details. He will be put to good use, and kept alive."

"In a fucking oven," Spoon almost screamed, almost drawing his weapon.

"Human… this world is just barely opening up its flower to you. Sit back, and find a way to absorb just what you've had hidden from your eyes. Sit. I'll have someone bring you a whiskey. You need a whiskey. Enjoy that you saved millions of innocent lives. Revel in your heroic deeds."

The minotaur ignored Spoon's hand on the pistol, and

entered the kitchen without a care in the world beyond getting his new arrival into his last oven.

This does not feel like a win.

Something that looked like an orc from the Lord of the Ring movies but wearing a shirt and tie pushed a tumbler into his hand, and Spoon drank the whiskey without thinking.

Chapter Thirty-Nine
Zeud

She flew.

Faster than she had ever soared the skies, she flew. One flap of her feathered wings grew her speed by steady, and enormous increments until she had to narrow her eyes against the onslaught of the winds she knifed through. The skies trembled at the power of her passing.

And as she flew, she kept her nostrils and mouth fused shut with the power of a thousand hydraulic presses. She'd held her breath since the skies over Austria, and somehow, she'd lost no energy, or consciousness as a result.

The woman's flesh, and her power inside me is releasing its fuel like bombs going off one after another. She had trapped SUCH energy. That she stayed in a single piece as long as she did is surely proof of miracles. Whatever stories they wind up telling of her, she was a hero of great regard.

The dragon soared, ignoring the worming, spiking pain that tried to claw its way through her muscles, bones, and the scales covering her body as best she could.

I can't keep my mouth shut much longer, and my body won't yield to the power, and explode. I'll have to release it, and I guarantee if I do, I'll carpet the lands below me in an

291

apocalyptic fog of radiation. I'll doom all the life below me. Soil and beast, water and tree. All of it shall be ruined by the radiation inside my belly. How much further must I fly?

She scanned for familiar landmarks. She searched the horizon in all direction looking for mountains, rivers, ancient forests — anything — that might tell her where she was. When she'd left Vienna she'd headed almost straight east, then turned northeast when she'd gotten over the center of what she thought was a lowly populated center of Slovakia. She had no idea, really. The world didn't have human map lines drawn on it. She wanted to go over areas where if she did exhale, or explode, the least amount of death and destruction would occur.

The task of searching for exactly where she needed to go was made worse by her intense speed. Normally she flew at a lackadaisical speed of perhaps one, or two hundred miles per hour, but this... this was a whole tier she'd never reached, not even when the volcanoes erupted over the Ur-City her dragon brother Tesser built by hand when the world had but one continent.

She saw nothing.

I'll... have to smell for the radiation. I know the scent of the blasted reactor is still strong, even though its danger has faded for the humans. But I must only inhale. She laughed. *Human politicians used to get in trouble for that. Funny. Let us try, and let us not ruin the lives of thousands below if I cough. The stakes are a bit different here.*

Zeud readied her lungs, and grit her ample, sharp teeth, and shot a single tiny snort of the eastern European air into her lungs. As the ice-cold wind frosted over the inside of her nasal passages, then disappeared down into her chest, she snagged the tiniest scrap of that rare, but unmistakable odor she'd learned to fear, and hate.

Radiation, and not terribly far. That way, slightly more east. My chest hurts. About to pop. Time is up. Let's see what I can do with this energy before it tries to destroy me from the inside out.

She flapped to fly faster as she tilted her direction of flight towards the tiny traces of what she believed to be Chernobyl. Her wings — feathered, fiery, and majestic beyond any ability for a human to describe or measure — set free trails of the fire that she was. Fire fueled by the captured energy inside her. Fires that propelled her like a rocket leaving orbit, shooting her through the skies so fast she erupted through the sound barrier with but a couple flaps, and then doubled that speed in just two flaps more. Ten flaps of her flaming wings later she was rocketing over western Ukraine at a speed that the men and women manning the radars in the region would later describe as, "a weird glitch."

Nothing could appear, fly that fast, then disappear.

Zeud could, and she did. A hundred miles before she flew over the top of the reactor and its massive concrete encasement she stopped her forward propulsion, and angled her wings to brake. The friction created by her transit scorched the skies, dropping twin clouds of ash to fall over the region near Pripyat, where she knew her human friend Abe, and their new friend Fiona had fled to.

As her chest threatened to burst, she took in another short inhalation, and smelled the sickness in the air. The latent corruption that the Russians let creep over their land, and destroy it.

It isn't corrupting me. My pendant.... She reached down with one of her clawed hands and felt the magically large amulet there. She lifted it, and looked at it. Tiny flakes of the black stone fell away like ash in the wind. She felt shock. *It's corroding. Melting away under the pressure. Shit. She looked around. I'll just let out... a tiny bit of the power. There.*

Zeud tilted her wings upward to slow her speed, and felt the wind grind against her bones and feathers as if she'd slammed into a wall. The force of the air she flew through nearly snapped her into smaller bits, but she held firm, and remained strong until her airspeed was manageable. She angled her flight, pivoting over to direct her landing halfway from Pripyat's apartment complexes, and came to a fiery, ground-burning rest in a field of grass that reached the top of her ankles. The reactor and its shining metal, rounded sarcophagus-lid was close by. So close she could jump to it. As the gentle, tainted grasses brushed against her scales, she opened her mouth, and screamed a mile long runner of molten air. The fire she breathed scorched, scalded, immolated, terrified the very atoms of reality its power was so great. She felt its heat on her teeth, and tongue, and even her own body—made of primordial fire—felt the incredible heat, and almost felt pain as a result. Flames—towering and furious—caught in every direction she breathed, and still, it hurt her.

To make fire feel pain?

She kept breathing, venting out the power she'd been capturing since Vienna, and felt relief as it spilled out over the little bit of nature she stood in, and splashed out onto the perimeter and near center of the actual reactor facility. A building with a red roof just thirty yards away erupted into flames and exploded into the air as if it had been filled with propane. The explosion echoed across the abandoned world, leaving a ghost of its former self in the ears of everything within miles. She watched as trees caught fire and disappeared into ash, then watched as iron, steel, and concrete did the same. Buildings crumbled from her fury. She felt the waves of destruction roll out from her in Biblical fashion, and she couldn't help but enjoy the moment a small bit.

When Zeud felt a small measure of relief, she shut it down, and reigned in the release, going down on all fours, feathered wings held high in the air off her back to exude more of the temperatures inside her, and she panted, sucking in breezes of Pripyat's now more-tainted air. The fresh oxygen stoked her healthy flames of life, and she felt clarity, and a measure of decent health return to her. Her claws stopped shaking, and she reared up on her hind legs, looking for any signs of where Fiona and Abe could be.

An exhausted, but relieved dragon of fire looked back over her shoulder at the closest urban area of Pripyat, where most of the dilapidated apartment complexes were, and immediately saw something equally biblical, and entirely out of place.

From an upper apartment window facing her, and the reactor, she saw a river flowing into the world. The shooting flood of water came out in a tiny spigot inside one of the windows, and fast spread into a twenty, or thirty foot wide stream of water that disappeared behind a building between the dragon, and the strange sight. An actual waterfall shooting out the side near the top of an abandoned building.

"Well that has the mark of Abe all over it," the dragon said, and leapt into the air. She left footprints of fire on the ground behind her, and crossed the distance between her and the closer building in just a few seconds. She came to a rest on the roof of the towering suburban structure, digging her claws into the flat gravel surface, puncturing holes into the harder roof below.

"Fiona is puking water everywhere," Zeud said to herself as she saw deeper into the room. "And Abe is there hooting and hollering at her like an idiot in the stands at a pitch. Abraham!" she bellowed across the courtyard in the center of several identical buildings.

"Hey!" he hollered. "You look like a comet! Fiona's releasing some of the energy she absorbed. We need to find a way to capture it. She can't stop and this stuff is guaranteed to be radioactive!"

She could flood the entire region, and if that water is radioactive… she'll ruin the ecosystem for another thousand miles and another thousand years. Killing her will do no good,

*and I can't fly her into space and throw her at the moon....
What would Kaula have done? What would Tesser or Garamos
do?*

She didn't bother thinking about what Kiarohn or
Fyelrath would do. Kia did nothing but fly around
incessantly for all time, stirring the lifewinds of the
world, and Fyelrath would try to drown the issue in even
more water, assuming she took any action at all.

*Kaula would use magic. She would either drain the energy
from her, or drain her from the world.*

*Drain her from the world. Where can we bring her that will
be safer than here? I cannot cross the Veil, nor tear a hole in it
to send her through, yet I can step sidewise into a pocket realm.
Like Chael's place. But to do that, I must have a tremendous
source of power, and physical place of strength and persistence.
A physical anchor, a magical anchor, and magical power to
rival Astrid or Kaula.*

*Power I have a plentitude of... but what place is the
strongest here? What place exudes strength, and could be a
vessel to house a shard realm?* She looked over her shoulder
at the human-engineered steel cap resting over the corpse
of the exploded reactor behind her. The half-circle
covered most of the old building, and contained the
cursed 4th reactor of the plant.

*That's the most anchored place here. The strongest edifice,
built to last most importantly by people filled with hope. Hope
is the key. It's... the only thing we've got, and it's stronger
than any creation made of matter.* Zeud looked down at the
marsh the woman had created in what had been an
abandoned

"What are we doing?" Abe screamed across the gulf
between buildings.

"Fiona," she said to the wide-eyed, strong but scared
woman as the magical river crashed out of her in a
scream. "I must send you to a place where your power
can leave your body, but do no harm to the world around
you."

She nodded, eyebrows tightened in pain, or fear.

"We must move you to the lid on the reactor, to the metal sarcophagus behind me. The grave of the great nuclear disaster here. You must release your energy at the sarcophagus as I release mine. I shall do my part with magic as I can. Abe, you must help as well. Speak words and work your spells as you can to and make us a hole in reality. Create a space that carves Fiona a home."

"I have no idea how to do that," he hollered back.

"No one alive does. Figure it out," Zeud said as she leapt into the air, crushing the roof of the apartment building as she leapt into the air. She glided across the gulf, over the stream of water coming from Fiona, and landed on the edge of the building's roof and side. She reached into the window with care, and picked up the woman making an ocean with the power inside her. Zeud held her in the air several stories above the growing pond below. *She's petrified. Look at her.* "We're going to the sarcophagus covering the reactor. As soon as we get close enough for you to hit it with the power inside you, set the power free, and imagine a place you can live in. A house, a city, a world. Imagine it as your salvation, and make it enjoyable. You could be there awhile."

She gave the dragon a tiny nod, and Zeud let go of the roof edge with her other claw, holding onto the side of the building with her rear talons sunk into its concrete side. She reached into the window and picked up Abe, then kicked off into the sky.

The agent screamed, but the sound seemed like joy, not terror.

Zeud let her jump gain her altitude, and avoided flapping her winds in any way. The spray of water hitting her and Abe in the face would be steam and murder if she let off anymore heat, and worse yet, she'd fly so fast Abe and Fiona might tear apart like tissue paper from the force of it all.

When they dropped down to the concrete grounds near the reactor, and approached the massive edifice covering the smoldering, evil terror of the cracked reactor core, the water spraying forth from the woman narrowed into a laser-tight beam, and carved an erratic stream of lines into the curved side of the lid. In a second of fire hose madness, Fiona doubled down on concentration in Zeud's hand, and the stream of tainted water turned into a cone of yellow, then blue, then white light that rumbled and vibrated the sky as it ate into the protective covering over the reactor. Zeud closed her eyes as they landed in the cleared out area beside the structure.

"Abe, do whatever you can," she said as she sat the two humans down. "Speak whatever words you think might help. Focus our energies into purpose as I do. Send her to a place to call home. A place where her power can be released safely. Help me create a world."

"I'll do something," he said. "I got it. I think." He began to chant. "Vade in domum tuam! Vade in domum tuam! Vade in domum tuam! Vade in domum tuam!" he repeated, with every cycle a bit louder than the last.

Go to your home. Yes... let's have her go to her home. "Don't stop, Abe!" She reached out, and shielded Abe with her wing from what was about to happen.

Zeud snarled, and allowed everything inside her out.

An apocalyptic blast of fire, light, and heat ripped out of her belly, throat and mouth, smashing into the side of the reactor's sarcophagus with the power of a million freight trains crashing, and a roar of noise louder than the center of the sun.

The energy releasing from Fiona wicked over to the fire and destruction releasing from Zeud, crossing like strings entwining with another, like threads on a loom. And as the two women released a tragedy's worth of power at the protective covering of the reactor, confusingly, it stopped harming it; instead, it pooled on the surface, creating a disc of white and orange light just a foot away from its sloped roof side. The disc grew, and grew in size, taking on a power of its own, a life, a presence, and eventually... the light changed to darkness, and a tunnel appeared into nothingness. A new space between, a void in the world created by their mountain of power.

Zeud stopped breathing fire for a moment, and looked down at the fierce, and powerful woman in her hand. She too no longer exuded a stream of power.

"Go now, and create the world you will call home," the dragon said.

Fiona didn't break concentration, but she nodded.

As if she were setting a dove free to fly into the sky, Zeud tossed the woman towards the hole in space and time, and she wicked out of existence, disappearing into the blackness.

With her energy no longer in this world, and no longer fed by the power within the dragon, the opening to Fiona's new realm snapped shut with a cacophonous boom. Only the metal roof of the sarcophagus remained, untouched by the power they'd just scarred it with.

Abe's chanting slowed, then ceased. She looked at him, and saw he'd been burned by their power. All of his exposed skin was reddened by heat or radiation.

Damn it. He caught too much of the spill. He must see the baku again, and soon. He'll be dead in a week.

They looked at the side of the reactor's shield, and all the damaged they'd done to it was gone. Taken away by the gate they'd created for Fiona to manifest her new world in.

"Where did she go?"

"To a world of her making, with our help, of course."

"How do we get there? How do we check on her?"

"Fiona is in a kind of limbo right now as she carves her space to live in. She'll show us the way when she's ready. A door, a window, a sewer grate, once she's spent enough time and energy, and vented enough power to create a—"

Zeud paused as a massive set of twin stone doors appeared at the base of the sarcophagus. Ringed by hieroglyphics, and obvious ornamentation of an Egyptian bent, the doors sat closed, but spoke of the realm beyond.

"She works fast, huh?"

"It would appear so. And it would seem she took the word sarcophagus, and its Egyptian origin literally in her imagination."

"Now what?"

The dragon shrugged. "Try knocking."

Epilogue
Zeud

The warmth cascading down from the sun in the center of the bright blue sky felt like heaven on Earth to Zeud.

Yet there was no sun, no blue sky, no Heaven above, and this was not Earth.

Spilling out like an ocean in all directions was a sea of sand. Dotted in a hundred tiny places with lush green palm trees, and tall grasses, and split into three wedges nearby by two crossing, meeting, kissing rivers was a world of Fiona's making. Buried deep in the distance, just over the horizon was the triangular shape of a mountain that reached about the clouds that clung to its side.

A closer triangle—a pyramid, actually—rose to an astonishing height. Ten, fifteen stories at least covered in white plaster or marble polished so smooth when the sun bounced off of it the glare could cook food. Topped with a giant black stone carved into the shape of a diamond, the obelisk built in Egyptian styling towered over a fertile, nearby river valley where a dozen smaller, western style homes were built in rolling neighborhoods. The idiosyncratic nature of the architecture styles looked odd, but the dragon had seen stranger mixtures in stranger societies.

The dragon lay in full form on a plaza made of volcanic stone. The scratchy platform had been formed into a gentle concave shape for her body to nestle in, and beneath the hard surface yet another layer of warmth emanated up, keeping her in a constant state of comfort. Near the plaza Zeud lay atop was a sprawling home, built from granite and marble in the style of the ancient Greek castles. Tall stone towers built alongside arcing domes, all with tall, open windows facing the rivers and desert. Palm trees grew everywhere, and where they did not, olives, figs, and grapes did. A huge area of reclaimed desert had the beginning of grass growing in it, ripe for the feeding of sheep, or goats. No animals wandered there yet.

It reminds me of Monemvasia. Such a beautiful castle. Though this... has the quality of a dream to it. Ethereal. I love it here. It is a special place, and born from such tragedy. I hope her deeds in this world match the cost needed to create it.

She lifted her long neck and craned her head up to look down into the central courtyard of the castle near the pyramid.

A pool lay at the castle's center. Round, and filled with water ten times as bright and blue as the clear sky above, it looked like the eye of a great, and beneficent god looking up into the world it had created, and loved.

Beside the pool, on a white linen towel atop the warm stones of the patio, lay a healthy, happy, and calm Fiona Gilmore. She had just retreated from the cooling waters of the pool, and she was still beaded with moisture. Several feet away, sitting in the shade of a white canopy was Abe Fellows. He was still red and raw from the exposure to Fiona's massive outburst of power, and from his time at Chernobyl and Pripyat, but he had not gotten worse in the weeks since the event. He had in fact stabilized, and gotten better here in Fiona's domain.

"How are you feeling?" the dragon asked the man as he sipped on a tall glass of iced tea.

"Better. Every time I go swimming I can feel the waters just wicking the radiation out. I mean that too. It feels so good. Ten, maybe twelve more dips in the water here and I think I'll stop glowing in the dark."

"Then what?" Fiona asked him. "Willing to move into one of the houses I'm building down by the river?"

"I'm more of a 'van down by the river' kind of guy, to be honest."

"That's not an answer," Fiona said as she relaxed on her towel.

"I'll consider it. We both know I struggle with commitment, and communication, so gimme a bit to think on it."

"I'm sorry about you and Alexis," Zeud said.

"Casualty of the job, and my mental health resulting," Abe said, not nearly as sad as he could've sounded. "It's for the best. She and I became what we did because we didn't know better, and we both were looking for love in the wake of such craziness, I guess. We were never a good match, and I think I allowed it to go to hell for a reason. Neither of you heard me say that."

"I hope you're more invested in your next relationship," Fiona said from her towel.

"I take it you heard me say that, then. Yeah, me too," Abe said before looking away from her direction. "Thank you for letting me heal here, in your house."

"Of course. But let's not call it a house. This my dear Abraham, is my Realm."

"That'd make you royalty," Abe shot back at her. "Are you insinuating you're a queen now?"

"You know," she said, "I've always been fond of the idea of being an empress. Like... of my own little empire."

"What would this realm's empire be? What kind of economy would it offer its neighbors? What kind of

303

government and theology would be welcome here, in the Land of Fiona?"

"Oh I'm curious about that," Zeud inserted from her elevated observation over the castle's walls.

"Looking to plop down another temple in your honor?" Abe joked with her.

Zeud snorted.

The woman chuckled. "Well, as you can see, we can offer anyone willing to relocate very discounted housing opportunities, as well as a essentially limitless supply of fresh food and water. We are aiming to offer any visitors a pleasurable experience with a semi-authentic Egyptian/Australian themed vacation. I also hope to offer radiation mitigation, for those people exposed. I also think I can store all radioactive waste here, and actually make it go away. I can absorb its power, then release it, making the realm larger, or building things in it."

"Tourist economy," Abe said. "No manufacturing base. Amateur hour. That'll be tough long term."

"Everyone's a bloody critic. I also think I might be able to make cabling to replace what we destroyed when we left Japan. Does that please you, great judge-y prick? I'm currently looking for an empire expansion manager, if you know anyone qualified or interested."

"Zeud you think Spoon would be interested in that kind of job?" Abe asked the dragon.

"I think he's busy back in America. He's reconsidering the offer of a more management –level position with Tapper. Apparently he might've had enough action of late, and wants a break. He's also trying to build support for finding a better way to release Seamus' energy. He's still in a coma, inside one of the minotaur's ovens. I hear the food is beyond compare, spicy no matter what Chael does to it, but still…."

"I guess that leaves him out," Fiona said, completely satisfied with the result.

"I guess I could ask around for ya," Abe said to Fiona, smiling. "I know some people."

"Don't ask too many people. I don't want to sift through applications," she said back.

"How long will this last though? Seriously?" he asked her.

She shrugged her narrow shoulders. "I don't know, but I can tell you this; To build what you can see, to create this little dimension, I only had to siphon off ten, maybe twenty percent of the power inside me, based on how I feel before and after. And, I can tell you that what you see will last. It won't fade away in a week, or a month, or even a year. This'll be here for decades."

"It should last forever," the dragon added.

"Wow. What's the plan for all the extra energy still inside you?"

"Learn a lot of Latin from someone who'll teach me, and figure out how to harness it into something useful. Then, maybe... I'll return to the real world, and face the music for what happened."

"They can't get in, right? I mean, the people most pissed at you are the Russians for shooting down their helicopter in Baikonur. Ukraine isn't really Russia, but borders in this region of the world are real soft for the Russians. Crimea, for example."

"I set the rules here, no different than how I manage my thoughts, or my healthcare. This realm is made of me, for me, and by me. Only those I deem willing are able to enter or leave."

"The few, the lucky."

"Maybe even the loved," she added.

Abe didn't respond to her flirt, but Zeud saw him smile.

"Well," the dragon said, breaking any tension the man could've been feeling, "the baku is on its way from Japan to assist either of you, with the Ukrainian government's blessing. They hope to give it a new home here where it can eat its full in the exclusion zone. I am led to believe through my contacts that the country is interested in handsomely rewarding many baku for moving here."

"I'll be happy to have it here," Fiona said. "If only to temper surges I get. I can only compare the experience to hot flashes. Very disorienting, and they feel dangerous. Right now I'm pouring all that energy into making the desert larger. Maybe I should make a lake..."

"They likely are a bit dangerous," the dragon answered. "But it seems you have a grip on it. So what now? What is it the great Abraham will do with his third, or fourth lease on life?"

"If I were a cat, I'd probably be going through my midlife crisis right now. I ought to be dead on several accounts."

"Answer the lady. What are you plans? Your empress commands you," Fiona said to him.

"Ha, well... If the empress insists. Well, I feel good, but I am still radioactive, based on the Geiger counter readings from this morning. Though, like I said, every swim here ticks it down a notch, so I would say I am rooted right next to this pool for at least another month."

"Your bosses at Tapper are okay with this?"

"Little choice in the matter for them. Mr. Doyle is happy with me being on the mend, and wants me to learn as much as I can about this shard realm, pocket realm thing, and to help Fiona in any way I can, so I'm still kind of working. I will say, I feel a lot better about my life right now. Stress here seems hard to hold onto."

"Good, good," the dragon said.

"What about you?" Fiona asked the dragon, sitting up on her bright white towel beneath the white sun above. "What's your move?"

"Ah yes. Well I am a guest of yours for the moment, and I am happy for this chance. Your realm suits me; it is bright, and warm, and full of energy. But, I am not meant for this place, and I must step back through the gates to the real world."

"What then?" the girl asked her.

"I promised the people of Japan that I would return to them to answer their questions, whatever that might look like. I'll give them a couple weeks. After that, I will go to Vienna. Speak with Dr. Tidwell. She has many good ideas about how to manage nuclear power, and I would like to hear them. I would also like to help Chael and Seamus in Frankfurt, as they deserve assistance. After that... I will see where the fires bring me. I will always have something that requires my attention. Hopefully, they will bring me near Henry. My heart longs for him."

"Now that's cute as fuck," Abe said.

"If I could blush, I would," the dragon said, and leaned back, lifting her head up and over the castle's walls until she stretched out again on the hard black surface Fiona had created just for her. She closed her eyes against the light of Fiona's sun, and let the heat rain down on her scales.

And, I must return to our Russian friend, and see to it that he is properly rewarded for the pendants he gave us. Poor old man might've caught the ire of people who believe they are his superiors, and I would hate to have anyone suffer on my behalf after being so kind and generous. I am sure the Russian government will want recompense for the loss of their helicopter, and the loss of lives. Never mind Japan's new suffering. I will go to Baikonur, after I visit Russia, and Belyakov. See the damage done, and repair what I can.

Now that I think of it... Siberia could use a forest fire right about now. Been awhile since the tundra was reborn under my gaze, and breath. Teach the humans there what power looks like. Show them how fickle their control of their realm is.

The fires in Zeud's belly sparked at that thought, and she knew she had a place to go, and a fire to set.

A large fire.

About The Author

Chris Philbrook is the creator and author of Adrian's Undead Diary, The Reemergence, Colony Lost, The Phone (as W.J. Orion), and the fantasy world of Elmoryn. Chris has several years of experience working in game development and editing as well as writing fiction for several major game design companies. He has a business degree as well as a psychology degree.

Chris has authored ten novels in the horror/post-apocalyptic series Adrian's Undead Diary, as well as four urban fantasy novels in The Reemergence series, and three dark fantasy novels in The Kinless Trilogy. His first science fiction novel; Colony Lost has received stellar reviews.. He has also edited two anthologies, and has had numerous short stories and novellas published in the horror world.

Chris calls the wonderful state of New Hampshire his home. He is an avid reader, writer, role player, miniatures game player, video game player, husband, and father to two little girls.

Can't Wait for More?

Look for Chris Philbrook's **FREE** short fiction eBook, *At Least He's Not on Fire.*

Find it on Amazon, Goodreads, or Smashwords today!

Amazon: *http://www.amazon.com/dp/B00JSGEKIK*

Goodreads: *https://www.goodreads.com/book/show/ 21948978-at-least-he-s-not-on-fire*

Smashwords: *https://www.smashwords.com/books/view/ 430970*

Made in United States
North Haven, CT
15 February 2022

16138708R00186